Praise for th

Silence of

"If you haven't read this
it a go. The mystery wi
be itching to start a knitting or crochet project of your own!"
—*Cozy Mystery Book Reviews*

"Good characters I hope to see more of . . . The characters are
developing well and the story line holds tight—and the book
ends with a cliffhanger question."
—*Kings River Life Magazine*

"What a fun read . . . The story is well plotted and there are
enough suspects to satisfy any cozy mystery reader."
—*MyShelf.com*

"Engaging . . . and quite difficult to put down . . . An excel-
lent read and highly recommended." —*Open Book Society*

Yarn to Go

"A cozy mystery that you won't want to put down. It combines
cooking, knitting, and murder in one great book!"
—*Fresh Fiction*

"The California seaside is the backdrop to this captivating cozy
that will have readers heading for the yarn store in droves."
—*Debbie's Book Bag*

continued . . .

Wound Up in Murder

BETTY HECHTMAN

BERKLEY PRIME CRIME, NEW YORK

An imprint of Penguin Random House LLC
375 Hudson Street, New York, New York 10014

WOUND UP IN MURDER

A Berkley Prime Crime Book / published by arrangement with the author

ISBN: 978-0-425-25265-9

PUBLISHING HISTORY
Berkley Prime Crime mass-market edition / July 2015

PRINTED IN THE UNITED STATES OF AMERICA

10 9 8 7 6 5 4 3 2 1

Cover illustration by Patricia Castelao.
Cover design by Rita Frangie.
Interior text design by Kelly Lipovich.

Acknowledgments

My first thank-you always goes to my editor, Sandy Harding, because her touch always makes my manuscripts better. I am forever grateful to my agent, Jessica Faust, because she has always been there for me.

Thank you to Linda Hopkins for doing such a great job helping me with the patterns. What would I do without you?

I appreciate my eternal cheerleaders Roberta and Dominic Martia. The Thursday group of knitters and crocheters offers me yarn information and friendship. Thank you, Rene Biederman, Alice Chiredijan, Terry Cohen, Trish Culkin, Clara Feeney, Sonia Flaum, Lily Gillis, Winnie Hineson, Linda Hopkins, Debbie Kratofil, Reva Mallon, Elayne Moschin and Paula Tesler.

And of course, thanks to my family, Burl, Max and Samantha. You guys are still the best recipe tasters!

1

"THIS TIME IT'S GOING TO BE DIFFERENT. THIS TIME I'm prepared. I know what the retreat is about. No more depending on one person to lead the workshops. And I have help with the other stuff, too." I looked to my audience to see his reaction. Julius, my sleek black cat, blinked his yellow eyes and jumped down from the bathroom cabinet. Did that mean he didn't believe me?

I put away the toothbrush and gave myself a last look in the mirror. Did I believe myself? What I said was true. I was definitely better prepared than I'd been for the first two retreats. Wasn't I going to a meeting with my two workshop leaders this very morning to go over the final details?

But me putting on yarn retreats? It's not what I—or anyone who knew me, especially my mother—would have expected, given my rather spotty career history. A semester of law school was enough for me to know that being a lawyer wasn't for me. I'd tried being a teacher, actually a substitute teacher at a private school. I did it for a couple of years and then I'd had enough. I baked desserts at a bistro for six months. I would have stayed longer but the place went out of business. Then there was the temp work. At least it wasn't boring. I gave out samples of new products on street corners in downtown Chicago and spritzed perfume on shoppers in several department stores. The best of the bunch was my time at the detective agency, where I was either an assistant detective or detective's assistant, depending on who you were talking to. If you were talking to me, the title would definitely be assistant detective. Mostly what I did was phone interviews, but I loved it. Everything might have been different if my boss, Frank, had been able to keep me on.

But you can't change the past. So in an effort to make a fresh start—that means when the temp work dried up, I'd had to move back to my parents' apartment in the Hancock Building and I needed to get out of there—I had relocated to my aunt Joan's guest house almost two thousand miles away on the edge of California's Monterey Peninsula. In no time, my aunt had helped me line up a gig baking desserts for a local restaurant called the Blue Door and making muffins for the assorted coffee spots in town. With the chilly temperatures and almost constant cloudy skies, coffee spots were big in Cadbury by the Sea.

So how did I end up putting on yarn retreats? Yarn2Go was my aunt's business, but just months after I'd moved into her guest house, she was killed in a hit-and-run accident. She left everything to me, including her business.

The next question is usually, what is a yarn retreat? The yarn part refers to a yarn craft, which so far has been knitting. I can practically see my mother's eyes flying upward at the thought. She's a cardiologist and it's pretty clear she thinks this apple has fallen very far from the tree. Her favorite line seems to be

"When I was your age [35], I was a doctor, a wife and a mother, and you're what?" It helps her case that until I inherited the business, I didn't know which end of a knitting needle was up.

Now after two retreats, I definitely know about knitting needles. Mostly that I don't really like the ones that are long and come in pairs. It's circular needles all the way for me. And although I can't knit as well as the retreaters, I'm holding my own and have samples of my work to prove it. And every time I finish something, I e-mail a picture to my mother. Yes, I might have an issue with proving that I can stick with something and finish it.

And it might be obvious I have a few issues with my mother. On the other hand, there is my father. He's a pediatrician and much easier to get along with. Of course, that could be because his patients are still in their formative years and he looks at me in the same way.

That covers the yarn part of the business. Now for the retreat part. It's really a vacation with a purpose. My group gets to learn something new, and has lots of time to hang out with other yarn lovers while they all work on their craft. They also get to enjoy the other activities put on by Vista Del Mar, the hotel and conference center where the retreats are held, conveniently located across the street from where I live.

But back to the present. Julius looked up at me from the floor. The cat kept surprising me, but then he was the first pet I had ever had. It had been all his decision. I had seen him around the neighborhood, but one day he showed up at my door and invited himself in. Did that make me his pet?

My impression of cats pre-Julius was that they were aloof and didn't really have a lot of interaction with their humans. Julius had made his presence felt from day one, and as the weeks had turned into months, he'd become my shadow when I was home.

He followed me into the room my aunt had used as an office. It had taken me a while, but I had moved into the main house. *Main house* sounds a lot grander than it is. For that matter, *guest house* does, too. The guest house was actually a converted garage, and the main house had just two bedrooms, one of which was this office.

My aunt's creations were all over the little room. My favorite was the crocheted lion that guarded the desk. Julius jumped up on the small love seat and curled up against another of my aunt's creations, a granny square afghan. How lucky that the bright colors were in the middle of the motifs with rows of black yarn around the edges. All that black yarn camouflaged the cat hairs Julius so generously deposited. He watched as I picked up the red tote bag with *Yarn2Go Retreats* emblazoned on the front. This bag and its contents were a sample for the upcoming retreat. I emptied the contents to look them over once again. There were several large skeins of yarn and then a number of smaller balls of yarn. All of them were in different colors and textures. A small plastic bag came out as well. It contained an assortment of beads and charms.

"We're calling this retreat Mystery Bags," I said in case Julius was interested. The plan was that each bag would have a different selection of yarn and embellishments. I put everything back into the red tote thinking about the upcoming meeting with my helpers to go over the plan for the projects. A large manila envelope fell off the desk as I picked up the tote bag.

I stared at it on the floor for a moment before retrieving it. I was about to put it back where it had been, but then I stopped and emptied the contents on the dark wood desk.

How many times had I emptied this envelope, looked at the contents and wondered what to do? The photo of the infant with a teddy bear was old and the colors faded, but I was certain the baby was a girl by the bow in her wisps of hair. A small white envelope had *Edmund's Hair* written across the front. Inside there was a clump of shiny dark hair with the roots still attached. Another much older envelope that had been sealed and opened had *Our Baby* written in faded ink. At the bottom *Mother's DNA* was written in fresh ink, no doubt referring to traces left when the envelope was licked to seal. And last was the ledger sheet from the long-closed Cadbury Bank. It was marked as a sign-in sheet to access safety-deposit boxes. What made it noteworthy was the fact that Edmund Delacorte had signed in for Box 273, and then a few lines down Mary Jones had signed in to access the same number.

"It was a money drop," I said. "It was a way for Edmund Delacorte to pay off his baby mama." I chuckled at the term that was so contemporary and would have sounded so odd on July 25, 1962, when this list was created. "Or at least I think it was."

Why did this matter all these years later? First you had to understand that the Delacorte family was like the royal family of Cadbury by the Sea. They had owned fishing boats, a cannery and a lot of land. Edmund Delacorte had been the sole owner of Vista Del Mar. He was married with a son when he died a couple of years after the date on the ledger sheet. His will had been very specific that Vista Del Mar was to go to his children. Barely a year after he died, his wife and son were killed in an accident. The hotel and conference center went back into the family pot. But if Edmund had fathered another child, she might be able to claim Vista Del Mar was hers as well as a portion of the family fortune.

I had no birth date, but it seemed likely that the baby

in the photograph was now in her mid-fifties. I thought that I could track down the mother. I checked the Cadbury census records, which were definitely old school, and found several women named Mary Jones. The problem was that their ages didn't fit with the age of the mother of the heir. I had even discreetly tried to find an employee from the long-closed bank who might have a memory of the woman. I already knew Edmund made his deposits just before the regular staff went to lunch, no doubt realizing there would be a rotating group who filled in during the lunch break, when his mistress came to pick up her money.

It was more than fifty years ago and the one former bank employee I had been able to locate had a foggy memory of someone coming in during lunchtime, but the woman always wore a big hat and sunglasses.

Julius gave me a look of reproach. Was he wondering what I was doing with the envelope anyway? The appearance of an heir would stir everything up. Did the Delacorte sisters want to find out they had to share their fortune with their brother's love child and relinquish the ownership of Vista Del Mar? The answer to that was easy, no. What about the rest of the town? They seemed to resist change, so I imagine they would probably prefer to leave things as they were. Maybe it was because I was new to the town and wasn't so concerned with keeping the status quo, but I thought Edmund's secret baby deserved the chance to get what her father rightfully left her. Even if I had hit a dead end.

"You are the only one who knows about this." I sat down on the small leather couch and stroked his neck. He leaned into my touch and began to purr. This living with a cat was an unfolding mystery. His displays of affection still surprised and touched me. "Well, at least I know you won't go blabbing to anyone."

He climbed into my lap and left a dusting of his short black hairs on my dark-wash jeans. "Mary Jones," I said with a disbelieving shake of my head. "Obviously it's a fake name." Julius looked up at me as if to concur.

"This is where my experience working at the detective agency comes in handy." Was the cat rolling his eyes now? Could cats even roll their eyes? "Okay so maybe I only did phone interviews and occasionally stood in for surveillance, but my boss, Frank, said more than once that when people used fake names, the initials were usually real. So all I have to do is find the right woman with the initials *M.J.* and hope she'll lead me to her daughter. That really narrows it down, doesn't it?" I punctuated my comment with a hopeless shrug.

Julius decided he'd had enough affection. He abruptly stood up and stretched, pressing his paws into my thigh before he jumped down. He looked back over his shoulder at me and blinked. Was that the cat way of saying a sarcastic "Good luck"?

Who knew if this M.J. was even still alive? She'd be in her seventies by now, and maybe she didn't want the world to know about her indiscretion. Without her, there was no way to know what the baby's name was, and all the DNA meant nothing. Why was I even bothering with it? Maybe everybody was right. Maybe it should be left under the rug.

"I'm talking to a cat," I said out loud in disbelief, throwing up my hands. Not that Julius noticed. With his tail held high, he walked out the office door and into the hall. I didn't have to be a cat specialist to know where he was headed—the kitchen with hopes of a breakfast of stink fish.

2

THE PHONE WAS RINGING WHEN I SHUT THE DOOR
a little while later. I knew it was my mother and deliberately
left without picking it up. Thankfully, she never called me
on my cell phone, too afraid I'd be driving when I answered.
Poor Julius looked a little forlorn as he sat in the window.
Instead of his favorite smelly fish, he'd had to settle for tastes
from my container of yogurt. You'd think he'd appreciate
that I was broadening his food horizons.

My yellow Mini Cooper was parked in the driveway next
to the converted garage that had once been my home. I had
stayed living there for months after my aunt died, feeling
strange about moving into her house. But finally I had
accepted that she would want me to have the place and I had
moved in. I was glad for all the space and now I just used
the guest house to store the supplies for the retreat. As
expected, the sky was white. By now I had come up with
various descriptions of the exact level of cloudiness. This

morning's was the standard issue. Flat opaque whiteness, no shadows, and light that would look the same all day.

My house was on the edge of the small town, but even so, I was in downtown Cadbury in about five minutes. The fact there was never much traffic helped.

I had put on two retreats so far and learned a lot in the process. I now knew I couldn't run the retreats on my own; I needed to be very familiar with the program and to be prepared for any disaster that might happen. In the past that had included murder. The meeting I was on my way to was part of my plan to be hyperprepared this time. No longer would I depend on only one person to handle the workshops. Now I was going to have two people, Crystal Smith and Wanda Krug, and I was going to make sure I understood the process as well.

I usually met Crystal Smith at Cadbury Yarn, the store she ran with her mother, Gwen Selwyn. But today since Wanda was going to be there, too, we'd decided to avoid all the activity at the store and meet at Crystal's house. Well, not exactly her house. It was really her mother's house, just like the yarn store was really her mother's business.

I found a parking spot on Grand Street, which was the main drag in town, and walked down a side street that sloped toward the water. Cadbury by the Sea was located on the tip of the Monterey Peninsula, and the ocean was visible from just about everywhere. In this part of town the houses were more like small cottages and were on top of each other with barely any yard. It made me grateful for the space around my place. The only open space was a small park with a beautiful old Monterey cypress tree. The foliage was a dark water retaining shade of green, and like all of them, the wind had shaped its branches into a graceful horizontal pose.

I had never been to Crystal's house before and had to

check the house numbers as I walked down the street. The houses were a mixture of styles, pastel painted small Victorians, Craftsman bungalows with long front porches and Spanish cottages with large arched windows and red tiled roofs. There was no strip of grass between the sidewalk and street, making the houses seem very close to the narrow roadway.

Crystal's address matched up with a sweet-looking dusty blue Victorian on a corner. It wasn't like the large grand old Victorians on appropriately named Grand Street. They took up whole corners and had elaborate gardens and also happened to now mostly have been turned into bed-and-breakfast inns. Crystal's place was a single story and much smaller but still had some of the touches like fish scale siding and a bay window. A white picket fence surrounded the small yard. Even with all the cloudy skies and fog here, there wasn't much rain, and water was at a shortage. Most people either left their small yards to go to native plants, which was a nice way of saying weeds, or like this one, had no lawn, but plantings placed around the yard filled in with wood chips. A pot of flowers brightened the bottom step leading to the small porch that ran up the side of the house to the door.

Crystal must have been waiting for me because she had the door open before I'd reached the top stair. "Wanda's already here." The words were benign, but her tone made it sound like Wanda was already ruffling feathers. She stepped aside to let me in. "C'mon inside and please don't mind the mess or the fact that it's a little crowded."

Even though I was relatively new to the town, I knew a lot of the backstories of the inhabitants. For example I knew that Crystal had run off with Rixx, a rock musician, when she was a teen. Eventually they got married and she had two kids. She'd stuck it out through his career ups and downs, along with his personal issues (i.e., drug problems) before Rixx (how pretentious can you get) traded Crystal in for a younger model. Crystal and her kids had moved back to town and in with her mother.

As we walked inside, I saw what she meant. The house was charming, but small and very full. I'd never met her kids and somehow pictured the girl and boy as being small, but when I saw the size of the boy's sneakers sticking out from under the couch in the living room, I realized they were teens. I instantly wondered how her kids felt about the way Crystal dressed. She had a whimsical way of mixing and matching—never wearing pairs of anything, even if it was earrings or socks. Her black hair naturally fell into tiny curls, which bounced when she walked. And her makeup— she could pull off the heavy dark eye makeup. I'd tried it and ended up looking like a raccoon.

She let out a sigh as I walked behind her. I wasn't used to seeing her like this. At the store she always seemed like a free spirit, but looking around the house, for the first time I realized the weight of her responsibilities. "We were hoping to do something like your aunt did and turn our garage into living space. Maybe someday."

I followed her into the dining room. The mystery bags had been Crystal's idea. She'd explained they had a family tradition of using odds and ends of yarn and leftover beads to make one-of-a-kind items. Eventually they had started making up grab bags of stray skeins of yarn and small amounts of beads, buttons and charms and selling them at the store. Sometimes they'd even had displays of the different things their customers had created with the mystery assortment.

A round oak table sat in the center of the room. Wanda Krug had been sitting, but stood up and took a step toward me in an eager manner when we came into the room.

"Good, you're here. We really need to talk about the plans for the retreat." Wanda struck what seemed to be her natural pose. She had one hand on her hip and held the other one out. I couldn't help it—between her short stout stature and the pose, all I could think of was the Teapot song with her arms being the handle and the spout. She glanced at Crystal, who was shaking her head at the comment.

"Wanda, we've already agreed on the program for the retreat," Crystal said. She viewed Wanda's job as just a helper during the retreat.

"And you're headed for disaster," Wanda added, looking at me. Both women were native Cadburians and only a few years different in age. It was hard to believe Wanda was actually the younger of the two. Between her manner and her wardrobe choices, like today's pale yellow polo shirt over loose-fitting navy blue slacks, she looked years older than Crystal.

It was a little unsettling that both of them were also about my age. I could practically hear my mother's voice with her oft-said words: "When I was your age, I was a wife, a doctor and a mother, and you're what?"

Crystal stepped up to the table and showed off the three recycled plastic tote bags that matched the one I'd brought. "This will give you an idea of how the contents of each bag are unique. My grandmother made the bags up with real leftovers, but since we were making so many, we actually ordered the yarn and supplies for them," Crystal said, emptying the contents of each bag and laying it on the table. Each one had three skeins of worsted weight yarn in different but complementary colors along with an assortment of small balls of yarn, some of which were novelty yarns, along with a plastic bag with assorted beads, and other embellishments.

"I have some samples of the kinds of things people can make," Crystal said, pointing out an arrangement on the sideboard. I was amazed at the selection of scarves with different colors and textures of yarn with random beads added in. A small purse had fun fur mixed in with the other yarn and a whole row of beads, which made it look flamboyant. There was also a lovely shawl. She'd put out some toys as well. A bear and a cat were made out of a mixture of yarns and dressed in little coats of many colors, but it was the doll on the end that really caught my eye.

"We will have patterns for all of these available," Crystal said. She saw me admiring the doll. "My grandmother made the bear for me, but she's all my idea." Crystal picked up the soft doll with her colorful dress and wild hair. A face had been created with bits of felt and the expression looked so concerned it made me laugh. "It's a worry doll," she said. When both Wanda and I seemed confused, she added an explanation. "It's my version of those dolls that come from Guatemala. The idea is that you tell her your worries at night and by morning they're all gone."

Wanda was still standing and looked over the selection of items. "It's a terrible idea. The people will spend the whole weekend trying to decide what to make. I say we just give them one scarf pattern and redo the bags so they all have the same supplies."

"That's no fun," Crystal said. I could see the anger flashing in her eyes and I suddenly realized hiring them to work together might have been a mistake. I had been so busy thinking about having two people to help with the workshop I hadn't considered the difference in their styles.

I knew both of them had been knitting since they were kids and were light-years ahead of me in ability. I had thought they would just get along. But Wanda kept voicing her opinion and Crystal didn't back down. The situation reminded me of my time as a substitute teacher. When the kids started acting up, I'd found the best way to deal with them was with a distraction.

"I'm sure you both know that there's another much bigger retreat going on this weekend, at Vista Del Mar, too. It's called My Favorite Year 1963. I'm not sure what it entails, but Kevin St. John did hire me to bake trays of sweets for the opening reception. He wanted something authentic from that time. Apparently cream cheese brownies were a big thing then."

"I hope we get some samples," Crystal said. Wanda agreed and suggested that I make a batch for our group to be sure. I breathed a sigh of relief realizing the old trick had worked.

"I heard Kevin St. John tried to change the dates of our retreat," Wanda said.

"He did," I said with an annoyed nod. "The My Favorite Year retreat came up recently. Supposedly the place they've been holding it in Cambria had a fire and they had to find a new venue. They needed facilities for a couple hundred people. The dollar signs lit up in Kevin's eyes. He shifted a bunch of reservations around so he could get their business. But I wouldn't budge. Just because he got a last-minute gig for some history club was no reason for us to be tossed out on our butts."

"It's more than this one retreat. He knows that if the event goes really well, Vista Del Mar could become their regular spot. I heard they have a number of events a year," Crystal said. "I can see why Kevin would want to please them. He's been rushing around town checking thrift shops for anything he can find from 1963."

"He's not just looking for things," Wanda said. "He rounded

up a local celebrity. I know because I overheard him talking about it at the resort."

Wanda was more than a great knitter and spinner; her real profession was golf pro at one of the nearby posh Pebble Beach resorts. She didn't really look the part, but she'd won numerous golf tournaments. Several months ago she'd been demoted to giving golf lessons to kids, but recently had talked her way back into her original position of giving lessons to adults and being available to play a round with the guests.

"Who?" Crystal asked. It amazed me how they'd forgotten their previous fussing.

"His name is Bobbie Listorie," Wanda said, sounding less than enthusiastic. "He's a singer. Some song—'Look into My Eyes' or 'In the Eyes,' or something like that—was a big hit in 1963. The resort where I work for peanuts pays him an absurd amount of money to hang around, schmooze with the guests and be available to make up a foursome on the golf course." Wanda shook her head with disapproval. "I don't get it. What's the big appeal with him? If they are interested in a good game of golf, they'd be better off going with me. But they gather around him like ants to honey." She shook her head again with dismay. "He usually does a few songs on the weekend in the bar. It's supposed to be impromptu, but of course, it's planned. You should see how the women go on about his green eyes." Wanda rolled her eyes. Clearly she had never been a groupie.

Crystal made a face. "You don't have to tell me about that. When I used to go on the road with Rixx, women would throw themselves at him when I was standing right there. I can just imagine what happened when I wasn't there." After that her expression brightened. "Kevin St. John has some other celebrities from that era coming, too," Crystal continued. "Someone in the yarn store said he found an old baseball player who played on the San Francisco Giants in 1963. You know the guy, he's the pitch man for that energy drink Boost Up. And last but not least, he rounded up Dotty Night. If my mother has pointed her out once, it's been a hundred times. She owns a hotel in Carmel and calls it the Dotty Night Inn. Her claim to fame, according to my mother, was starring in a string of movies during the sixties. She was always a perky good girl who got the guy. The big one from 1963 is *Bridget and the Bachelor.*" Crystal rolled her eyes. "Not exactly like that reality show *The Bachelor.*"

Now that they both had cooled down, I brought up our retreat and the solutions I'd come up with while we were talking about Kevin St. John's efforts for his retreat. It was my call anyway.

"Here's what I propose," I said. "We keep Crystal's bags as they are. We offer a pattern for a scarf." Wanda nodded, looking triumphant without realizing I wasn't finished. "And we offer them the pattern for the worry doll." Wanda's expression dimmed and Crystal smiled. "And if anybody wants to make something else, we do our best to help them."

I was shocked when they both agreed.

3

"YOU LOOK FRAZZLED," LUCINDA THORNKILL SAID
when I walked into the Coffee Shop. It was just a short walk
from Crystal's and I had arranged to meet my best friend
and boss for a coffee drink after I met with my two helpers.
The plain-sounding name for the coffee place was just what
the Cadbury town council insisted on. So there was no Ye
Olde anything in this town. They wanted everything to be
called what it was, rather than any cutesy name. It even
extended to my muffins. When I'd first started baking muffins for the various coffee shops, I'd called them things like
Merry Berry, The Blues and Simplicity until I saw that the
places that sold them had changed the names to the essence
of what they were after some council member complained.
So they became mixed berry muffins, blueberry muffins and
plain vanilla ones. I think the fuss about the muffin names
was a bit much, but I had begun to understand their point about
not having any "ye olde" anythings. They wanted the town

to feel real instead of some place that catered to tourists even though the natural beauty of the area attracted travelers from around the world.

"What was I thinking when I hired Crystal and Wanda to work together?"

"I was going to say something when you first told me, but you seemed so certain about it," Lucinda said. It was hard for me to think of Lucinda Thornkill as my boss, even though she and her husband, Tag, were the owners of the Blue Door restaurant, where I baked the desserts. She was really my best friend in town. It helped that we were both transplants to Cadbury and it didn't seem to matter at all that she was much older than me. Or that everything she wore or carried had a fancy designer name on it and the only designer piece I had was an Armani jacket my mother had given me as a gift.

"I think I have it worked out so they are both happy, at least with the retreat plan." I let out a sigh. When it got down to the wire of putting on the retreat, I got nervous. Maybe because of past problems. Lucinda slipped off her Burberry jacket and hung it on the back of the chair.

"You know you can count on me to act as a host during the meals." Lucinda had let her hair grow and wore it pulled back in a ponytail. She'd started getting some gray streaks and was counteracting them by coloring her hair. Not that anyone would notice. The stylist had done a masterful job of blending in some golden strands with the dark shade of brown so it appeared very natural. It figured that someone so into designer wear wouldn't be a do-it-yourself colorist.

"I feel guilty letting you pay for the retreat and then work it as well."

"I love helping. Isn't that part of the definition of friendship? And I'm so accustomed to working in a restaurant, I think it would make me more nervous to not work the meals."

I suddenly felt guilty for not telling Lucinda about my so far unsuccessful search for the Delacorte heir. Maybe it was time to share. I must have been shifting my eyes around as I thought about it because her face registered concern.

"Is there something on your mind?"

"Yes," I said. First, I tried to explain my reticence by saying, "You've lived in Cadbury longer than I have, and I thought you might be concerned about shaking things up." Then I told her about the contents of the envelope. "It probably doesn't matter anyway because I've reached a dead end—the most I know is that the mother's real initials are possibly M.J."

Lucinda shrugged off my concern. "I think this town could use a little stirring up. The Delacorte sisters have oodles of money, so if they had to share it, it wouldn't be the end of the world." Lucinda's eyes began to dance with wicked merriment. "And just imagine how upset Kevin St. John would be if the mystery heir felt differently about owning Vista Del Mar than the Delacorte sisters do and didn't let him act like the lord of the place anymore?"

"I see your point," I said with a smile. "I could keep looking for the heir, on the q.t. of course."

"And I could help," Lucinda offered. She made a nodding gesture toward Maggie, the proprietor of the Coffee Shop. "Maybe she knows something."

Maggie finished with a customer and came from behind the counter, stopping at our table. As always, she was wearing something red—today it was a bright red tunic. She'd had more than her share of tragedies—she had lost her daughter and shortly afterward her husband—and I thought she wore the red to put on a bright front to keep up her spirits.

"Cappuccinos coming up," she said to me with a smile. Hers was the original coffee spot in town and everybody's favorite. Her coffee was great, but I think they came mostly because of her. She made everybody feel at home and it was kind of the news exchange spot. That was a nice way of saying she heard all the local gossip.

"You better make it a double for her," Lucinda said and then told her who I'd just been meeting.

Maggie's blue eyes went skyward as I told both of them about the retreat project problems. "It should be quite a weekend. Kevin St. John has been running around town like a crazy person for that 1963 retreat he arranged. He stopped in here for a coffee the other day and wanted to know if I knew any special coffee drinks that were popular in 1963, so he could put them on the menu in Vista Del Mar's café. You know, I've known him since he was a kid."

Lucinda and I traded glances, both thinking about what we'd just said about him. "Did he wear those dark suits when he was a kid?" I said, rolling my eyes at the image.

"No. But I will say he looked old even when he was young." Maggie gave me a sidelong look. "Is there something else?"

There was, but I couldn't figure out how to bring it up without saying what we were doing. Lucinda followed my lead and we both shook our heads.

"Okay, then. I'm off to make your drinks." She went back to the counter and began working at the espresso machine as more customers came in.

She delivered the large frothy drinks a few moments later and made sure we were happy with them before she went back to deal with new customers. They were perfect, of course, and she had made me a double. After a few sips the drink perked me right back up.

"What do we know about the secret heir besides what her mother's initials might be?" Lucinda asked.

"I think she's somewhere in her mid-fifties. There was no date on the picture. I'm just going by the date on the ledger sheet and assuming she was born sometime before it, but who knows how much before." Lucinda listened to me and then made a gesture toward Maggie again.

"I thought Maggie was older than that," I said. "But then, I don't know for sure. And we can't really just ask her. Think about the question. We don't say, 'How many years since you were born?' We say, 'How old are you?' I can see why people of a certain age feel it's a rude question." I paused for a moment. "Come to think of it, I don't like people asking me. Maybe it's only an okay question for young kids who don't fixate on the word *old*."

Lucinda chuckled. "You might be overthinking that question, but I do agree that asking her directly would seem odd."

"It is such a relief to talk to you about what I have. Up until now, Julius was my only confidant," I said. "I don't think he cares that there is someone who is entitled to the ownership of Vista Del Mar and a portion of the Delacorte fortune unless it involves him getting an extra serving of stink fish."

"Do you think Edmund's mistress ever tried to come forward?" Lucinda asked.

"I thought about that. She would have had to deal with the Delacorte sisters' mother. There was no DNA stuff back then, so even if she went to Mrs. Delacorte, she probably would have been brushed off." Suddenly the impossibility of it all sank in. "Who knows if Edmund's woman is still alive? And the baby, who we know is likely in her fifties, probably has no idea who she really is. We don't even know if the heir is still in town. This is worse than looking for a needle in a haystack."

Maggie cruised by again and asked if we needed refills. No matter how hard I tried to pay her for the drinks we'd had, she refused. She always said it was professional courtesy.

Lucinda was already gathering her things. "I have to get back to work," she said, draining the last of her coffee drink. "Tag gets crazy if I'm not putting the specials in the menus at least an hour before we open for lunch." She got up and picked up her bag.

"Have fun," Maggie said with a wink.

"You mean when I go to Vista Del Mar?" I asked. Maggie laughed and shook her head.

"I'm talking about your date with Dane this evening."

"Don't worry. We have it covered," Lucinda said. "Our cook is making them a special meal with oysters. And we all know they're aphrodisiacs," she teased.

"It's just dinner and then we both have to go to work," I protested. I could feel the color rising in my face. I was doing my best to make it sound casual. Dane Mangano lived down the street from me. He was a member of the Cadbury Police Department. In other words, he was a cop. Since the streets of Cadbury weren't exactly mean, he spent a lot of time doing things like getting overzealous tourists out of the fish tanks at the Monterey Bay Aquarium.

He had taken it upon himself to try to keep the local teens from getting bored and in trouble by offering free karate lessons in his garage. He cooked for them, too. And for me.

I might have been a master at muffins and dessert, but when it came to regular food, I wasn't very interested in cooking it and was happy to eat a frozen entrée. Dane cooked homemade tomato sauce that made me salivate just thinking about it. We had an exchange going. He left me plates of spaghetti or lasagna, and I left him muffins and cookies.

We'd been sort of circling each other. Even when my

mother had visited, she'd noticed a spark between us. Not that she approved. Normally her disapproval might have been enough to make me jump into his arms, but I had been resisting the definite something I felt for him. With my history of leaving people and places, it seemed like the best idea. And he was my neighbor. If we got together and then broke up, it would be very awkward.

Dane didn't seem to be bothered by any of my objections. Finally, he'd worn me down and I had agreed to dinner in a neutral place. I was trying my best to make it seem like it was no big deal.

"Whatever you say. But we have a table all reserved for you two," Lucinda said as she went to the door.

I drank down the last of my cappuccino and was going to leave myself, but I had a thought about Maggie. Maybe I couldn't ask her age, but I could ask her about her parents. It was funny that someone who so easily talked about everybody in town was closemouthed when it came to her own life. It took some doing, and in the end I didn't find out much except that she'd been named after her mother, who was now living in a retirement community in Phoenix. She had never really known her father. He'd been in the army and was killed in Vietnam. So now I knew her mother's name started with an *M*. I wondered if the story about her father was just a cover-up. Could Maggie really be a Delacorte?

4

THE SKIES IN CADBURY WERE ALMOST ALWAYS cloudy, but there were different versions. Sometimes the clouds were a filmy white, letting some blue show through; other times they were tinged with gold from the sun trying to melt them. But most of the time the sky was spread with an even coating of white, which was how it looked when I pulled my Mini Cooper back into my driveway.

The cappuccino had left me with an energized buzz, and I immediately began work on the cream cheese brownies for Kevin St. John's retreat. The old recipes I'd found all started with brownie mix. I never used mixes of any kind, so I simply used my brownie recipe and added in the cream cheese part of the recipes I'd found. In no time the wonderful fragrance of chocolate swirled around my kitchen. Julius came in to see what was going on, but brownies did nothing for him and he left a moment later.

Of course, I tasted the finished product before I packed

them up. It was the first time I'd made them and I wanted to be sure they were okay. Wow. They were so good, I decided to add them to my dessert repertoire for the Blue Door.

A short time later, with the brownies boxed up, I headed across the street to Vista Del Mar.

As soon as I went past the two stone pillars marking the entrance of the hotel and conference center, I felt as if I'd entered a different world. My house was on the edge of town and there was a rustic wildness to the area, but the grounds of Vista Del Mar took it to another level. There wasn't a hint of a manicured lawn or border of flowers. Over a hundred acres of gentle slopes were left to grow wild. Tall lanky Monterey pines grew everywhere between the weathered brown-shingled buildings that housed the guest rooms. And trees that had died were left on the ground to decompose naturally. The buildings were over a hundred years old, left from the center's beginning as a camp. I thought the weather, the wild grounds and dark wood buildings all added up to a moody atmosphere with a slight touch of sinister.

I'd barely cleared the driveway when the hotel van pulled in. I did a double take when I saw that it wasn't the usual white one with *Vista Del Mar* painted on the side and a Monterey cypress next to the words. This one was white and there was a temporary sign on it with the hotel name. I was no car expert, but it was clearly a vintage model. And then I got it. Kevin St. John must have rounded it up for the Favorite Year 1963 retreat. Then I noticed some old cars parked in the small parking area nearby. The old Chevys and Buicks looked light-years away from the current style, but oddly enough the van looked almost the same as the contemporary model.

The van stopped outside the building called the Lodge. I'd always thought of the large one-story building as being the heart of Vista Del Mar. It was where guests went to register and to gather. Like all of the buildings, it was designed in the Arts and Crafts style, constructed from local materials and meant to blend in with the landscape.

The doors opened and Bree Meyers bounced out of the van. I thought of the first time she'd come to one of my retreats. She'd been a basket of worry. It was the first time she'd left her young sons and the first time she'd gone anywhere on her own. Now on her third retreat, she had a new aura of confidence.

"I'm ready, willing and able to help any retreaters who are worried about being here alone, or worried about anything," she said. Her blond frizz of curls seemed to have gotten puffier, but she'd stayed with the comfortable jeans and gray hoodie with her kids' school name emblazoned on the back.

Scott Lipton climbed out next. He had his knitting tucked under his arm. No more hiding it in a briefcase. "I want you to know the woman next to me on the plane commented on my knitting," he said. "I will offer knitting lessons to anyone who wants them." He had loosened up and changed from business-looking attire to more of a preppie look with khaki pants and an oxford cloth shirt.

Olivia Golden got out last. Her almond-shaped face glowed with happiness and it was hard to remember how sad and angry she'd been on the first retreat.

"I'm ready this time," she said, opening the top of a duffle bag. There were piles of plastic bags containing folded sheets of paper with instructions and small balls of yarn. Olivia had learned to battle her own troubles by thinking of others. At the last retreat she started having our group knit squares, which got sewn together into blankets and then given away to people in need. She'd had limited supplies then, but she knew that we'd agreed to include any guests of Vista Del Mar in the square making this time, and so she'd come prepared.

"I got my local yarn store to donate all this," she said. She had needles as well.

I called the three my early birds because they came a few days before the official start of our retreat. I realized I should really call them by what they had become—my helpers.

"Let's go inside," Bree said. The rest of the van had already unloaded and the people had gone in. I had hoped to give them a little heads-up about what else was going on at Vista Del Mar, but Bree had the Lodge's door open and was on her way in before I could say anything.

I joined them and then we all crashed into each other when Bree came to an abrupt stop. I understood when I looked up. There was an archway with a sign that read, YOU ARE NOW ENTERING MY FAVORITE YEAR 1963. A crowd was gathered just inside the archway. I did a double take. A lot of the women were wearing white pillbox hats and pastel shift-style dresses along with heels. Whoever wore heels to Vista Del Mar?

"What's going on?" Olivia asked.

Before I could answer, a man came through the crowd and joined us. "Welcome. C'mon in. Registration is right over there. Then you can just mingle." His hair was cut into a short neat style and he wore a suit and tie. There was something charismatic in his even features and engaging smile. A younger woman accompanied him. She reminded me of a Modigliani painting with her elongated face framed in short dark blond hair. I did a double take at the nubby gray suit she was wearing. The pumps just accentuated her thick ankles. She seemed to be trying to keep up with the man, but still ended up a step behind.

Through the throng of people, I could see that multiple tables had been set up and a line of people snaked around them.

"Norman Rathman," he said, pointing at his name tag. Underneath his name it said, *President and Founder, Favorite Year Club*. He offered his hand to Scott since he was the closest to him. "You seem like a new member. If you need any help, this is my assistant, Sally Winston." The woman with the long face nodded her head in recognition. "I hope you're ready for a fun fling into the past." He gave my black jeans and shirt the once-over and his face clouded. "You do know that we're all dressing in the style of that time."

I stepped forward to say something, but Kevin St. John swooped in first. He stood between us and Norman, and did his best to hide us from sight.

"They're not here for your event." The manager of Vista Del Mar was in an extreme mode I'd never seen before. He directed my three early birds to the registration counter to get their room keys. "I'm sure I mentioned to you that there is another much smaller, really tiny retreat going on here this weekend, too. They were already booked," the dark-suited moonfaced manager said. There was a quiver in his voice. Was he actually nervous?

I was stunned. This man had been nothing but trouble since I took over my aunt's business. She had never said anything about him, so I don't know if he gave her problems or just saved it all for me. The basic issue was that he wanted to have complete control of the hotel and conference center and arrange all the retreats himself instead of offering space to people like me and letting us plan our own events. When I kept refusing to turn the business over to him, he finally gave up. Then he realized I could be helpful to the place. My retreats always have a lot of impromptu gathering of knitters and he'd seen it as another activity to offer the guests. So, anytime there was any knitting going on in a public area, all guests were welcome to join in or even get a knitting lesson.

Norman Rathman didn't look happy. "My understanding was that we had the whole place. The point of our events are that we are completely steeped in a past year."

"That's the beauty of Vista Del Mar," the manager said. "If ever there was a perfect place to put on an event like yours, it's here. The furnishings in this room are still true to its original style. And since we've gone unplugged, there are no people hovering over laptops or staring at tablets or cell phone screens." He pointed toward the row of vintage phone booths that had been added. He segued right into the accommodations. The guest rooms had no telephones or televisions, only old clock radios—the kind that installing meant just plugging in. Kevin St. John did have a point. The place was like a blank canvas when it came to making it appear like any time in the last fifty years.

There was, however, a sound system and I noticed music playing over the buzz of conversation. I couldn't make out anything beyond the beat. Norman seemed to notice it as well. "Who put together the playlist?" he asked.

Kevin St. John's tense look turned to one of pride. "I did."

The president of the Favorite Year Club let out a disapproving sigh and pointed up in the vague direction the music was coming from. "If this is any example of your arrangements for the retreat, I'm very disappointed. Manfred Mann didn't come out with 'Do Wah Diddy Diddy' until 1964. Maybe I better have a look at the list of songs."

Kevin looked stricken and gave me a dirty look, no doubt because I had just witnessed his dressing-down. "I'll take care of it immediately and check all the songs," he said, quickly stepping away and going toward the business area.

"Remember, earlier is okay, but later than 1963 isn't. We're not putting on a retreat for clairvoyants," Norman said with a warning tone.

I glanced around the large main room of the Lodge, realizing I hadn't asked Kevin St. John where he wanted me to leave the cream cheese brownies. I noticed that the crowd was made up of people of all ages. For some, 1963 was a memory, and for others, it was an ancient time when the TV show *Mad Men* took place. Interspersed with the crowd, I noticed several easels holding posters, and one that had a blown-up version of a baseball card. I caught sight of a table being set up with drinks and snacks at the back of the room, but then I saw someone else who grabbed my attention.

"What is she doing here?" Norman Rathman said just as I was having the same thought. I turned toward him and quickly ascertained the *she*'s we were referring to were different. His *she* was a woman in the corner of the large room near the gift shop and both Norman and Sally Winston were staring at her. I couldn't help but think of that saying if looks could kill, that woman would be dead. Was it because of her outfit? She must have gotten the year of their event wrong because the gauzy print skirt sprinkled with sparkly spots that caught the light and white tunic top looked to me to be more the style from the hippie era or the present day. The look had never gone out of fashion. Even from this distance I could see her large dangle earrings. They seemed to have tiny pieces of something shiny that reflected back the light. She had a scarf tied around her dark hair. Busy talking to someone, she didn't seem to even notice Norman and Sally's presence, let alone their reaction to her. After a moment I noticed they moved off in the other direction.

The *she* I was referring to was in the seating area around

the massive stone fireplace. The early birds had just rejoined me, now with their room numbers and keys. They stuck with me as I moved toward the woman in the seating area.

"I guess you figured out that there is a 1963 retreat also going on this weekend," I said with an apologetic smile to the three of them.

"It should be fine. It doesn't matter what they're wearing," Scott said. "If any of them want to learn how to knit, I'm still game."

The four of us stopped at the reddish brown leather couch. The coffee table in front of it had a selection of *Life* and *Look* magazines with 1963 dates. There were several books as well. The titles were unfamiliar to me, but I guessed *The Bell Jar* and *The Spy Who Came in from the Cold* were from 1963, unless Kevin St. John had screwed it up.

"Oh, good you're here," Madeleine Delacorte said, looking up at me. I tried to hide my discomfort as I greeted her. I was sure she was glad I was there because she wanted me to do something. She was one of the Delacorte sisters, the family I'd described as local royalty. She and her sister, Cora, were the last of the family, and they controlled the estate and owned Vista Del Mar.

I had thought of Madeleine Delacorte as the quiet sister, until recently. She'd been more than quiet, and at times I actually wondered if she talked at all. That is, until she'd gone through a transformation, which she somehow connected to me.

It had turned out that Madeleine had been a knitter, and thanks to the last retreat, she had rediscovered her love of the craft, as long as she did it with me. I had been surprised to learn that she was actually the older sister, and while I genuinely liked her and was happy to spend time with her, I felt a sense of obligation. She and Cora were the ones forcing Kevin

St. John to continue giving me a great deal for the retreats. And she was used to having someone accompany her, which more and more, had become me.

"I didn't expect to see you here," I said to Madeleine after introducing her to my group. That was a nicer way of saying, "What are you doing here," which was really what I wanted to know.

"Are you kidding? As soon as I heard what Kevin had arranged for this weekend, I had to be here. Nineteen sixty-three was a great year for me." While she talked, she kept glancing at the crowd and smiling. "Look at the gloves that woman is wearing." I followed her gaze and did a double take at the long white gloves one of the women was wearing. "And all the pillbox hats. Everybody wanted to look like Jackie Kennedy then. It's good they've made a point of celebrating the summer of 1963. It was still a happy time." Her smile dimmed. "Then that November, it all changed."

She came back to the present and looked at my group. "Casey has told me all about you. Now who's who?" She laughed as she pointed to Scott. "Well, of course I know which one you are. But you two . . ." Her voice trailed off as she studied Bree and Olivia. "Casey said one of you has young kids. That has to be you," she said, pointing at Bree. "You look like a kid yourself, though I guess it is all relative. Compared to me, you are." She nodded toward Olivia. "So that means you are the one who has turned great unhappiness into a new purpose in life. I think your name is Olivia Golden."

Madeleine turned to me. "See, you're not the only detective around here."

I blushed at the reference and told her I was hardly a detective. "I love that you are a sleuth. It's so fascinating. This town was pretty dull before you moved here."

I blushed again as she patted the seats around her and urged my group to sit.

Madeleine had gone from mousy quiet to almost bossy, and the three of them followed her suggestion. I was about to excuse myself when Madeleine looked across the room with a start. "I'd know those green eyes anywhere." Green eyes? I'd heard that before from Wanda when she'd been complaining about the singer the resort she worked at had hired. I followed Madeleine's sight line. A man in a suit that seemed to change colors when the light caught it was standing in the front of the cavernous room. He had his arm over one of the large posters and was posing for pictures with the retreaters. Most of them were using real cameras. The kind that used film that had to be developed. They seemed like relics from the stone age compared to the instant gratification we'd gotten used to with digital photography. Norman plowed through the group and snatched a cell phone out of someone's hand with a severe shake of his head. I actually saw his point. There was something out of sync about seeing someone trying to manipulate her cell phone camera through elbow-length black gloves.

Bobbie Listorie's hair seemed a little too dark and full and didn't quite work with his tanned complexion. If he was a singing sensation in 1963, he had to be around Madeleine's age. No one ever spoke of the two sisters' ages, but I thought they were into their seventies, though seventies weren't what they used to be. Nobody fits the image of an old granny in a rocking chair anymore, or some old grandpa clacking his false teeth. The singer appeared quite fit, but then Wanda had said he played a lot of golf.

"Sing for us, Bobbie," some people began to plead. He did a whole act of trying to appear humble and then promised he'd perform on Saturday night.

Sally Winston, the 1963 retreat leader's assistant, was standing near me and I overheard her telling the people around her about the singer. I thought she was doing it more to be the center of attention than offer necessary information. Did anyone really care that he'd started out being part of a duo with his cousin? But I was impressed that their retreat had actual researchers.

The early birds seemed anxious to go to their rooms and drop off their stuff. They were familiar with the place, and as they left, I heard them talk about meeting shortly for a knitting session. The building their rooms were in had a comfortable lobby with a fireplace and was a perfect place to hold their get-together. I wondered if Madeleine wanted to join them, but she seemed too immersed in the scene from the other retreat to even notice their departure.

Madeleine grabbed my arm and got me to sit next to her. "I can't believe Bobbie Listorie is really here. I have to talk to him and show him this." I noticed that she had taken out an old 8 by 10 photo, which she put in front of me. It showed Madeleine in the middle of two men and all three were holding up champagne glasses. "That's him," she said, pointing at one of the men. "And that's my brother, Edmund."

As she went on about how special the night was, I looked more closely at the photograph. The second man was Bobbie Listorie, who was much thinner and younger looking, with no pouches below his eyes and a chin that didn't sag below the dimple in it, but his basic body shape was the same. Yet I was really more interested in Edmund Delacorte—who wasn't so much handsome as dashing. Madeleine was all aflutter about Bobbie Listorie for a few more minutes, but then she began to talk about her brother.

She started on a story I'd heard before about how her brother had bought Vista Del Mar and saved it. By then it had gone from its original incarnation as a camp to a run-down resort. Edmund had loved the place, and instead of modernizing it, he had refurbished the place and captured its original rustic charm. "Edmund would appreciate how much Kevin St. John cares, but he'd probably tell Kevin to lighten up." Madeleine's eyes started to dance as she looked at me. "Edmund was so much fun." My attention lagged as she talked on about how her mother was so concerned that the three siblings behave so properly and act as an example to the people of Cadbury and would have been horrified if she knew what she and Edmund had done on a trip to San Francisco.

"We went there because he was giving a speech about saving Monterey Bay. But he also took me to Fisherman's Wharf and we ate fish and chips with our fingers. I took off my scarf and let my hair blow all over the place on the ferry ride to Sausalito. We ran and jumped on the cable car as it was going up Nob Hill. And finally we ate moo goo gai pan in Chinatown before we went to Bobbie Listorie's show. Edmund had connections everywhere. That's how we ended up drinking champagne backstage."

"Did Edmund's wife go with you?" I asked. Madeleine's eyes clouded.

"No. She was nothing like my brother." The Delacorte sister stopped for a moment to consider her words. "You see my mother had big plans for Edmund to run for governor and she helped him find the right sort of wife." It was pretty clear that Madeleine hadn't really liked her, but understood why her brother married her. It was a strategic match for his political aspirations.

Madeleine seemed to have something else on her mind. She checked the area around us and then leaned closer. "I'm going to tell you something that nobody else knows." I leaned closer to her in anticipation of the big secret. But when I heard what it was, I felt like rolling my eyes in frustration. I was hoping she'd divulge something about Edmund's woman on the side, but instead it was just a story about how she'd seen Bobbie Listorie perform another time. She seemed so excited about it I couldn't really follow the story and just smiled and nodded in response. When she took a breath, I tried to change the subject.

"What about Edmund's family?" It was another case where I knew the answer, but was curious on her take. She blinked a few times at my off-subject question.

"He had one son, James. Barely a year after Edmund died from an infection, his wife and son were killed in a car accident. There was a rumor that he had a mistress and another child . . ." Her voice trailed off. "There is just no proof. Cora was certainly happy when that whole story died." Madeleine looked at me directly. "Edmund had specified in his will that Vista Del Mar was to go to his children. So if there had been a secret child, they could make a claim on the place." She glanced around the interior of the Lodge as if she was imagining a new owner. "Who knows what some stranger might do to the place."

"You keep talking about Cora's reaction to a secret heir. How would you feel about it?"

Madeleine took a moment to think about it. "I suppose it would depend on who the person was." She seemed suddenly puzzled. "Why are we even talking about this? It's a dead subject." And just like that, she went back to talking about how excited she was to see Bobbie Listorie again. She seemed pretty interested in Jimmie Phelps, too, which surprised me. He was the baseball player from 1963 that Crystal had mentioned. Had Madeleine been a Giants fan?

A woman with bright platinum hair had just come in and

Madeleine squealed. "Dotty Night is here, too. She was one of the only actresses Mother approved of. She barely got to kiss her leading man." Madeleine seemed intent on watching the three special guests of the retreat.

I made a move to get up. "I have to drop these off," I said, holding up the dessert carrier. "Then I'm going to go."

Madeleine appeared stricken. "Oh, there is a mixer in a while and I was hoping you would stay and then you would take me over to meet them." She gestured toward the three celebrity guests.

"I saw the two men outside before talking to that woman." Madeleine indicated the woman in the gauzy skirt and big earrings. "I went over to join them, but they ignored me." She let out a frustrated sigh. "They were talking about the concert and fireworks show at the baseball park, but Bobbie had it all wrong. I was going to say something, but I'm not used to breaking into a conversation. It would be completely different if you introduced me."

Inwardly I rocked my head in frustration. Madeleine had come out of her shell and even changed her look. Her dark hair was cut in a swingy bob and she was wearing one of her first-ever pairs of jeans. But she still required a certain level of attention. She was accustomed to someone accompanying her to sort of clear the path.

"I really have to go," I said.

Madeleine let out a disappointed sigh. "What's the rush?" Then her eyes lit up. "That's right. I heard you have a date with that handsome cop."

I felt color going to my face. Did the whole town know I was having dinner with Dane? "It's not really a date. It's just dinner." I caught Madeleine's eyes as they did a tiny disbelieving roll. "I'm sure Kevin St. John would be glad to make sure you meet everybody," I offered.

"I suppose he would do it because we own the place," she said, sounding disappointed. "But you'd do it because we were girlfriends."

When she put it that way, what else could I do? "Okay," I said. I didn't really mind helping Madeleine meet the celebrities or make new social connections. It was actually exciting watching her start a new chapter in her life. Maybe it gave hope to me. "How about this. I'll go home and change for my whatever it is. Then I'll come back for the mixer and help you meet them."

Madeleine's face lit up in a big smile. "Perfect."

I wish she hadn't said that. It seemed like she was daring fate.

5

SINCE I WAS GOING TO DO A GIRLFRIEND THING FOR Madeleine by handling her introduction to the singer, baseball player and actress, she wanted to do a girlfriend thing for me and offered to come home with me and help me figure out what to wear. Girlfriends? I hadn't exactly thought of our relationship that way, probably because of the age difference. I was thirty-five and she was seventy-something. It surprised me, too, that it seemed no matter how old women got, they still used that term. Anyway, I appreciated her thought but I had convinced Madeleine to stay at Vista Del Mar.

Much as I had argued to the contrary, it was really a date, although a short one with a defined ending since we both had to go to work afterward. I rummaged through my closet wondering how there could be so many clothes but nothing to wear. There was a package stashed at the back of the closet. A gift from my mother. I opened it and looked at the long cotton turquoise dress before shoving it back in the box.

I wasn't twelve anymore with my mother picking my clothes. The thing was, I kind of liked the dress. But it didn't seem to be me. I took it out and held it up against myself and looked in the mirror.

Julius had come in and was making figure eights through my ankles before sitting down next to me. "What do you think? Should I wear it?" I asked. He blinked a few times and then I swear it was like he nodded. Was I really going to wear something my mother sent me?

I generally wore black or blue jeans. Nothing really girly. The dress was linen with spaghetti straps and had long narrow lacy inserts on the front and back and slid on easily. I had to admit that it fit perfectly and looked great. I added a black crocheted choker with a pearl in the middle that my aunt had made and found a pair of sandals. Bare shoulders didn't work with the weather here, so I finished it off with a triangular-shaped shawl made with colorful yarn that complemented the color of the dress. Another of my aunt's creations, of course.

Because of the white sky, the light looked the same as it had hours ago. As I went back across the street, I needed to look at my watch to tell that it was late afternoon. Once I was back on the grounds of Vista Del Mar, I noticed people coming down the sloped roadway toward the Lodge. Their attire surprised me. Because of the camplike feel and weather of Vista Del Mar, most of the guests usually dressed in casual clothes like cargo pants and jeans topped with Windbreakers or fleece jackets. Now I watched women in black sheath dresses totter in heels over the asphalt. The men wore suits or sport jackets. It made me glad I wasn't around in 1963.

"Hey, Casey," a voice called from the small parking area. I turned just as Sammy got out of his black BMW. Seeing him wearing a tuxedo didn't really surprise me. It was what he wore when he was performing as the Amazing Dr. Sammy. He caught up with me and I saw him giving my outfit the once- and twice-over.

"You look nice," he said. He paused for a breath. "What's the occasion?"

Could he be the only one in town who didn't know about my dinner with Dane? I hoped so. Sammy was Dr. Sammy Glickner and my ex-boyfriend. He'd relocated to Monterey claiming it was because he loved the area and had nothing to do with me or any possibility of us getting back together.

He joined a local urology practice for his days and then pursued his real passion—magic—at night. I'd had mixed feelings when he'd gotten a regular gig performing table magic on weekends at Vista Del Mar. It was a more appreciative audience than he'd had at the biker bar in Seaside, but it put him in the middle of my business.

I liked Sammy. I liked him a lot. Just not as a boyfriend.

I gestured toward the Lodge building and mentioned meeting Madeleine and the mixer without actually saying that was what I'd dressed for.

"Kevin St. John hired me to mingle and do tricks. He insisted they had to be classic tricks. The kind that would have been around in 1963." Sammy seemed pleased. "Those are the fun corny tricks." He patted his sleeves and the magic wand sticking out of his pocket.

He opened the door and let me go in first. The crowd had swelled and people were standing around in small groups. Some were examining the row of placards that had been set up along the back wall featuring news stories of the time, lots of old pictures, and magazine ads for old products. The biggest crowd was at the end hovering around the movie poster of *Bridget and the Bachelor*, a blown-up rendition of Jimmie Phelps's baseball card and finally a poster of Bobbie

Listorie's 1963 album cover. It probably helped that the three celebrities were standing next to their posters.

Trays of food had been set out, including my cream cheese brownies cut into bite-size pieces.

"Well, it's showtime for me," Sammy said. "How about a hug for good luck?" He held out his arms. He had a hulky teddy-bearish build and he always gave more than he got in the hug department. There was no way I could say no to the puppy dog adoration in his eyes, so I stepped into the hug and added a kiss on his cheek.

"Thanks," he said, his eyes shining when I'd stepped away. "Maybe we can grab a bite of dinner after my show." He seemed to be making an effort to make it sound casual.

I mumbled something about having to work later and escorting Madeleine. His face fell a little, but not nearly as much as it would have if he'd known about dinner with Dane.

We parted ways and Sammy went into his act. He was a natural performer with his warmth and basic friendliness. By the time I found Madeleine in the sitting area, he'd already started performing to a small clump of people.

"There you are," Madeleine said, waving me over. "Bree, Scott and Olivia are here, too," she said. "I told Kevin St. John that your group should have access to all the big events this weekend."

"How'd he take it?" I asked. Kevin St. John had been somewhat used to answering to Cora, but now he had two Delacorte sisters he had to please. I'm sure he didn't like it that Madeleine hung around Vista Del Mar so much, either. It cut into his ability to act like the lord of the place.

I wanted to get the introductions that Madeleine wanted over as soon as possible, so I could leave. I held her elbow and cleared the way through the crowd toward where the three celebrity guests were holding court.

Kevin St. John was at the front of the room introducing Sammy, and for the moment the three celebrities were alone. "I have someone who'd like to say hello," I said, taking Madeleine by the hand and moving her in front of them. As soon as they heard the Delacorte name, they all turned on the charm. But she only had eyes for Bobbie Listorie. She held out the photograph from years ago and started to gush.

"My brother, Edmund, took me to your show. We came backstage afterwards."

I watched as he smiled and took her hand. "Of course I remember," he said. "You were wearing that lovely dress. It was a special occasion, wasn't it?"

Madeleine gushed more. "You do remember. It was for my birthday. That was my favorite black dress."

While they talked, I watched. It was amazing how much Bobbie Listorie still resembled the old picture of himself, but then he'd kept the same slicked-back hairstyle, wore a similar-styled suit, his green eyes still sparkled and the dimple in his chin was hard to miss. I wasn't sure if he really remembered Madeleine or not, but he certainly convinced her he did.

He squeezed her hand and I thought she might faint. "I was there for that show you did at Candlestick Park, too."

"That was a pretty special night," Jimmie Phelps said, stepping closer. "It was the only time we had a baseball game and a concert on the same day. Then you must have been there for the fireworks." He seemed genuinely friendly, unlike Bobbie's more calculated demeanor.

"They were really something," Madeleine began before Bobbie joined in.

"They were beautiful, weren't they? I love a good fireworks show," Bobbie added. "You know, I'm going to be playing Vegas. Two weeks to start with in the lounge at the Sahara

Sands. The Bobberino is going to be back where he belongs."
He winked at Madeleine and she fluttered her eyes and
smiled. It was cute the way she was flirting.

"Don't leave me out of all this," Dotty Night said. She
reached out and took Madeleine's hand and said how nice it
was to meet her. Madeleine was thrilled with all the attention
and I decided to stay a little longer

Across the room, Sammy was working the crowd. He
had gone up to a couple and made a coin appear from the
woman's hair. Just then I noticed some loud voices. Norman
Rathman was talking to the woman in the gauzy skirt I'd
seen before. *Talking* wasn't quite the right word. It was more
like yelling. "You have to leave." He didn't seem to notice
that everyone was looking at them.

"You're going to ruin everything," he said in a sharp tone.

I felt someone pushing through the crowd behind me and
recognized Sally Winston. She looked toward the confrontation. "Oh, no," she said, viewing the couple. "I knew she was
going to cause trouble."

My detective antennae went up, and I couldn't help asking her who *she* was.

"That's Diana Rathman, Norman's wife," Sally said.
"They're in the process of getting a divorce."

"Time for the Amazing Dr. Sammy to come to the rescue.
I can turn these two into love birds," Sammy said to the crowd
as he joined the battling couple in the center of the room. He
took a hammy bow and pulled out his magic wand. "I know
why you're upset," he said to Diana. "You wanted him to bring
you flowers." Sammy did a few waves of his hand and then
snapped the magic wand and a bouquet appeared. He tried
to give it to Norman's wife, but she pushed it away.

"Oh, please," she said, annoyed. "What's next. A row of
scarves?" With that she grabbed the sleeve of his jacket and

pulled out a chain of brightly colored silks. A gasp went through the crowd and I felt for Sammy. The crowd might have figured out that he did have things up his sleeve, but to have someone so blatantly point it out had to be embarrassing.

Sammy didn't miss a beat. "Thank you," he said with a gesture toward Diana. "Let me introduce my new assistant." The crowd loved it, but Diana scowled at him. Sammy tried to carry on and took out a deck of cards. He fanned them out and held them toward the crowd, asking someone to pick a card.

I figured he had everything under control and I really had to go. I passed Kevin St. John making his way through the crowd to them. I looked back before I went out the door just as Diana Rathman flipped the cards out of his hand. Poor Sammy. How embarrassing.

6

THE DINNER BELL WAS BEGINNING TO RING AS I rushed down the driveway of Vista Del Mar. Meals were included and served in the Sea Foam dining hall. It was one of the features that made the resort a great place to hold retreats. When I glanced behind me, the crowd was coming out of the Lodge door and heading toward the dining hall. I went across the quiet street to get my car.

Even though Dane lived down the street, we'd agreed to meet at the restaurant since I'd be sticking around afterward to do my baking and he would be heading to the police station and his shift. When I looked down toward his place, his red Ford 150 wasn't in his driveway.

Just before I pulled away in my Mini Cooper, I gave a last glance toward the house. Julius must have heard the car and jumped on the kitchen counter. I saw the black cat looking out the kitchen window. I was glad he was inside. It was useless trying to make him an indoor cat and I'd arranged it so he could come and go as he pleased, but now that it was twilight, I didn't like to think of him as wandering alone outside.

Lights were coming on as I drove to downtown Cadbury by the Sea. I had dropped off my muffin-making supplies at the restaurant earlier in the day. I was still a little nervous about this dinner with Dane and tried to distract myself with thoughts about the fuss between Norman Rathman and his wife. He seemed to want her to leave the conference yet she wanted to stay. I had a feeling she was going to win out and I wondered if there would be repeats of their scene all weekend. I hoped not. The distraction ended, and before I could come up with something else to think about, my thoughts returned to Dane. I had been drawn to him since the very beginning no matter how much I tried to deny it. But something had always gotten in the way of us doing anything more than flirting.

He came from a different world than I did, for sure. I had two parents who probably focused too much attention on me. I'd found out recently that he'd never known his father, and his mother was an alcoholic who still hadn't tamed her demons. Dane had acted like the man in the family from the time he was a kid and had taken care of his mother and his sister. His sister said everybody had thought he was this tough bad boy type but in reality he was the one keeping his family together. He'd even been the one to take his sister shopping for her first bra. It was obvious he had a lot of character, even if he came off as a little cocky. How could you not be attracted to someone like that? And did I mention that he was hot?

I turned off the motor and sat for a minute. Was I really doing the right thing? Was I opening a door that should be left closed? All kinds of messy scenarios played in my mind. "Shut up," I told myself. "It's only dinner."

There was a line of people waiting for tables on the porch

of the Blue Door. The restaurant was always busy from the time they opened until I came in to do my baking. For good reason. Lucinda and her husband had turned the old house into a charming place with wonderful food. Lucinda was standing by the front counter when I came in. It was habit, but I looked at the array of desserts on the covered pedestal dishes. One of the waitresses was just taking a slice of the flourless chocolate cake I'd baked the night before. There was a quarter of it left. The pound cake next to it was in a similar state.

"Don't worry, your desserts are moving. We always run out of them before we run out of customers," my friend said. She looked at my dress and gave me a discreet thumbs-up. "He's already here," she said with a knowing smile.

When I said the Blue Door had been a house before it had been a restaurant, I probably should have specified small house or cottage. The dining area was spread through what had once been a living room, another small room beyond and the sunporch on the end. I was hoping we'd be seated on the sunporch. There was only room for a few tables and it was probably the most private spot in the place.

But Lucinda pointed to a table in the former living room in front of a window that looked out on Grand Street. Dane looked up and our eyes met, then his gave my outfit the once-over. He stood up as I approached the table and pulled out my chair. Since I'd seen him either in his uniform or something casual like jeans and a hoodie, I guess that was what I expected him to show up in. But he had on a dress shirt and a sport jacket and he smelled of woodsy cologne. He'd gone whole hog.

"I thought you might have stood me up," he said, looking at his watch with mock seriousness. He pointed at the chair. "But now that you're here, let's get this date started. Sit."

I had this horrible urge to take off when he said the word

date. What had I gotten myself into? What were we going to talk about? Maybe this was the time to tell him what I'd learned about Edmund Delacorte's love child. He had nothing to gain or lose if a Delacorte heir showed up, but I was sure he'd have an opinion. I could tell him about the information I had and see what he thought I should do with it.

"I'm sorry I'm late," I said before telling him about the mixer and Madeleine wanting me to be her escort. I went on about the 1963 retreat people and how one of them had tried to ruin Sammy's show. Dane listened with interest, then he reached over the table and took my hand.

"We're really doing it this time. Just you and me. Our first real date."

There is something else about the Blue Door. The tables are very close together. In other words, what Dane said was heard by everyone at the tables around us.

"Aw, how sweet," I heard someone say from the next table. "You two make such a cute couple."

"Don't they," I heard someone else say before explaining that I was a dessert baker and he was a cop.

"Oh, to be young and in love," a white-haired woman said. It was followed by more comments wondering about our future together. A man walked by and nudged Dane. "Looks like you've found a keeper."

There were more comments like was I going to bake my own wedding cake and would we have the reception at the Blue Door.

I don't know about Dane, but I was slumping farther and farther down into my chair. I hadn't considered what it was like to date someone in a small town. Everyone was in our business and apparently not afraid to let us know.

Even Lucinda and her husband, Tag, weren't much better. Tag hovered, wanting to make sure everything was just right, and Lucinda kept dropping comments about what a cute couple we made each time she went by.

"What have we done?" I said in a whisper. It was really more what had I done. I was still uncertain about how long my future was going to be in Cadbury, and I was trying to keep myself unfettered.

"I should have realized what we were in for," he said. "Let's try to make the best of it. I promise no more hand touching and I won't throw any adoring looks your way," he said with a teasing laugh.

We ended up eating dinner like two strangers, barely talking except to ask for something to be passed. There was no way I was going to bring up the contents of the envelope with so many ears taking in everything we said. It was a relief when we got to coffee. We were going to share a dessert, but decided not to. It would just give more fodder to our fellow diners.

Lucinda refused to bring us a check and then stepped away as Dane looked at his watch. "Duty calls. I'm sorry this didn't turn out the way it was supposed to."

"It's not your fault. I'm not used to being watched and having people tell you what they're thinking."

Dane laughed and started to reach toward me, but retracted his hand. "How about you walk me to the truck," he said.

It had grown dark and the stores were beginning to close as we walked out onto the main street. As soon as we were outside, both of us relaxed. "I should have known. Next time will be better," he said.

"Next time? Maybe this was a bad idea. I'm not so sure about being the topic of town gossip."

Dane grabbed my arm. "You look for an excuse to back away, don't you?" I looked down. He knew about my history of not staying with things very long.

"At least give me a second chance." Before I could respond, he'd put his arms around me and pulled me to him. And then he kissed me. Not that I minded. It was everything I thought it would be and more. Like sticking my finger in an electric socket, but in a good way. Boy, was I in trouble, or maybe not. Suddenly we were flooded by light and I heard a voice over a loudspeaker in a singsongy tone.

"Dane and his girlfriend sitting in a tree. Looks like they're k-i-s-s-i-n-g."

"Aw geez," Dane said as we stepped apart. When I looked at the curb, a police cruiser had pulled over and trained its spotlight on us. The cop stuck his head out of the window.

"Way to go, Mangano."

HOURS LATER WHEN EVERYTHING WAS CLOSED UP for the night and the streets were deserted, I carried out all the containers full of muffins. In honor of the 1963 retreat, I had baked classic blueberry muffins with no cute second name from me. I had left a change of clothes with the muffin ingredients and was now wearing comfortable jeans dusted with flour and a beige fleece jacket that had a nice blueberry stain on it.

Dane had gone off to work. He had desk duty and was probably sipping coffee at the police station a few blocks away. My feet echoed on the empty sidewalks as I dropped off the muffins at the local coffee spots. It didn't matter that they were closed. They all had a place to leave deliveries. I picked up the empty containers from the previous day and loaded them back in the car.

It had been a very, very long day and the concept of a long sleep sounded appealing. Finally, I started up the Mini Cooper and headed for home and my last delivery—to the café at Vista Del Mar.

Without thinking, I pulled into my driveway. The head-lights illuminated the stoop outside my kitchen door, where I noticed a dark hump of something. I cut the motor and left the headlights on as I got out to see what it was. Or who it was, I thought, as I realized that it was a slumped figure.

"Sammy?" I exclaimed as I got closer. At the sound of his name, his head shot up, then wobbled.

"Case, am I glad to see you," he said in a slurred voice. He put his hand in front of his eyes to block the bright light, but I could still see that his features looked vague. Was Sammy drunk? I'd never known him to be much of a drinker, other than a glass of wine or champagne to celebrate something.

I went back to the car and shut off the headlights and he lowered his hand. "Thanks," he said. He made an effort to stand, but slipped back down before he could manage it. Before I could ask him what was going on, he grabbed my arm. "Case, I've done something terrible." He stopped abruptly and said something about feeling a little queasy and then mumbled to himself that he was a doctor and should know what to do about it.

He seemed to want to explain something about the magic act earlier, but he wasn't making much sense. He certainly wasn't in any condition to drive himself and I wasn't so sure how he'd react to riding anywhere, since he wasn't feeling well. I considered letting him sleep it off at my house, but rejected that idea since mine was the only room set up as a bedroom.

I glanced across the driveway at the guest house my aunt had created out of her stand-alone garage. I had lived there comfortably while she was alive. The furniture was all still there. Lately I had just used my former home to put together and store the mystery bags for my retreat. I had discovered it was better to keep the bags away from the playful paws of a cat.

I steered Sammy toward the door and opened it for him. When I flipped on the light, I saw all the bright red tote bags lined up on the counter that blocked off the tiny kitchen area and also served as a place to eat.

"You're the best, Case," Sammy said as I helped him inside. "Like I always say, you're the only one who gets me." The words all ran together and I probably wouldn't have understood what he was saying if it hadn't been something he said all the time. He was leaning all over me and clearly still very drunk as he muttered on about breaking some illusion and that it was wrong, but he had to do it. It sounded like it had to do with his magic act and I wondered if something more had happened after I left. I had to prop him up against the wall, so that I could pull down the foldaway bed. It had barely touched the floor before he fell across it mumbling a thank-you, which quickly morphed into a soft snore. I managed to get his feet on the bed and take off his shoes. I pulled the colorful afghan my aunt had made for me over him before shutting off the light and walking back outside. Julius was in the window and had watched the whole thing.

"It's not what you think," I said. "It's just one night until he sobers up." The truth was I somehow felt responsible for Sammy. If I hadn't moved here, he wouldn't have followed me. Of course, he insisted that he'd relocated here and joined a urology practice in Monterey because he liked the area and it had nothing to do with me. Sure, right. And he wouldn't have gotten the gig doing magic at Vista Del Mar if I hadn't been doing the retreats there. So whatever had gone wrong that made him get drunk was more or less my fault.

I started to walk toward my back door and remembered the muffins. Rather than pull the car out, I decided to walk the supply across to Vista Del Mar. There were no streetlights here on the edge of Cadbury and it was pitch dark, so

I grabbed my flashlight as I took out the plastic container of blueberry muffins.

The grounds of Vista Del Mar were quiet and the windows in the guest rooms all were dark. Even the small lights that illuminated the edge of the roadway had been turned off. Though the lights still blazed in the Lodge. Since it functioned as the lobby and registration for the place, it stayed open 24/7. Inside the cavernous room was empty. I waved at the sleepy-looking clerk leaning on the huge registration counter. I left the plastic container outside the door of the shuttered Cora and Madeleine Delacorte Café and made my way back across the room. It had been Kevin St. John's idea to give that name to the café. He knew whom he had to please.

And now to bed, I thought as I walked back into the dark night. I had just started down the driveway that led to the street when I heard a rustle in the brush. There were no buildings on this part of the grounds, just land with shrubs and grasses left to grow as they wanted, which meant there was a tangle of undergrowth below the stand of tall Monterey pines.

I automatically trained my flashlight where the noise had come from. A deer stopped in its track, momentarily stunned by the light, and then it loped away and disappeared in the brush. I started to move the flashlight back to lighting my way, but the beam of light reflected off something glittering in the distance. My curiosity was instantly stirred and I thought about finding out what I was seeing. But then I reconsidered and turned the flashlight back to where I was headed.

Did I really want to go stumbling through the undergrowth? Who knew what I might step on? I shuddered as I thought of something that I'd heard. There was a rumor that not only trees that fell were left to decompose naturally, but any animals that died on the grounds were left as well.

I took a step toward home, but stopped to run the light over the undergrowth one more time. There seemed to be multiple spots picking up the light and shining it back, making me even more curious. Still the idea of tripping over twigs and through dead grass seemed like a bad idea. That is, until I noticed an old path leading back into the area.

I pointed my flashlight ahead to light the way, hating to admit that the bits of sparkling light were drawing me toward them like a moth to a flame.

I could feel my heartbeat pick up in anticipation as my feet crunched twigs and dry grass on the path. I got to a clearing and the spots of brightness were just ahead. I began to notice there was something colorful around them and quickened my step.

It all came into focus now and I recognized what I was looking at. I don't know what I expected the source of the glittering to be, but certainly not tiny mirrors on a gauzy piece of fabric. There was another source of reflection. Something metallic with a lot of detail. An earring? I stepped even closer and then shrank back in horror as I realized there was a woman sprawled on the ground. I shone the light on her face. It was Diana Rathman, the woman who had ruined Sammy's show.

7

I CHECKED FOR DIANA'S PULSE AND FOUND NONE.
There were bruises on her neck and red spots on her neck,
face and around her eyes. By now I knew those were the
signs of strangulation. But I was hardly a doctor and rushed
to call the paramedics in the hopes I was wrong.

I was operating on adrenaline now and without thought
propelled myself to the Lodge to use their phone since now
that Vista Del Mar was unplugged my cell phone was useless. The sleepy clerk snapped to attention when I said there
was an emergency. I called it in and then left the clerk to
notify Kevin St. John.

I was waiting in the long driveway of Vista Del Mar when
the rescue ambulance came down the street. There were no
lights flashing or siren breaking the quiet of the night
because there was no need for either at this hour. The streets
of Cadbury were dead and there was no traffic to warn out
of the way. And no need to stir up the sleeping guests.

I showed the ambulance where to stop and then pointed my flashlight down the path toward the woman. Kevin St. John arrived just as a police cruiser pulled in. The headlights of the ambulance illuminated him as he got out of his tan Buick sedan. I did a double take when I realized that it was the first time I'd seen him in anything but a formal-looking dark suit. I had to choke back a nervous laugh when I saw the red and blue spatter print of his pants. I didn't know what the technical name of the style was but they ballooned around his legs and seemed to have elastic at the ankles.

His close-cropped hair looked tousled, and his expression got grimmer when he saw me.

"Ms. Feldstein, so you're connected to yet another mishap," he said in a terse tone. "Who is it this time? One of your early arrival retreat people?"

"You really shouldn't jump to conclusions," I said. It was hardly a time to feel a sense of triumph, and yet it was hard to keep that feeling totally out of my tone as I told him who I had found.

The manager swallowed hard. "You're telling me that Norman Rathman's wife is over there?" He swung his arm in the general direction of the path without looking. When I nodded, he swallowed hard again.

"That's right, Mr. St. John, it is not one of my people. It is one of your people. Norman Rathman is the head of the Favorite Year Club and the person who let you arrange their retreat?"

I'm not saying Kevin St. John had no empathy for the woman in the bushes or her family, but I'm sure the look of upset on his face was also connected to his hope that Vista Del Mar would become the regular venue for their future retreats.

The adrenaline from finding the woman was beginning to wear off and my legs felt rubbery. The fact that I'd been up for way too many hours didn't help, either. I knew the cops would want some kind of statement, and I looked around hoping I could be done with it and go home.

"You're here," I said, surprised, as Dane approached me. "I thought you were on desk duty."

"Can't stay away from trouble, can you?" he said in a teasing voice.

"Or maybe trouble can't stay away from me," I countered in a tired voice.

"As soon as I heard where the call came from and from who, I got somebody to take over for me." He looked at me closely, examining my face as he offered his arm for support. "Are you all right?"

"More or less," I said, letting out a sigh. The paramedics had the back of the ambulance open and were loading in a gurney. They were clearly not in a hurry, which confirmed that I'd been right about Diana's lack of a pulse.

Kevin St. John and another cop were conferring. "About tonight," Dane said. "I'm sorry for the way things turned out. But I think we should give it another try."

"Maybe not," I said. The expression drained from his face and his eyes grew dark. "It's nothing about you," I said quickly. "I like you—a lot. I just have a lot on my plate with all the baking and this retreat that starts tomorrow. I mean, today." I glanced down and saw the hour on my watch.

Dane's usual cocky stance had gone south and he shifted his weight with displeasure as I continued. "It doesn't mean anything has to change. I'll still leave you desserts and you can still leave off plates of your delicious pasta dishes. No way do I want to give up the chance for your lasagna oozing with cheese or anything with your homemade tomato sauce."

I was a little surprised by his response. Basically he just ignored what I'd said. "You want to call it quits after one dinner? I'm sorry for my immature cop buddy and his stupid remark, but other than that and a few comments by other diners in the restaurant, I thought it went pretty well." He looked at me directly. "If you want to avoid all the stares, we could just have dinner at my place."

"I don't think so," I said, feeling the pull of his presence even in this situation. "It was okay when we were just neighbors, but as a date—no way."

"We could try going to the movies," he offered and I rolled my eyes at his persistence.

"I just don't want to start something I'm not sure I can finish. And having the whole town watching is too much pressure." I was avoiding looking at him, afraid my resolve would melt. "I'm doing you a favor. I'm a real heartbreaker. Just ask Dr. Sammy."

"Hey, Mangano, over here," his partner shouted. I followed behind Dane as he went along the narrow path into the brush, both of our flashlights illuminating the way. The other officer was standing at the edge of the small clearing where I'd found Diana, holding a roll of yellow tape. For a moment they discussed where to position the yellow tape that marked the crime scene. There was something on the ground. "Look what I found," the other cop said as he pointed toward a long piece of brightly colored silk. I felt my breath stop. It was Sammy's long streamer of silks.

8

MY MIND WAS REELING OVER THE APPEARANCE OF the silks. Though no one had said the words, I was pretty sure they were the murder weapon. No one had said the word *murder* yet either, but they had said she appeared to have been strangled, and let's face it, that's not something she was likely to have done to herself or by accident. I didn't get off just giving a statement to Dane and his partner. Instead, as more cops came and set up a tent over the area where Diana had been found, we adjourned to the Lodge.

It felt strange to be in the large room in the middle of the night. Kevin St. John had somehow managed to change into something that looked more managerial. Maybe he kept a suit of clothes there. Someone had awakened Norman Rathman and he was sitting slumped on one of the leather sofas. He had hastily put on the suit he'd worn earlier. It appeared really strange now with the dress shirt hanging out. I recognized the elongated face of his assistant, Sally Winston, who was seated on the piano bench in another area. Had they been found together, or did she just follow wherever he went? I had been offered a chair next to my muffin container near the café. I eyed the CLOSED sign on the café door and wished I could get a cup of coffee.

I was also beginning to feel a little panicky. In a few hours, I'd be back in this same room welcoming my retreat group. Visions of me nodding off at the registration table danced anxiously through my mind. And contributing even more to my feeling of anxiety was seeing Sammy's silks.

A cop finally had come by to take my information and my statement. I simply told him what I had seen and done. I hesitated when I got to the end. There was no reason to mention what I'd seen on the ground after Diana was removed. But I couldn't get the image of the brightly colored prop out of my mind. What had Sammy done? I got up to leave. "Not yet," he'd said, gesturing back toward my seat.

The officer didn't explain why he wanted me to stay but I thought I knew the answer. When the door opened and Lieutenant Borgnine came in, I realized I was right. He glanced around the room and his gaze stopped at me. There was a flicker of "oh no" in his expression. Not that it was a surprise. And the feeling was mutual.

Lieutenant Borgnine had moved up to Cadbury after spending years working for the Los Angeles Police Department. I think he viewed working in Cadbury as retirement with pay since the crime rate was very low in the small town. Murder had been unheard of for years. And then suddenly there seemed to be an upturn in the homicides, which unfortunately seemed to coincide with my moving to town. It wasn't my fault, honest. There was a little more to the tension between us. Let's just say he'd been wrong and I'd been right on a number of cases.

He was just a little taller than me with a firepluglike shape. His hair was salt and pepper, heavy on the salt, and cut so short it was more like stubble around a generous bald spot. The rumpled gray-toned sport coat seemed to be his uniform. I still hadn't figured out if he had a number of them that all looked the same or he just always wore the same one. The surprise was, he had jeans on instead of his usual slacks. They weren't the form-fitting kind of jeans that Dane wore. I'd classify Lieutenant Borgnine's loose-fitting pair as grandpa jeans.

He had zeroed in on me and crossed directly to where I was sitting. "I dressed in a hurry," he said in a curt voice, apparently noticing that I had focused on his pant choice. "Let's get down to business," he said, taking out his notebook. "I understand you found the victim." He was doing his best to sound professional, but there was a tinge of disappointment as if, if there had to be a victim, he wished anybody else in the world had found her.

I nodded and he continued. "Is the victim one of your retreat people?"

"No," I answered.

"Any personal involvement with her?" Again I said no and he seemed a little relieved. "Then you'll just answer any question without a problem." He said it more as a statement but left it hanging like a question. Maybe we'd had a little problem in the past of me asking him too many questions and answering too few of his.

I wasn't looking to be disagreeable. In fact, I wanted to give him the information about her as quickly as possible, hoping he'd let me go without bringing up the long tail of silks. I was hoping that the lieutenant would think it was just a scarf she'd been wearing.

"Diane Rathman is the wife of the president of the organization putting on the My Favorite Year 1963 retreat." I still used the word *is*. Wishful thinking maybe? "I don't know her. In fact, I have never even spoken to her." I mentioned that I'd been with Madeleine Delacorte, hoping that he was like the rest of the town and viewed her as local royalty. "I overheard a conversation with her husband, Norman Rathman, and he seemed surprised that she'd come. And not so happy about it, either." As I said it, I dipped my head toward where Norman Rathman was sitting. I wanted to imply something without saying it. To somehow make it so that Lieutenant Borgnine would think it was his idea there was something going on between Norman Rathman and his assistant. I thought he'd be less resistant that way. "That's his assistant, Sally Winston." I did a similar move with my head toward the woman sitting on the piano bench. "She didn't seem happy to see Diana, either."

When I'd started working for the detective agency, my boss, Frank, had given me a short lecture on investigating. I'm not even sure why he bothered. I was only temp help and he had me doing phone interviews. But the information had stuck with me. Did I mention that working for Frank was my favorite of all temp jobs, and if he'd had more business, I'd probably still be in Chicago working for him? One of the things he'd said was that most killers knew their victims, usually very well, and the cops always considered spouses first. I'm sure Lieutenant Borgnine knew that and would get there on his own, but I wanted to point him in that direction on the slight possibility he wasn't thinking of it.

I made a move to get up, thinking we were finished, but he gestured for me to stay put. "You gave that up a little too easily," he said, studying my face. "What's going on?"

"Nothing," I said, putting up my hands in capitulation. "She's not one of my people, so there's no reason for me not to tell you everything I know about her or her husband or even the assistant." I couldn't resist and had to add, "Isn't it odd that Norman's assistant is here? I mean, did Kevin St. John feel obligated to notify her? Or maybe she and Norman were having a late-night meeting to discuss the next day's activities. I heard that Norman and Diana were getting a divorce. Probably a messy one. But that's not an issue anymore, is it?"

"Ms. Feldstein, I knew your cooperation was too good to be true. Just because you worked for a PI once upon a time doesn't mean you're qualified to investigate—anything." He sat forward and moved a little closer. "I understand there was some kind of altercation between Dr. Sammy Glickner and the victim."

I tried to do the cop face thing and not react to what he said, but his words hit me like an arrow and I instinctively drew back. Did that mean that someone had identified the scarf as Sammy's?

What to say, I thought, trying to come up with something that wouldn't sound defensive. The lieutenant smiled. "Don't worry, there's nothing you need to say. There were plenty of witnesses."

He abruptly snapped his notebook shut with a satisfied expression, but even so I noticed him give his right temple a slight massage. I'd heard that I'd given him a headache before, and it seemed that even when he thought he'd won, he got one anyway. And he'd probably blame me.

The night was fading when I finally went home. I'd never seen Vista Del Mar at dawn before. Other than the cop cars and the tent that had been erected over the spot where Diana had been found, the place was still. The low-hanging clouds absorbed even the sound of the rustle of the wind. Normally, I would have been fascinated by this last moment of quiet before the place began to stir, but today it only made me more apprehensive.

I glanced at the guest house before continuing on to my kitchen door. What had Sammy done? Then I mentally shook myself. Of course, nothing. Sammy was a big teddy bear who said he was a lover, not a fighter. He'd been heckled before. He'd survived doing silly magic tricks at a biker bar in Seaside. Surely one woman ruining an illusion wouldn't put him over the edge. Would it?

Julius was waiting for me when I came in the kitchen door. He rubbed against my legs in his version of a welcome. Then he sat down and looked up at me with his yellow-eyed stare. It seemed like some sort of reproach. Was he trying to ask where I'd been all night?

I didn't waste any time fussing with him and went right for the stink fish in the refrigerator. I had it wrapped in multiple layers of plastic inside a plastic bag and still the fishy odor escaped. He smelled it, too, and rubbed against my ankle, this time appearing to be saying thank you.

He was noisily eating when I went for the phone. I calculated the time difference. Even so, it was still early in Chicago, but Frank had to be up, didn't he. I punched in the number and waited.

Frank answered with an abrupt hello. I'd barely gotten my greeting out when he interrupted.

"Feldstein, is that you?" He didn't wait for my response before he continued. "Oh, no, an early morning call from you can't be good. What's wrong now?"

Frank was my former boss, the PI in Chicago. He had nothing in common with the sexy TV detectives, but then I doubted any real private investigators did. I always said he resembled the Pillsbury Doughboy more than James Bond. This wasn't the first time I'd called him for help and I knew I'd have to endure his grumbling before he gave me advice.

I was proactive this time and didn't wait for him to ask if I was still living in the place he referred to as "that town that sounds like a candy bar."

"So what is it this time?" he said. "It can't be another murder." I swallowed hard, trying to think of a way to put it so it wouldn't sound so bad. At last I croaked out a yes.

"Feldstein, you better give me the details. How do you know the victim?"

"I don't know her at all," I began. "It's more about who the cops are going to focus on. It's Sammy," I said.

"Sammy?" Frank repeated. "Is he the cop down the street you keep flirting with?"

"No, that's Dane," I said.

"I can't keep up with the men in your life. Who is this Sammy?" Frank let out a little grunt, trying to sound like he was frustrated by the whole thing. I gave him the run-down on how Sammy fit in my life, explaining that he was my ex-boyfriend from Chicago who had recently relocated to Monterey. I detailed that he was a doctor of urology who did magic on the side.

"The magic part is important," I said before describing how, in the midst of Sammy's magic act, the victim had intervened and pulled the trail of silk scarves from Sammy's sleeve. When Frank heard that the same trail of scarves had been found at the murder scene, he sighed. He sighed even more heavily when he heard that Sammy had showed up drunk on my doorstep mumbling that he'd done something terrible.

"Maybe you should just find him a good lawyer," Frank said.

"But I'm sure he didn't do it," I protested.

Frank tried to tell me that it didn't matter what I thought. "Feldstein, it sounds like he had a motive—she made him look bad in front of a crowd. He had the means, the silks you seem to think she was strangled with were his prop, and he could have easily had opportunity. You describe that place as dark and eerie. He could have been waiting behind a tree when she walked by and then . . ." It sounded like Frank snapped his fingers to re-create the sound of a breaking neck.

I let out an involuntary *ewww*.

"I'm telling you, Feldstein, your best bet is to lawyer him up before the cops even get to him." When I protested further, I could hear Frank mumbling to himself about unrealistic amateur detectives. "Okay, have it your way, defend the guy. Then why don't you just settle down with him. A nice doctor for a husband, isn't that every woman's dream?"

"You sound like my mother. Getting Sammy off the hook has nothing to do with wanting to marry him. Where should I start?"

"Feldstein, you know what to do. I know you only worked for me a short time, but I like to think I taught you a lot and I have given you advice since. Think about it."

"I suppose I should start by talking to Sammy. Maybe he has a great alibi. And I should find out what happened to the silk piece . . ." My voice trailed off as I thought about it.

"See, I told you, you know what to do. But even so, you might want to have a lawyer in the background, just in case." Just before he hung up, he told me to let him know what happened.

I sat back with the phone in my lap. I planned to think about my options, but instead drifted into a light sleep. I was vaguely aware that Julius had jumped on the couch and had cuddled next to my thigh. And then the phone in my lap rang and shattered my sleep.

"Hello," I said, snapping to attention as I answered.

"Casey, I didn't wake you, did I?" my mother said. "I have an early day and I wanted to reach you before I left. Your father and I want to wish you luck on your upcoming retreat. Everything going okay?"

At least she hadn't started in on me about going to cooking school, reminding me it was all on hold, just waiting for me to say yes. My mother was convinced that I wouldn't keep up with the retreats and she had dangled cooking school in Paris to me as an alternative. Her thinking was that at least then I would have some credentials that made me a professional baker. I admit it had sounded appealing, particularly when I ran into snags with my aunt's business. But so far I had not taken my mother up on the offer.

"Everything is going great," I mumbled in a sleepy voice. "It will be fine. I have everything covered this time." With each word, I spoke a little clearer. I just wanted to reassure her and get off the phone before I said too much.

"What's wrong, honey?" she said. How did she know something was wrong? Was it something in my voice? I thought I had sounded so confident. I don't know how my mother did it, but it was like she had some kind of radar that picked up on trouble.

I hated to let on, but when she called me honey, I melted. All the fussing between us and her reminding me that my life seemed headed nowhere went out the window. "It's Sammy," I said. Then the story tumbled out.

There was a long silence before my mother began to speak. "And his parents were upset about his magic show." She sighed and let out some disconcerted noises. "He didn't do it, did he?"

"Mother, we're talking about Sammy. He rescues spiders and takes them outside."

"But you said he was drunk." She paused a moment. "You're right. Even drunk I can't imagine Sammy strangling somebody. You have to do something. You seem to have a knack for investigating. Find out what happened before they arrest him. His parents would be devastated if he called them from jail."

Was my mother actually giving me the thumbs-up on my sleuthing? I was about to thank her for the confidence, but then she added the kicker. "Casey, he's only in all this trouble because of you. He's only there because of you."

9

IT WAS TIME TO SET UP FOR MY RETREAT. I
hesitated outside the guest house before opening the door
softly and wheeling the plastic bin in. Sammy stirred a little
as the wheels made a squeaking noise.

I was trying not to feel too guilty about what my mother
said. The worst part was I couldn't argue with it. I didn't
admit it to her, but I had already come to the same conclu-
sion. Sammy would never have moved here if I wasn't here,
so it was really all my fault he was in trouble. He was snoring lightly and had a peaceful look on his face.

"I'm sorry," I said, standing over him. "Don't worry, I'm
going to get you out of trouble." He opened his eyes a little
and looked up at me.

"That's all right, Case. I know you always come through.
You're the best." His voice still sounded under the influence.
He reached up. "Want to snuggle?" His arm fell back on the

bed and his eyes closed again as he mumbled something about how loud a noise his arm had made.

"Sammy, you don't understand. Something happened." I realized my words were hitting deaf ears. He'd already gone back to sleep and was snoring again. I straightened the afghan and went to collect the mystery tote bags.

SAMMY DIDN'T STIR WHILE I LOADED THEM IN THE bin, or even when the wheels squeaked as I rolled it to the door. He had no idea of what was brewing around him.

The grounds of Vista Del Mar were still quiet as I walked down the driveway. There were just a few stragglers coming down the roadway from the guest room buildings, headed toward the Sea Foam dining hall for breakfast. For a moment I considered joining them. The pot of coffee I'd downed on an empty stomach after talking with my mother and catching a few hours' sleep had left me feeling jumpy. The whole thing with Sammy added to my anxiety, along with the fact that my retreat was about to begin. As I neared the Lodge, the breeze carried the smell of hot food from the dining hall.

The kitchen staff excelled at breakfast and I imagined a stack of pancakes with a pool of melting butter. They always had eggs, breakfast meats and fresh fruit, too. The food might help the jumpy feeling, but I was pretty sure it would make me feel sleepy. Given the choice, I decided to endure my nerves.

I wondered how Diana Rathman's death would affect the 1963 retreat, and at the same time I was glad it wasn't my problem. It was enough to be concerned with twenty people coming for a weekend of yarn craft led by two women who I'd come to realize didn't exactly get along.

The interior of the Lodge was empty and the noise of the bin as I rolled it across the wood floor echoed in the huge room. All the decorations for the 1963 retreat were still up and there was something more. An old TV had been brought in and left in an open space between the table tennis and pool tables at the back and the seating area around the massive stone fireplace.

The space set off for my registration was behind the TV and in front of the windows that looked toward the sand dunes running between the hotel grounds and the beach. The Vista Del Mar staff had already put up two tables and provided some chairs. I arranged the bags out on one of the tables. Crystal had made up some extra bags just in case. It had been fun putting the supplies in them—deciding what kinds of yarn to add and picking out the beads from the big box we had. We'd put some charms and special beads in each one. I had made binders for everyone, too. I'd begun to understand that presentation was everything. The papers with the schedule and assorted information appeared far more impressive in a notebook than just stuck in the tote bags.

I set out the sign-in sheets, the name tags and holders, and a dish of foil-wrapped chocolate candy. I liked to start things off with a sweet touch. The setup had gone far quicker than I'd expected, and the jumpy feeling of my empty stomach had gotten worse. I decided to stop in the Cora and Madeleine Delacorte Café for a quick bite.

Since everyone was in the dining hall, the place was empty. Almost. I was surprised to see Dane in uniform leaning against the front counter. "Are you still here or here again?" I asked.

"Still," he said. "Nothing very exciting. I was just making sure no one started poking around in the tent set up around the crime scene." He dropped his voice at the end even though there was no one to hear but the guy behind the counter. And I was sure he already knew about it.

"Anything happening with the investigation?" I asked.

"Not that I know of. Lieutenant Borgnine is being very closemouthed, particularly to me." The counter man interrupted and asked for my order. I glanced at all the sweet things and even considered one of my own muffins, though that seemed a little weird.

"I'm not sure. Maybe one of the smoothies." I saw Dane shaking his head at my choice.

"Why don't you have a breakfast sandwich, my treat." He proceeded to give me a lecture on the importance of a good breakfast. My stomach grumbled in agreement and I nodded to the man.

"Any idea why Lieutenant Borgnine isn't talking?"

Dane let out a heavy sigh. "He knows I talk to you. He's probably afraid you're going to get in the middle of things again and he doesn't want me helping you. Though I don't know why you would. The victim isn't one of your people." He led me to a table by the window and we both sat.

The sandwich was delivered and I started to eat so fast, Dane had to tell me to slow down. "I don't understand how someone who bakes so well can be so lame about regular food."

"Hey, I started brewing a pot of coffee instead of using instant," I said between bites. He gave me an approving nod and I smiled, glad that he seemed to have accepted what I'd said the night before. I debated whether I should tell him about the silks. "There is a way I might be sort of involved with Diana Rathman's death."

Dane's eyes opened wider. "Oh, so you want to confess," he teased.

"Ha, ha, very funny," I said with a joking eye roll. Then

I got serious. "There might be something that looks bad, but isn't what it seems."

Dane held up his hand. "Don't say anything more, please. Whatever it is, it's better if I don't know it. Lieutenant Borgnine has already warned me that I'm not supposed to help amateur investigators—in other words, you."

I remembered Frank's advice on how to get information from Dane—flirt. I started batting my eyes and twirled a strand of hair. "C'mon, tell me what you know. You're not going to listen to him, are you?"

Dane watched in amusement, barely holding back a laugh. Once again I'd come across more as funny than sexy. Not the reaction I was going for. I said Frank gave me the advice; I didn't say I was good at it.

"Nice try, but your attempts at flirting are still too obvious. However, if you'd like to practice, I'd be glad to be your coach," Dane said with a wicked smile. He looked disappointed when I changed the subject.

"You can probably answer this, though. Do you know how it's going to affect the 1963 retreat?"

"Yup, I could answer that if I knew. But I don't." He looked at his watch. "I better check if I'm done for the day. I need my beauty sleep." He got up from the table and gave my arm an affectionate squeeze. "Next time I promise, no audience," he said. And then pursed his lips in a kiss in case I didn't get his meaning. So maybe he hadn't given up.

I finished the last of the sandwich and headed back into the main room. It had gone through a big change in the short time I'd been away. The quiet had disappeared and there was a buzz of activity. The TV was on and playing a Jack LaLanne exercise show. A group of the 1963ers were in front of the screen exercising along with Jack. One of them was wearing a Jack LaLanne–style jumpsuit and ballet slippers. Others just wore timeless-looking shorts and T-shirts. A couple of women had on black stretch pants with stirrups that went over their feet along with T-shirts. Exercise attire was certainly a lot easier to wear now.

Jimmie Phelps was bringing in a load of boxes on a dolly. It was amazing how much he'd retained the athletic build pictured on the old baseball card. He just had less hair with more silver in it. Bobbie Listorie was helping him. His attempt to keep the same look as he'd had in his younger years seemed to be based on keeping the same hairstyle and wearing the same type of clothes. And as Madeleine had said, who could miss those beautiful green eyes.

Kevin St. John was standing in front of the massive registration counter. I recognized the woman talking to him as Sally Winston, Norman Rathman's assistant. Their body language said there was some kind of dispute going on. I edged closer to hear.

"Norman Rathman would be here himself, but he's in shock. We haven't made an announcement to our people yet. But we think that under the circumstances, once we tell them, they should be given the option of leaving with a complete refund."

Kevin St. John seemed to be trying to retain his cool, but I could see the frustration building. "That's completely against our policy," he sputtered. Just then Lieutenant Borgnine joined them.

"Did I hear something about people leaving?" he said, looking at Sally Winston. She apparently thought she'd found someone who understood and proceeded to plead her case.

"Sorry, Ms. Winston," the policeman said. "I have to insist that everyone stay put until we finish our investigation."

"And when will that be?" she asked in a shrill voice.

"Certainly by the end of the weekend," he said. "In the meantime I would suggest you try to keep the weekend going as planned." He gestured toward the exercise group. "And your people needn't worry that there is some crazed killer on the loose. We're sure that it was personal to the victim." He let it all sink in for a moment before he continued. "I know we spoke last night, but I'd just like to clarify a few things while I have you here." He waited until she gave a nod of agreement. "Norman Rathman didn't seem to be aware his wife was missing. Do you know anything about that?"

Sally suddenly looked like she wished she was anywhere but there. "Norman and I were going over the program like we do at the beginning of these events. He's a bit of a perfectionist. Diana said she didn't want to disturb him and had arranged for her own room." She did her best to turn the tables on the police lieutenant. "I can assure you that he loved his wife very much."

My eyes were almost jumping out of my head, they opened so wide in disbelief. She was lying. She'd told me they were getting a divorce. I wanted so badly to butt in and tell the lieutenant, but I knew all it would do was get me in trouble. Where he was concerned, a low profile was best.

I couldn't believe what she said next. She complained that they were ruining the illusion of the 1963 retreat, and if they were going to have police officers wandering around, the least they could do was wear uniforms from 1963 and hide their cars if they couldn't get old ones.

Lieutenant Borgnine looked at her at if she was crazy. His answer was a mere shake of the head before he walked away.

"I'm sure everything will be fine," Kevin St. John said to Sally. "It's important to keep things as normal as possible."

As he said that, Jimmie Phelps began to unpack one of

the boxes. He took out some cardboard pieces, and as he assembled them, I saw that it was a life-size cardboard cut-out of him with a tray attached to the front. A prominent sign read, GET A BOOST WITH BOOST UP. Jimmie lined up rows of red-colored cans.

"What are you doing?" Sally Winston demanded. "That Boost stuff wasn't around in 1963. In those days there were only caffeine tablets. Now please take that down."

Jimmie Phelps looked at Kevin St. John. "Our agreement was I would stay here for the weekend and mingle, along with putting on a softball game, if Boost Up could be a sponsor."

Kevin St. John looked really uncomfortable. "Well, yes, I did say that . . ." Just then Bobbie Listorie chimed in, "And you said I could sell CDs."

"CDs?" Sally shrieked. "There were no CDs in 1963. It was all vinyl LPs. She grabbed one and examined the cover. "This isn't even one of your old albums."

"You've got to move with the times." He pointed out that the CD was all covers of ballads from the last ten years. She seemed upset and he looked to the manager. "The only reason I'm here is they're having a private event at my usual place." He did a couple of winks as if there was something wrong in mentioning the name of the posh resort where he was paid a retainer. Or maybe it was that he didn't want to say that he was paid a retainer to hang out and schmooze. "The point was to give the guests here a chance to take home a souvenir of the Bobbarino." He threw a seductive look Sally's way.

"What's going on? Are we having a meeting?" Dotty Night said, coming in with a box of DVDs. Her platinum hair was so bright, I thought it might glow in the dark. Sally took one look at what Dotty was carrying and got even more upset and fussed that DVDs weren't around in 1963.

"But these movies were," Dotty said. She set down the selection of movies on the table alongside Bobbie Listorie's CDs. She rechecked that the desk clerk would take care of the sales before she put out a gigantic brandy snifter and a small pad of paper. She stuck a printed note to the large glass that announced a drawing for a weekend at her inn in Carmel. Next to that she put up a small poster with a picture of the place and a stack of brochures. Sally Winston's eyes were bugging out at everything on the table. "You didn't think we were doing this just for the glory of it all, did you?"

Sally stormed off as Dotty Night commented on how odd it was that Sally had such a slender shape but such thick ankles. Adding that somebody ought to tell her that wearing capri pants only drew attention to them.

The three celebrity guests finished and then headed to the café saying they would be available to talk over old times with any of the guests.

Kevin St. John was left standing by himself. I know it was childish, but I had gotten so much grief from him whenever there was a problem with my retreats, I couldn't resist going over and gloating just a little. He had always tried to put me on the hot seat, and this time it was reserved for him.

But I didn't have to say a word. He knew why I was there. "Casey, there have just been a few snags in the Favorite Year retreat. But the sign of a true professional is that they can smooth things over. No matter what has happened so far, I'm sure by the end of the weekend, Norman Rathman will want to arrange to have their next retreat here."

Was he delusional?

10

NOW THAT EVERYTHING WAS SET UP, I WAS GOING
to sneak across the street and take a nap and I was almost
to my back door when Madeleine Delacorte drove up my
driveway in her golf cart. As soon as she saw me, she steered
next to me.

"Casey, I went over to Vista Del Mar to see what was
going on with the 1963 crowd and I heard someone died. Who
is it? Are you going to investigate? This is so exciting. The
town used to be so boring." Then she patted the seat next to
her. "Get in and you can tell me all about it."

I suggested she park the golf cart instead and we could
talk inside, but she was insistent that we'd have more privacy
this way. "There are ears everywhere," she said, her eyes
dancing. Again, I marveled at the change in her. No longer
was she walking one step behind her sister carrying her handbag Queen Elizabeth style. It was as though she'd just peeled
back a decade or so and was suddenly living with both hands.

I wasn't sure of her driving abilities and offered to take over the wheel, but she was insistent. I got in and we took off. Basically we drove on the narrow roadway that wound through the grounds of Vista Del Mar over and over while I told her everything I knew.

So much for my naptime.

"Thank heavens nothing happened to Bobbie Listorie. I can't wait until Saturday night. I know he's going to sing "It's All in the Eyes." And I'm so glad it wasn't anybody connected to our retreat. It's going to be such fun not knowing what's in your bag and then making something with it," she said, finally steering the golf cart in her designated parking spot. "They're here. Our retreaters are here," she said as a van rolled past us and pulled in front of the Lodge.

By the time we'd walked over to the building, the van was unloading. I rushed ahead as the newcomers stood around getting their luggage. Madeleine kept right up with me as I went inside.

The old TV was no longer playing *The Jack LaLanne Show* and the exercise crowd had dispersed, replaced by a small audience on folding chairs. They didn't seem to mind, but the black-and-white picture seemed so strange and rather blurry to me. A vintage episode of *American Bandstand* was playing. I stopped to look at the teenagers dancing. I couldn't believe the prim round-collared blouses and the pageboy hairstyles.

The pool and table tennis tables were both in use at the back of the room. Someone was pinning a note to the message board back by the gift shop. And all of them were dressed in some version of the retro style. Seeing all those cat's eye–shaped glasses was enough to make me do a double take.

The early birds were hanging around the registration tables waiting for me. It was easy to pick them out. They were the only ones wearing contemporary clothes. The first thing I did was tell them about Diana Rathman's death, explaining that it had nothing to do with us and assuring them there was no crazed killer on the loose, repeating what Lieutenant Borgnine had said about it being personal. They knew who she was from the scene she had made with Sammy. I didn't mention anything about his string of silks being found at the murder scene.

"We already heard about it," Olivia Golden said. "I'm glad it wasn't one of our people. And I'm glad that police lieutenant isn't going to be grilling me this time." She let out a sigh and I could see why. She'd been in the lieutenant's crosshairs in the past. Then Olivia leaned in close and dropped her voice. "I don't know if you're doing your own investigation, but if you're interested, I saw the victim having a pretty cozy conversation with him." She used her elbow to indicate Jimmie Phelps. Olivia looked around us to see if anyone was within earshot. "I didn't mean to, but I kind of overheard what they were saying. It seemed like they had some kind of history. Like she knew him from a while ago."

By now the arrivals for our retreat had checked in and gotten their room keys and were heading over to our tables. I knew I would never remember all of their names, even with name tags, so I sorted out who was who by identifying features. For example, one of the women had her hair in a funny topknot and another was holding her knitting, and whenever she stopped, her needles would start to move. I referred to her as the knitting fanatic. There seemed to always be at least one retreater who wore oversized T-shirts with either clever sayings or pictures of something near and dear to her. I noticed a woman in the group with an electric blue extra-sized shirt that had *I Knit Therefore I Am* emblazoned on the front in white letters.

They were all pulling their suitcases and looking around the huge room with puzzled expressions. The TV playing the old show and all the people in vintage clothes must have made them feel like they were in the Twilight Zone. It would have made it seem even more so if the TV had actually been playing an episode of the eerie show.

I'd have to explain.

"It looks like we're ready for business," Olivia said, coming around to the back of the table. "I'll take the first third of the alphabet," she said.

"I'll take the middle," Scott Lipton said. I was going to suggest I take the last part, but Bree Meyers grabbed the spot first.

"And I'll be on the lookout for anyone who seems a little lost," she said, reminding me that her job was to help anyone who was having trouble coping as she had on her first retreat.

"Isn't that nice that they are all helping us," Madeleine said before pulling up a chair and sitting down. I'm not sure what she considered her job to be. Observer maybe. I was left to be the greeter.

"Sorry I'm late," Lucinda Thornkill said as she joined our little group. She stowed her suitcase under the window that looked out on the wooden deck. She'd gotten stuck with the lunch setup at the Blue Door restaurant. "Tag acted like I was going a million miles away for a hundred years," she said, referring to her husband.

Madeleine listened from her spot. "Maybe that's because it took you two so long to get together." Lucinda seemed surprised at her comment, until Madeleine reminded her that the story of how they got together was on the back of the restaurant's menu. "I love a happy ending."

My friend smiled as an answer. There was no reason to bust Madeleine's romantic image and bring up Tag's shortcomings and how she needed to get a break and come to the retreats.

Lucinda pulled me aside and started talking about the case of the secret baby.

With all that had happened, I had forgotten about the envelope of evidence. "That is so yesterday's news," I said to Lucinda. "Obviously you haven't heard yet about the death here."

"Death? Who?"

I pulled her farther away from the others and gave her the details and one more. I told her about Sammy's silks being the murder weapon. I also told her how I'd found him drunk on my doorstep the night before, mumbling about something he'd done. "I left him sleeping it off in my guest house."

"Casey, we have a problem," Olivia said, interrupting my conversation with Lucinda. A woman in pedal pushers and a T-shirt with her hair in pigtails was standing by the table.

"She'd like to be part of our group, but she isn't on the list."

"Scarlett Miller," she said, putting out her hand. "I know I didn't sign up in advance for your program, but I saw women with knitting stuff getting in line and I thought, that's for me. It's my husband who is really gung ho about this Favorite Year Club. I come along for the ride. I would much rather hang out with yarn people than try to pretend I'm in a time machine. So how about it? Can I join your group?"

"Let's let her in," Madeleine said from her chair.

"That's what I was going to do," I said, turning to Madeleine. "It's fine. I brought extra bags just in case." The bonus was the new member, Scarlett Miller, explained the 1963 retreat to everyone else in my group, saving me the trouble.

Once the main group registered, there were only a few stragglers and I manned the table alone. They all went off to enjoy their free time until lunch. I think Madeleine would have hung out with me, but her sister, Cora, showed up.

Cora was wearing a designer suit, pumps and loads of green eye shadow and was carrying her handbag Queen Elizabeth style. The funny thing was the suit was a classic style and fit right in with the 1963 people. She looked at her older sister with a horrified expression.

"We're supposed to go to the luncheon and meeting of the Women's Club of the Natural History Museum to discuss the Monarch Butterfly Parade. That is not the proper attire."

Madeleine looked down at her jeans. They were hardly the washed-out, soft-with-age variety. Hers were rather formal looking, particularly with the belt and the tucked-in blue shirt. She looked like she was about to object, but Cora spoke first. "I was afraid you were wearing a getup like that and I brought a change of clothes." She gestured toward the area behind the registration desk and said she'd left them in the private bathroom back there.

Madeleine balked about going, but in the end gave in. "The meeting about the parade is really important. We're discussing the Butterfly Queen," she said to me.

I understood. One of the things that made Cadbury by the Sea special was that thousands of monarch butterflies came every October and stayed until February, gathering in a grove of eucalyptus and Monterey pines. There was a strict no-touch-the-butterfly rule and anyone molesting a monarch could be fined $1000. The parade in October welcomed them back and was a major event for the town.

"I'll be back here for the first workshop," Madeleine said, holding up her tote bag as her younger sister made unhappy sounds.

The sun had decided to make an appearance. The whole interior of the Lodge seemed brighter with the blue sky outside. The change in weather didn't seem to have affected Lieutenant Borgnine. He had his usual look of displeasure

as he came out of the Cora and Madeleine Delacorte Café
with Norman Rathman. It was the first time I'd seen the
retreat leader since we'd all been in the Lodge in the middle
of the night.

His assistant, Sally Winston, had talked about him being
in shock, but he didn't look that way to me. Several of his
people who had been watching the old shows on the TV saw
him. Norman definitely had charisma, and two women
floated over to him like he was a magnet. I only saw the
body language, but I thought that was sometimes more telling than what was said. They looked like they were offering
their sympathy about his wife. Then he gave each of them
a full body hug. After that he seemed to ask them something
and there was an animated conversation among the three
while the lieutenant stood by with a dour expression.

I wanted to send telepathic messages to the cop, reminding him that spouses were always first in line as suspects.
Particularly when the death solved a problem for them, as
in no longer needing to worry about a messy divorce.

The lunch bell began to ring. This was the first official meal
of my retreat, and I wanted to meet up with my group to explain
how the meals were handled. The line had already begun to
go inside the Sea Foam dining hall when I came outside. I was
glad to see that Lucinda was toward the front of it.

When I got inside the large open structure, she had
already commandeered tables in the corner of the room near
the large stone fireplace. What a difference having help with
the retreat made. She had so much experience with the restaurant, it was second nature for her to arrange the seating
and make everyone feel welcome. The early birds split up
and each one of them hosted a table, which helped, too. I
went around and greeted everyone before directing them to
the food line in the back of the room.

I was glad Dane had talked me into the breakfast sandwich because now I was too keyed up to eat.

When lunch ended, we directed all of our people to the meeting room we'd be using the whole weekend. It was time for the first workshop and the first time Wanda and Crystal would be working together. Fingers crossed they would get along.

Our meeting room took up the whole small building called The Pines. I had never used this one before and was glad to see it had the same inviting feeling as the others. There were windows looking out on the grounds and a cozy fireplace. Coffee and tea service had been set up on a counter that had a sink. I usually brought some cookies or baked goods to go along with the drinks, but with all that had gone on, I had simply forgotten. But there was always tomorrow.

The group came in and found seats around the two long tables that paralleled each other. They all set their bags on the table and then waited. I didn't say idly waited. Most of them had brought projects with them and used the time to work on them, so there was the soft clack of needles.

Madeleine came rushing in and then stopped short when she realized we hadn't started yet. She had changed back to the jeans from the stuffy outfit her sister had brought for the meeting. The only sign of it was the handbag she carried Queen Elizabeth style. Lucinda had figured out by now that Madeleine expected extra attention and pulled out a chair for her. I looked at my watch, nervously wondering where my workshop leaders were.

I went to the front of the room and welcomed everyone again and spent a few minutes saying how happy I was that they were all there, hoping the two women would show up. I let out a major sigh of relief as I saw Wanda and Crystal through the window as they came up the walkway.

They walked right to the front of the room next to me and I introduced them. "Wanda Krug has been knitting since she was a child," I began. "She is also an accomplished spinner, handy with a crochet hook and a world-class golfer." Wanda took a little bow with her head at the last statement and I heard a ripple of interest go through the group. I could see the group giving Crystal the once-over as I introduced her. The two women were like day and night. Wanda was the picture of conservative dress, and Crystal was like a rainbow of colors, heavy eye makeup and earrings and socks that didn't match. Not that even I saw the socks, I just knew they were there. Wanda appeared like serious business, and Crystal looked like fun.

"Crystal Smith and her mother, Gwen Selwyn, own Cadbury Yarn. Like Wanda, Crystal has been working with yarn since she was a small child. She is the originator of the mystery bag idea. I'm going to let her explain the whole plan to you."

As I said that, I noticed Wanda appeared perturbed and adopted her teapot pose.

Crystal stepped into the spotlight and greeted the group. "I hope you're ready for something exciting," she said. "At the end of the weekend, you will be finished, or close to it anyway, making something unique." She had a bin with her and began to unload the contents on the table. "This idea started as a way to sell off odds and ends of yarn at the store. We began bundling them into bags. The bags always had the same amount of yarn, but the selection was different in each one. When we started doing this, there wasn't the selection of novelty yarns like there is now. It was my idea to include them. Then odds and ends like beads or charms were added. In the beginning it was up to whoever bought one to figure out how to use everything, but in time we realized that it was helpful to show samples of what could be made and even offer some patterns." She set out the selection of scarves, small bags, toys and finally the worry doll.

Wanda was getting hot under the collar and I could see she wanted to interrupt. Crystal seemed to figure it out and then changed her patter. "With the limited time we have, we don't want you to spend too much time trying to decide what to make, so Wanda and I have come up with a plan." She went to take a breath and Wanda jumped in.

"The plan is to give you a scarf pattern to use. Since what you all have to work with is different, even with the same pattern, yours will be unique." While she was talking, she brought out a stack of papers with the pattern and several samples of the scarves. As she'd said, each one of the scarves did look different despite the same instructions. Wanda was wound up and it didn't seem like there would be a break in her speech, so Crystal broke in.

"But in case you don't want to make a scarf and would like to make something different, we have the directions for her." She held up the worry doll and the group all smiled. Crystal explained that the doll even had a use. She finished by saying, "And if neither of those ideas please you, I have patterns for all of these." She gestured toward the array of things she'd brought.

There was a buzz of conversation and everybody got up from their seats to have a closer look at Crystal's samples. I heard someone mention that the bear looked loved, which was a nice way of saying well used. "It's had a few owners," Crystal said with a smile.

Wanda seemed about to jump out of her skin and simply interrupted. "Wanda Krug here," she said, reintroducing herself as if anyone didn't know. "Crystal has some wonderful ideas, but you ought to know that the worry doll and the other toys aren't meant for young children." Wanda held up a bead and mimicked choking. "In the old days they never thought about stuff like that." She gave a dismissive nod toward the bear. "All those choices are probably a little overwhelming for all of you. Right?" A number of women nodded their heads and Wanda seemed triumphant. "That's why I think you'll be happiest if you go along with the scarf plan."

Crystal let Wanda have her say without reacting.

The one thing they were in agreement on was that everyone should empty their bag and see what they had to work with.

There was a buzz of conversation as they checked out their yarn and saw what their neighbors had. One of the women stood up. "I understand different yarns, beads and even some charms, but how am I going to use this?" She held a large earring in her hand.

"That's Diana Rathman's earring," Scarlett, the defector from the 1963 group, said. "She was wearing it last night."

11

SCARLETT WAS OUT THE DOOR ON HER WAY TO
fetch Lieutenant Borgnine before I could stop her. I wondered how he'd react to an adult woman dressed like a kid
in the early sixties, but then he probably would be dealing
with a lot of similarly clothed people this weekend.

The group seemed to freeze, not quite knowing what was
going on, but that didn't last. After a moment there was a
hum of conversation, and I heard just enough to figure out
that my retreaters were getting the scoop on who Diana
Rathman was and what had happened from the early birds
and Madeleine. Particularly Madeleine.

"I was practically there when it happened," she said to a
woman wrapped in a red shawl.

"But what is the dead woman's earring doing in one of
the bags?" another asked with a shudder.

Madeleine had center stage now. Who would have figured

that someone who had been so quiet would flip so far the other way?

"I think that when the killer went to strangle her, the earring must have snagged on their clothes. Maybe they didn't notice it until later and needed to get rid of it." She looked to me. "Don't you think that's what happened?" The Delacorte sister turned back to the rest of the group. "You might not know it, but Casey is quite the sleuth. She learned it all when she worked for a detective agency in Chicago."

The early birds knew all of that already and nodded in agreement. The rest of the people looked at me with new interest.

"Sounds to me like we're getting a mystery bonus with our yarn work. Are you one of those amateurs that always bests the cops?" a woman with piles of light brown ringlets said.

I was embarrassed by all the attention, and was trying to divert it by rocking my head in a self-deprecating way, which meant I totally missed the arrival of the lieutenant. Unfortunately, he was there for the woman's comment.

He showed off his badge, gave me a harsh sideways look and responded to the remark. "No one is besting anyone here," he said. "I can assure all of you, the Cadbury by the Sea Police Department is totally in control of the investigation and will bring the culprit to justice."

His gaze moved over the crowd at pretty much the same time mine did. If I was a betting woman, I'd say they all looked like they were betting on me. The lieutenant must have got the same impression because he glowered at me.

"Where is this piece of evidence?" he said curtly. Scarlett pointed to the earring on the table and repeated that Diana Rathman had been wearing it the previous day.

"She must have been wearing it when she got killed," Scarlett said.

"And it was in one of those bags?" he said, eyeing all the red tote bags on the table. Scarlett rushed to point out the bag belonging to the woman sitting next to her. He turned to me with a disconcerted grunt. "Ms. Feldstein, suppose you tell me where these bags have been."

"They were in my guest house until I brought them over here this morning. Then they were sitting out on the table in the Lodge." I was relieved when he ignored the part about them being in my guest house, but then he didn't know that Sammy was sleeping there. And I was pretty sure he was still in the dark that the so-called scarf used to strangle Diana was actually one of Sammy's silk streamers.

"Was anybody watching them?" I shook my head and mentioned that, after I'd set them out, I'd gone to the café.

"When I came back in the main room, it was full of people," I said. "Any of them could have dropped the earring in."

"I'll draw the conclusions here," he said. He took his pen and pushed the large earring to the edge of the table. He'd taken out a small paper bag and knocked the earring into it.

"Wait a minute," the woman who'd had the earring in her bag said. "I touched it, so my fingerprints must be on it. Is that going to make me a suspect?"

Lieutenant Borgnine gave a little rub to his temple, which implied he had a headache coming on. "No, it won't make you a suspect. Come with me and we'll take your fingerprints so we can eliminate them from whatever we find."

"You better take mine, too," Scarlett said. "I picked it up off the table so my fingerprints must be on it, too."

The lieutenant shook his head and waved for her to join them.

"You know, no one questioned me and I was there last night when the dead woman was arguing with her husband," Madeleine chimed in.

"Really?" he said, stopping in his tracks. I'm sure he knew who she was. He gave his temple a stronger rub this time. I suppose he probably thought that people who volunteered to be questioned didn't usually have any useful information, but he pulled her aside anyway.

Madeleine turned to me. "Casey, please come with me. I've never been interrogated before."

I so wanted to say, "And you're not going to be interrogated now," but I suggested everybody take a break, even though we'd just started, and we'd reconvene in half an hour. The lieutenant sent Scarlett and the other woman with a uniform who was walking by.

Madeleine seemed disappointed when we stopped at a bench outside. "I thought it would be something more formal than this," she said. He shrugged and rolled his eyes at her comment. She sat down and the lieutenant remained standing and opened his notebook. "Okay, then ask away," Madeleine said.

I think he tried to hide the groan, but I heard it. "Why don't you just tell me what you saw."

"I'm sure you realize that I didn't really know the victim. There I was trying to talk to that wonderful singer and she just interrupted. Like I wasn't even there. She seemed like one of those people that stirred things up in a bad way. I saw her arguing with her husband, and then, what she did to the Amazing Dr. Sammy."

I froze as he suddenly seemed to take notice of what she was saying.

"What exactly happened?" he asked.

"Why, she ruined his trick and embarrassed him in front

of everybody. He seemed to take it pretty well, but I just thought what she did was uncalled for." Madeleine went on as I grew more worried about what she might say. Then I looked at the cop and almost laughed. He was doodling on his pad of paper. To him he was just doing her a courtesy. Like I thought, he dismissed the importance of anyone who volunteered to be questioned. Even so, someone was bound to tell him about the incident when he was paying attention.

I GOT BACK TO THE ROOM EARLY AND WAS WAITING when Scarlett and the other woman came back from having their fingerprints taken. Seeing that the rest of the people weren't back, the woman went off to the café. Scarlett stayed with me and Madeleine.

"Thanks for adding me to your program. I'm already having more fun than I usually do at the Favorite Year retreats." I guessed Scarlett was well into her forties, but her slender build and round face made her appear younger. The pigtails helped, too, but it was also her manner.

"Did you know Diana Rathman very well?' I asked Scarlett. I figured before I asked it that she probably did judging by how quickly she had recognized the earring when it fell on the table.

"We weren't besties or anything, but I've known her for a long time. Norman Rathman and my husband are both in the history department at CalStateCentCst." She noted my puzzled look. "Sorry. That's the abbreviation for California State Central Coast University. You know how it is, I'd see her at faculty events." She pulled out a chair and went to sit. "Do you know the whole story about how the Favorite Year retreats started?"

I shook my head and she continued. "Norman and my husband both taught contemporary history classes and they discovered a great teaching tool that made the lessons come alive, by literally making them alive. It had started with small events like a potluck dinner with foods from an era, and the showing of media from the time. They morphed into all-day events and became more like stepping back into the time. The students enjoyed them and started bringing friends along. Finally, Norman got the idea of turning it into a club, and instead of putting an event on during a single day, it became a long weekend with a particular year being re-created. He also turned it into a business. Everybody knows professors don't get paid much so this was a good way to earn some extra money. Diana helped with a lot of the arrangements. She and Norman were co-owners of the club."

Reading between the lines, it sounded like Scarlett's husband might have gotten the shaft when it became a business. I asked her about it, but she said her husband was glad to just work for them rather than be an owner. "Diana stopped coming to the events a couple of years ago. Nobody is supposed to know, but their marriage is falling apart. That's why I was so surprised to see her. She must have decided to come at the last minute."

I wanted to ask her if she had any idea why Diana had decided to come to the retreat, but she veered off Diana and started talking about Norman Rathman.

"He was not happy to see her. He added it to the list of things that had gone wrong with this retreat. He bent my husband's ear about all the problems and Jason, in turn, dumped it all on me." She smiled at me. "You can see why I was so anxious to join your group." I asked her what the problems with the retreat were and she was only too glad to pass them along.

"You probably don't know, but the place Norman usually holds the retreats had a fire and he had to relocate it here. It's not his way to give over any control and he was upset from the get-go about the way the manager of this place handled things."

"Really?" Madeleine said. "You know my sister and I own this place."

Scarlett went through a laundry list of complaints from the wrong music, to inviting the celebrity guests, to our retreat going on at the same time. "Norman is such a stickler for accurate details. But he was very happy with the phone booths and unplugged nature of the place. Personally, I like the activities the manager added. It's fun seeing a movie from that year with the star there to talk about it. And I have to believe it's a big thrill for the guys to have a softball game with a real baseball player. Having that singer do his hit from 1963 at the dance makes it exciting."

"I know what you mean," Madeleine said in a wistful voice. "You have no idea the memories that's going to bring back." She told Scarlett that she had heard Bobbie Listorie do the song the actual year it was a hit. As soon as the words were out of her mouth, she looked around nervously. Did she think her sister was hiding behind a tree?

"What about Sally Winston?" I asked.

"So you noticed. I'm not sure what is going on between them. She's an instructor and has been his assistant in the club business for a while. I'm sure you noticed that Norman has a lot of charisma. The students hang on to his every word. Sally is fine with being his helper. Maybe Diana got tired of being outshone by him."

I had waited before bringing up my last question. She was talking freely now and I thought this was the best chance to get something useful from her. "Do you have any idea who would want to kill Diana?"

As I thought she would, she answered without hesitation. "Having her out of the way certainly makes things easier for Norman. There's no question anymore of who gets what. He gets it all. But maybe there is somebody else. I heard she was pretty wild before she married Norman. It was the seventies; I guess everybody was."

Our conversation ended as the group began to filter back in and take their seats. Lucinda caught my gaze and I mouthed that I'd tell her later.

What the group did next surprised me. They all started trading balls of yarn and beads from their bags. There wasn't really a reason to stop them, so I let it be even if Crystal seemed disappointed.

It turned out that the main event of the first workshop was for each person to decide what they wanted to make.

At the end of the session, the group had broken into Team Wanda and Team Crystal. Wanda's group agreed it was a good idea to all make the same thing and something basic like a scarf. The Crystal Group mostly wanted to make the worry doll, but one person wanted to make a small purse. The early birds split between the two teams. Lucinda and I stuck with Crystal's team so we could make the worry dolls.

I didn't know about the others, but I really needed one of those dolls to hand off my worries to.

Madeleine seemed a little frazzled by the choices and just stuck with me. Wanda managed to woo her over to the scarf team, but the Delacorte sister insisted on sitting with me. I knew it had to do with me acting as her aid, but it was impossible to be upset with Madeleine. On the one hand, she might have looked at me as her assistant, but at the same time she seemed to be in such awe of my talents.

Wanda checked her watch. "Time's up for today," she said, gathering her things. Crystal seemed in less of a hurry to leave. The table was littered with everyone's supplies and assorted patterns. Wanda was out the door in a flash. Crystal hung back and suggested we leave everything as is and continue on in the morning.

I mentioned there was a nature walk put on by Vista Del Mar starting in a few minutes if any of them were interested. Madeleine nudged me. "Tell them that they can take part in the activities put on by the other retreat." But before I could say anything, she turned to the group. "I'm kind of your hostess, since my sister and I own Vista Del Mar. I was the one who arranged for all of you to be welcome at the things being put on by the 1963 people. That's what I call them, but I think the official name of their retreat is My Favorite Year 1963." She let out a little titter of laughter. "I don't suppose you really care what their real name is as long as you know who I'm talking about." She took a breath. "Tonight there is a screening of *From Russia with Love* in Hummingbird Hall. There's also going to be folk singing around the fire pit." She looked back at me. "Do you have anything planned for our people?"

Olivia Golden stood up and answered for me. "After dinner I'm going to be in the Lodge and anyone interested in making squares for charity is welcome to join me."

The woman wearing the T-shirts with witty knitting sayings stood up. "A bunch of us are going to get together in the lobby of the Sea and Sand building. It's bring your own project."

When she finished, everyone got up and began to file out in small groups talking among themselves. Lucinda and Madeleine hung back. Lucinda and I straightened things up while Madeleine watched. Finally, we walked to the door together.

"I suppose you're going home now," I said to Madeleine when we got outside. "All the planned activities for our retreat are over." At least I hoped that was her plan. I didn't mind spending time with her and even sort of looking after her, to a point.

"No, I'm absolutely not going home now. If I do, I will just have to listen to Cora lecture me on how inappropriate everything I'm doing is. I know I shouldn't let her boss me around, but it's hard for me to stand up to her. It's a lot easier if I'm just not with her." Madeleine must have picked up on the downturn in my expression. "Don't worry, Casey, I'm not expecting you to be my escort tonight. I appreciate that you introduced me to Bobbie. I was a little intimidated by meeting him again. But I'll be fine tonight. I'm not even going to sit at Cora's and my special table at dinner. I'm going to eat with the rest of our group. Then I'm going to the movie they're showing." She had a happy smile as she said she was going to the café to get an espresso drink, like it was something very naughty.

Lucinda and I watched her walk down the path. When she was almost out of sight, Lucinda turned to me. "Okay, tell me everything you know."

We went in the other direction almost to the edge of the grounds and found a solitary bench. We were at the top of the slope, and from there we could see over the sand dunes all the way to the water. The sun had done another disappearing act, and the breeze felt cool and fresh.

I filled her in on what Scarlett had said about Diana Rathman, and the fact that Lieutenant Borgnine didn't seem to have Sammy as a suspect yet. "The most important thing I got from talking to Scarlett was that Diana Rathman seems to have come at the last minute and even her husband didn't know she was coming. She hadn't been coming to the retreats for several years. What made her suddenly come to this one?"

Lucinda pulled her Ralph Lauren jacket a little tighter. "If we figure that out, maybe we'll know who killed her."

I sent Lucinda off to join the others, and I headed across the street to my place. She offered to come with, but I wanted her to enjoy the retreat as much as possible, and I thought Sammy was really my problem.

Sammy had been in the back of my mind all day. I regretted that I hadn't talked to him more when I picked up the tote bags. I was worried that he might have awakened and left. I knocked on the door of the guest house softly before I unlocked it. I heard something like a groan as a response. Inside the light was dim and I barely made out Sammy's hulking shape sitting on the edge of the bed. When I got closer, I saw that his head was down, almost between his knees. He looked like he felt awful.

"Hey, Case," he said in greeting and then went back to moaning and groaning and muttering to himself. "I'm a doctor. I should know what to do for a hangover." Then he let out a laugh that sounded more like a croak. "That's what happens when you specialize in the other end of things. I should have been a GP, then I'd know what to do."

I didn't know what to do, either. He still seemed a little slurry and I wanted him 100 percent before I started asking him questions. I made sure all the shutters were completely closed before turning on a low light. Sammy responded with more groans as he shielded his eyes.

"I'm going to make us some coffee," I said, going to the door.

"I'll come with you," he said, standing too quickly. He wove back and forth before falling back onto the bed. "Maybe not."

I returned a few minutes later with a pot of coffee and a couple of mugs, a pitcher of water and some burnt toast. Sammy looked at the offering. "Gee, Case, I knew you weren't much of a cook when it came to regular food, but that toast looks beyond eating and kind of empty. You know, so burned it's black, and missing butter and jam."

"I deliberately burned it. I may not go in for making gourmet dishes, but I can make toast. It's amazing what you can find on the Internet. The burned stuff is carbon and is supposed to filter the alcohol out of your system. I think butter and jam would get in the way."

"Whatever you say." He picked up one of the pieces of toast and tried to eat it, but he couldn't get it down. He did drink several glasses of water and began to nurse a mug of coffee. He looked a little better. I felt rotten interrogating him in the condition he was in, but I had to know what had happened.

"Do you want to tell me about last night? Like what happened before you landed outside my back door," I said. His head bobbed back and forth and he began to massage his temples.

"Is that what happened? I was wondering how I got here. Did we spend the night—"

"No, nothing like that," I said, interrupting him.

He hung his head dejectedly. "Maybe it is just as well. I wouldn't have remembered it." I prodded him some more for details of his evening after I left.

"I was pretty upset," he began. "That woman kept heckling me."

"And," I said, trying to keep him talking.

"I probably could have handled it, but I heard about your date," he said in a dejected tone.

"It was only dinner, and it was just a onetime thing." I thought of adding that since Sammy and I weren't a couple, I was certainly free to go on dates, but he looked so bad, I didn't have the heart to say it. I was glad that I hadn't said more when I heard his relieved sigh before he continued.

"If only she hadn't messed with the card trick. She wouldn't let up. You're sure it was just a onetime thing?" Sammy said.

"Forget about my date for dinner, then what happened?"

"Apparently people drank a lot in the early 1960s, and part of the mixer was a martini bar. I was feeling pretty upset by then, and I just took a whole shaker of them and went to the beach."

"You must remember something else," I said, trying not to sound as frantic as I was beginning to feel.

He rolled his head a few times and moaned. "I don't know. I vaguely remember wandering around in the dark."

I kept at it. "Did you talk to anybody? See anybody?" He shrugged in response and looked like he was thinking about lying down again.

"Case, I don't remember. If I did something embarrassing, I'll apologize later."

"What about the silk streamer she pulled out of your sleeve. What happened to that?"

Sammy shrugged. "What's the difference?"

"Last night you told me you did something terrible. What was it?"

"I pride myself on not letting down my professional persona. But I couldn't help it. When she messed up the card trick, I lost it. I called her Miss Crabby Pants and said she was fired as my assistant. Case, I've never lost it like that before." He held his head again. "Could we talk about this another time?"

"No," I said. "We can't. There's something you don't know. That woman who wrecked your show was found dead last night. Strangled with your silk streamer."

At that moment it seemed like I had found the cure for a hangover because Sammy stopped massaging his forehead, sat forward and seemed suddenly completely alert.

"You think I did that?" He shook his head. "Did I do that?"

Then he looked bewildered. "I couldn't have, could I?" He viewed his surroundings. "Are the cops looking for me?"

"I know you, Sammy, and even drunk I can't imagine you strangling anybody. So even if you don't know, I know. And the cops aren't looking for you, yet anyway." I mentioned that I was pretty sure they still thought the streamer was a scarf Diana was wearing. "There's something else. She was wearing big filigree earrings, and one of them turned up in the tote bags I had sitting in here. Do you know anything about it? Like maybe you found it stuck to your clothes and dropped it in there."

He shrugged. "Oh, Case, I don't know. If I had it, my fingerprints could be on it." He turned to me. "You have to find out what happened."

"Nobody knows that you're here. Why don't you just stay here for now—until I can get this sorted out."

"I can't let you do that. You could get in trouble. Oh, my gosh, I'm a fugitive."

"Almost a fugitive," I countered.

"If my parents find out, they'll kill me. As you might imagine, they were against my whole plan to move, er, stay in Cadbury for a while." But then his demeanor changed. "Be sure to let your mother know I'm a fugitive," he said as his eyes brightened.

"Almost a fugitive," I repeated. "Sammy, this is serious. It's not about trying to show my mother you're some kind of bad boy. Besides, she already knows about it."

"I bet she thinks I'm all wrong for you now. Dangerous." He struck his version of a bad boy pose, but his good-natured expression and puppy dog eyes blew the illusion.

12

I HAD GONE BACK AND FORTH BETWEEN MY PLACE and Vista Del Mar so many times and I was so tired that I had lost track of time. The white sky didn't help since the light looked the same all day. It was even hard to remember what month it was. The weather didn't seem like August. Or at least not the Augusts I'd known all the years living in Chicago. Summer there meant sundresses and a sweat fest. I zipped up my beige fleece jacket as I walked down my driveway. Summer, winter, spring and fall were all pretty much the same here—cool and damp. I was still getting used to the uni-season climate and had a wardrobe of fleece jackets in many colors since they were basically my year-round outerwear of choice.

The dinner bell had already rung and there were just a few stragglers with me on the walkway toward the Sea Foam dining hall. The building up ahead was mostly windows and I could see the tables full of people.

I was once again grateful that meals were included with the rooms at Vista Del Mar. It was so much nicer than just having a restaurant connected to the place. This way everyone ate together. The big round tables and cafeteria-like setup for the food service made it feel like the guests were one big group. And the food was good.

I wasn't worried about being late for the meal with my group. Lucinda had taken on the job of acting as a host at the meals. With her restaurant experience, my friend was a natural for the job. I still wondered how much of a holiday the weekend was for her, but she insisted it was about a change of scenery, or in this case, a change of where she offered pitchers of ice tea.

The din of conversation and the smell of hot food greeted me as I walked inside. My stomach gurgled in response to the delicious fragrance and reminded me that I hadn't eaten since the breakfast sandwich. In a true gesture of sacrifice, I wasn't going to eat now, but get my meal packed up so I could take it to Sammy.

He'd finally eaten the burnt toast I made, not to filter the contents of his stomach as much as to put something in it. Could I have come up with a cure for a hangover? As soon as it sank in that Sammy might be a murder suspect, all traces of his headache and bad feeling left and were replaced by the gnawing of a hungry stomach.

Okay, I felt responsible for the mess he was in. He would never be living in Cadbury if it wasn't for me, and certainly part of his getting drunk had to do with my dinner with Dane. The least I could do was give him a place to hide out and bring him some food. I still wondered if he realized how much trouble he was in. All he seemed to care about was how my mother would view his situation.

Lucinda had taken over a group of tables near the large

stone fireplace. When I caught up with her, she was circulating with a pitcher of ice tea and pointing out the food line at the back of the large room. As usual, she was wearing something designer. The Eileen Fisher pants outfit appeared comfortable and stylish. I felt underdressed in my black jeans and tunic-style shirt, but then I always did compared to her. And I still had a night of baking ahead of me.

"Why don't you get your food," my friend said.

"I think I will," I said. "And thank you again for your help. It is such a relief to know that I have you and the early birds helping out now. I practically have a staff," I joked. This was certainly a change from the temp work I'd done before moving here. I had repeat retreaters and people assisting me. That meant I was going to stick with something this time, didn't it?

I didn't let on what my plans for the food were. It had nothing to do with not trusting her and everything to do with I didn't want to stick her any further into the middle of the mess. If I had it to do over, I never would have told her Sammy was in my guest house. I knew that she would protect him, but I hated putting her in a position where she would have to lie if Lieutenant Borgnine asked if she knew where he was.

The line was long and I decided to cut to the chase and asked for mine in a to-go box, explaining I knew I wouldn't finish it all. *Or eat any of it*, I mumbled to myself, wondering if it would be so terrible if I took a few bites. The meatloaf and mashed potatoes looked particularly tasty.

I was on my way back to the table when Scarlett approached me. She was holding a plate of food and looking in the direction of our group. "Would it be okay if I sit with you guys?" she said, giving a dismissive glance to her husband and the rest of his tablemates. "I wish there had been events like this when I went to the other Favorite Year things." She had changed out of the pedal pushers and was wearing a rosy pink with white polka dot shift-style dress. I saw a pair of long white gloves hanging out of her bag. It made me glad that I wasn't around in 1963. Who would want to wear gloves unless it was to keep your hands warm?

"Of course, you're officially one of us now anyway. You're a dual retreater." We started to thread our way through the tables. Now that I knew Sammy didn't remember anything from the previous night, I hoped I could find an alibi for him. But then, I couldn't ask for it directly. Why not start with Scarlett. "So then you've been to a lot of these Favorite Year retreats?"

"How about all of them and I have the wardrobe to prove it. I have raided all my relatives' attics and hit all the local thrift stores. To a lot of the people, the appeal is it's like a weekend-long costume party." She glanced back toward the table where her husband was sitting. He was wearing a boxy-looking black shirt with white embroidery. "It makes you wonder what people were thinking of when you see some of the old styles. You should have seen the outfits from the My Favorite Year 1977. Norman actually wore one of those white three-piece suits like John Travolta did in *Saturday Night Fever*. He even wore the heeled shoes and he did his rendition of the dance routine from the movie."

I looked at Norman as she spoke, imagining him in the outfit. He seemed to have all the attention of the people at his table. They honestly seemed to be hanging on to every word he said. "Last I heard he was in too much shock to deal with his people. I guess he recovered. He hardly looks like someone whose wife just died," I said.

Scarlett followed my gaze. "I see your point. It makes you wonder." I led the way to a couple of open chairs near the early birds. She pulled out a chair and sat down. I just deposited my food and went about working the tables.

It turned out I didn't have to worry about picking at Sammy's dinner. I spent the whole time circulating and working the crowd. For once Lucinda got to sit down and eat.

I waited until the last of our group was finished and the dining hall had emptied before I left. Outside, the light definitely looked like evening, but with the cloud-lined sky, it was more like someone was turning down a dimmer on the day than the brilliant light of the sunset. My plan was to take the food across the street to Sammy. But as I passed the Lodge building, Olivia Golden caught up with me.

"You're coming in, aren't you?" she said, taking a step toward the building that I thought of as the heart of the place. "You know the agreement. If we meet here, all guests are welcome to join us. And if they want to learn how to knit, we'll teach them. I think Scott is a little nervous and it would be good if you joined us."

I understood. It was one thing to knit yourself and a total other thing to give lessons.

"It's not just the lessons. He's come a long way since hiding that he was a knitter on the first retreat, but people still do stare," Olivia said. She looked at me for an answer. All the early birds had gone through some kind of transformation since the first retreat, but Olivia's had been the most dramatic. She had literally turned her frown upside down. She had bristled with anger on that first long weekend. Now, she'd turned all that negative energy from her ex's remarriage to something positive. She'd learned to help herself by helping others.

Instead of her eyes flashing with hostility, they glowed with good feeling and her mouth seemed to naturally rest in a pleasant smile. Gathering the squares to make into blankets for needy people had really turned her life around. More than once she'd brought up how each square carried the good feelings of the person who'd made it. What could be nicer than being a recipient of a blanket with such good vibrations attached?

I held up the food container and said I was just going to take it across the street.

"It'll be okay for a few minutes. I just think you should be there for the beginning of our first knit gathering. I know Scott would feel better if you were there."

She was right; the food would be okay for a while, and if my presence made Scott feel better, so be it. We walked into the Lodge together. It was buzzing with activity. The table tennis and pool tables were both in use. There was a line for the phone booths and a crowd around the message board outside the gift shop. The corkboard was Kevin St. John's substitute for texting. By now, it was a little better organized than when Vista Del Mar first went unplugged and the messages were all over the place without any sense of order. Now the board was divided into alphabetical quadrants, more or less.

A group of the 1963 people were gathered around a long table having a discussion. I noticed copies of a book called *The Group*, which I assumed was connected with the year they were spotlighting. The café was crowded with customers looking for espresso drinks.

The amber-colored glass lampshades gave off a friendly glow around the seating area. And the chandeliers hanging from the open-beamed ceiling were reflected in the dark wood floor.

Scott had already staked out another long table and chairs for the knitters. A smaller table was set up for a game of cards next to it. Since it was unoccupied, I set the food container on it. Scott was standing up waiting for people to join him. I thought I'd work the room and see if anyone was interested in doing some yarn craft.

I was surprised to see Norman Rathman standing with

Sally Winston in the midst of a small group of people. I was curious about the conversation and pretended to be interested in a copy of *Look* magazine on the table next to the couch.

"We're all so sorry for what happened," a woman in a full skirt said. "But we're glad to have you back with us."

Norman reacted by touching the woman on the arm and thanking her. I noticed that he had a way of looking at her as if she was very important to him. It was definitely part of his charm. It was interesting that while I was sure he was wearing clothing in the appropriate style from 1963, the off-white cable-knit sweater over khaki slacks were a lot more attractive than some of the old shirts the other men were wearing. "Sitting in my room didn't help. And to be treated like the prime suspect at a time like this was just terrible." The group all murmured sympathy and he put his hand up. "It's okay now. That police lieutenant is looking elsewhere."

"Really?" a man in a plaid sport shirt said. "What happened to change things?'

Norman shook his head, apparently referring to the ineptitude of the cops. "They finally thought to show me the scarf that was used to . . ." His voice grew strained with emotion. I had a hard time buying that it was genuine. There had been nothing but hostility between him and his wife when I'd seen them together. I knew their marriage was breaking up, but not who wanted out. Was he putting on an act now?

The group had drifted toward the front of the room as they talked. Was Norman going to finish the thought or leave it hanging? I moved with them, wanting to hear what he was going to do. In an effort to hide that I was eavesdropping, I pretended to be very interested in the displays the three celebrities had put up near the registration counter. Jimmie Phelps had the most professional one, but then the energy drink company was sponsoring his being there. I was pretty sure that meant they were paying him. It seemed like it was a success as the supply of energy drinks had dwindled. I pretended to flip through the CDs that Bobbie Listorie was offering. There were a few old ones, but the largest number of copies seemed to be of something he'd done recently. The title read, *Bobbie Listorie, My Life in Song*. There was an attractive photo of him on the cover straddling a chair and looking straight into the camera. Dotty Night had a small display of DVDs, but most of the space was given over to photographs of her inn, along with postcards with all the information. The picture made it look charming, like an inn out of a fairy tale. It wasn't anything like Vista Del Mar and looked like the perfect place for a romantic weekend.

Norman knew how to draw out a story. In all the time I'd been looking at the stuff for sale, he still hadn't come out and said anything more about the "scarf." Instead he'd talked about how bad he felt for missing out on so much of the day's activities and how upsetting it was dealing with an inept police department at a time like this.

Finally one of the people standing around him realized he'd never finished the thought and asked him what they'd found out about the scarf.

Sally Winston was standing quite close to the leader of the retreat, though not touching him. She kept bending her angular face toward the group as though she was anxious to join in the conversation, but somehow was restraining herself, and let Norman Rathman speak.

"What they found out from me was it wasn't a scarf at all. It was that long colorful thing. It looked kind of like hankies sewed together." He seemed to be getting frustrated that they didn't understand. "It was the magician's whatchamacallit. The thing Diana pulled from his sleeve when she ruined his trick."

The group sucked in their collective breath and a titter of conversation broke out. "So, they have a new suspect," the man in the plaid shirt said, nodding with comprehension.

"I hope they put out an all-points bulletin or whatever it's called for him and leave me alone. The situation is difficult enough for me without being worried I'm going to be handcuffed and arrested," Norman said. The others began to discuss what motive Sammy would have had and how they thought the crime had been committed.

Well, there went the grace period of the cops not knowing the silk streamer was Sammy's. Now they'd be on the hunt for him.

"Let's try to focus on something more positive," Sally said, interrupting them. "We still have a whole long weekend of events planned." Her face grew animated and she pointed toward the double doors of the Lodge that led out onto the wood deck and the grounds beyond. "There's going to be a campfire and folk song sing-a-long in a few minutes at the fire pit. And after that we're screening *From Russia with Love*," she said, quickly adding it had a little more meat to it than the Dotty Night movie being shown the next night. The assembled group started to make their way toward the exit, but Norman and Sally stayed put.

I did, too, curious to see how they changed when they were alone. She gave him a sympathetic look and reached out to touch his arm, but stopped herself. She turned to check out the area and her eyes stopped on me. I quickly averted my gaze from her face to look at the floor and noted for the first time that she really did have remarkably thick ankles for someone with such a willowy build. I started to edge away and just heard the tail end of their conversation.

"You should join the others," Norman said. "People might get the wrong idea."

I realized the same thing could apply to me, only the wrong idea would have been a little different—namely that I was spying on them, which of course, I was. I needed to attend to my people quickly so I could get across the street. The table had filled in my absence and there was no reason to try to recruit any more guests. I noticed a little perspiration on Scott's forehead as he sat at the end of the table with his first student. I stood next to them, hoping I wasn't too late to offer him moral support.

"Toby is a friend of mine," Scarlett said. I had so focused on Scott I hadn't noticed her sitting next to his student. Scarlett handled the introductions and Scott took the opportunity to wipe his brow. The rest of the people at the table were already knitting and looking at the sheets Olivia had given out with directions for the squares. Lucinda was with them and glanced up and made a move as if she was going to change seats, but I shook my head.

"It looks like everything is under control here," I said after watching for a few minutes. I went to retrieve the container of food I'd left on the next table, but Scott's head shot up. He looked panicked, and while he didn't say the words, I got that he wanted me to stay.

I could empathize. Yes, I knew how to knit now, but the thought of trying to teach someone sent me into a cold sweat. The woman seemed to be having trouble learning how to cast on and he tried to patiently show her again. There was no question having Scarlett watching them and chattering away was making it harder for him.

Instead of picking up the cardboard food container, I sat down and motioned for Scarlett to join me, saying there was more space. She picked up her square in progress and sat down next to me. Out of the corner of my eye, I saw that Scott had given me a thank-you nod.

"This is much better," she said. "More room to get comfy." She started to work a stitch.

"No martini bar tonight," I said, glancing around at all the activity going on in the room.

"That's was just for last night," Scarlett said. She finished the stitch and looked up.

"So then you were there?" I figured as long as I was keeping her out of Scott's way, I might as well see what I could find out. I was hoping it would be something to help Sammy with an alibi.

Scarlett had indeed been there. Her husband, Jason, who she pointed out was coming across the room with his guitar for the folk singing, had served as the bartender.

"Did Diana join in the drinking?"

Scarlett thought for a moment. Now that she'd taken her hair out of the pigtails and teased it into a bouffant-style reminiscent of Jackie Kennedy, she looked her age, which I now guessed was in her fifties, around the same age as Diana. "I hadn't thought about that. She wasn't in here." I saw Scarlett's gaze go to the windows on the side of the building that looked toward a boardwalk that led through the dunes to the beach. "I was walking out there when I saw her." Scarlett strained to remember. "And she was with someone. I remember now thinking that it was a man but I couldn't make out who he was. They hadn't gotten to the boardwalk. They had stopped in the grassy area with the trees." I knew just where she was describing. It was on the other side of the roadway that led past the Lodge and was called the grass circle. It was one of the few spaces that had almost a lawn. She got frustrated. "Since I didn't know what was going to happen to her, I didn't pay that close attention."

"Do you think it was the magician?" I asked, almost afraid of her answer. I didn't see any reason to bring up my relationship with him.

She shrugged as she said, "I don't know if it was him. Now that I think of it, I didn't see Diana's face, either. I knew it was her because her earrings and clothes had all those reflective decorations and they caught the light." Across the table, Scott tried showing Toby another way to cast on and she was having more success. "I'm sure Diana must have seen me going by, but she didn't say anything. I suppose that was why I didn't greet her. To be honest, I was trying to keep my distance from her. I heard that Diana was going through some midlife thing and reevaluating her life. Thinking about the road not taken." She looked at me intently. "It's probably hard for you to understand, you're still so young. And free." She sounded a little wistful. Should I tell her the truth, that according to my mother, my life was splattered all over like a Jackson Pollock painting and that having all those choices of direction were not necessarily a good thing. No, let her keep the fantasy.

Scarlett didn't seem to notice that I didn't respond to her comment and she went on talking.

"I hadn't really thought about it until now, but since my husband more or less works for Norman, I didn't want to get in the middle of anything with his wife." She was still holding her knitting needles and the beginnings of a square. Scarlett's eyebrows creased with concern. "Do me a favor. Don't mention what I saw or what I just said to anyone, particularly that lieutenant. I don't want to get caught up in the investigation." Abruptly, she wound the yarn around her needles and got up to go.

I had no problem agreeing to that.

13

ONCE SCOTT GOT TOBY PAST CASTING ON AND
working on her first row of knit stitches, I figured it had to
be okay to leave. I grabbed the food container and stood up,
anxious to go.

Lucinda caught up with me. She knew there was something wrong without me saying it. I really appreciated having
a friend like that. It didn't matter that there was a difference
in our ages or that she was my boss as far as baking desserts
was concerned. We could read each other's moods.

"What is it?' she asked. Despite what I'd thought about
not wanting to involve Lucinda in the Sammy situation, I
told her all of what I'd heard.

"I was hoping that Scarlett might have been able to give
Sammy some kind of alibi, but seeing some unidentified
man with Diana near the walkway to the beach only looks
worse for him."

"Oh, dear," she said. "That's not good." She looked at the box in my hand. "You're taking that to him?"

I told her about feeding him the burnt toast and she laughed. She was about to let me go, but then snagged my arm. "I suppose this isn't a good time for this, but I thought of a way we could find out the identity of the secret baby. Since you don't know when the baby was born and only the possible initials of the mother, checking public records is impossible. But how about this? We could make a list of the people we know who could be the love child, like Maggie from the Coffee Shop, Crystal Smith's mother and Wanda Krug's mother, then we try to eliminate them."

"I'm not so sure that's a good plan," I said. "It's like trying to find the needle in a haystack by taking away one piece of hay at a time."

"But maybe in the course of talking to them, something else will come up that will point us in the right direction."

Her suggestion about finding the heir had momentarily distracted me, but I suddenly remembered the food container in my hand. "I'm putting it on the shelf for now. Sammy's troubles are a little more immediate."

"Let me know if I can do anything," Lucinda said. "You can always knock on my door. No matter how late." I gave her a one-armed hug and thanked her and said I would check on the group again in a little while.

I rushed out the door on the driveway side of the Lodge and walked right into Lieutenant Borgnine. I excused myself and started to pull away.

"Ms. Feldstein, I was hoping to find you," he said in an all too pleasant tone. When had he ever been happy to see me? "I know Dr. Samuel Glickner is a friend of yours. Do you know where he is? There's a matter I'd like to discuss with him."

Did he really think I would fall for that? I didn't want to give anything away by my behavior. The secret was to act as difficult as I usually did. My first thought was just to say a curt no and be on my way. But that would be going too much the other way.

"What do you want to discuss with him?" I asked, forcing my eyes into what I hoped looked like a wide-open innocent expression and not a crazed psycho look. Without a mirror I wasn't sure. I don't think it mattered anyway because now that it was dark outside, my face was in shadow, as was his. The light coming through the window of the Lodge barely illuminated the round shape of his head and the lighter parts of his stubbly hair.

I almost smiled when I heard him making his usual grumbly noises and he began to rub his neck. "Can't you just give me a simple yes or no answer?"

"Okay, then, no," I said. "Now, if you'll excuse me." I made a move to leave.

"What's that?" he said, noticing the to-go box of food.

"My leftover dinner. I'm just going to drop it off." I pointed off in the direction of my place.

"Really," he said with interest. Not missing a beat, he continued, "You know, it's pretty dark out here and we did have one person strangled. It would be terrible if something happened to you. I would feel better if I saw that you got across the street safely."

Boy, was he laying it on thick. He was clearly up to something. I tried to talk him out of it, but it was like trying to get rid of a piece of tape stuck to your shoe. No matter what I did, he was still there.

We walked across the street in silence and went up my driveway. I kept my eyes averted from the guest house and headed directly to my back door.

"Okay, you did your duty. I'm home safe and secure." I paused at the back door, but he didn't move.

"If you're just going to drop it off and come back across the street, I'll wait for you and walk you back."

I put the key in the lock and opened the kitchen door and he followed me inside. I flipped on the light and went to put the box in the refrigerator. Poor Sammy wasn't going to get his dinner after all.

I got ready to turn around and leave, but my escort glanced around the kitchen and toward the hall. "This is a nice place. What do you have—two bedrooms?"

"Something like that," I said, taking a step toward the door.

"Mind if I look around? I'm curious about the design of these places on the edge of town."

Aha, so that was what he was up to. I was sure it had less to do with architecture and more to do with finding Sammy. But I had nothing to hide in the house but my unmade bed and the need to vacuum up the cat hair, so I shrugged and told him to be my guest. I'm afraid I was too easy about letting him do it, which he took to mean that Sammy wasn't hiding in my house. He stepped into the hall and glanced around quickly before announcing that he'd seen enough.

Julius heard me come in and walked into the kitchen. He did a figure eight greeting around my legs and then seemed to notice we had company. What did the black cat do? He plunked himself down in the space between me and Lieutenant Borgnine. Though I could only see the back of Julius's head, the way he was thumping his tail made me think he was giving the lieutenant a hostile stare with his yellow eyes.

Maybe it was because I had never had a cat before, but I'd always had a stereotypical view of them as sort of background pets. Doing things like lounging on the back of a sofa and ignoring what was going on in their human's life. I

thought they were very into themselves. It had never occurred
to me that they would be protective of the people they lived
with, but Julius was certainly giving off that vibe. Though I
wondered what exactly he would do—shred the lieutenant's
pant leg?

Whatever Julius was doing, he'd made the lieutenant
nervous because I saw him give the cat a wary glance. "If
you're ready," the cop said. He was careful to walk around
Julius as he went to the door.

I was relieved to be outside in the darkness and walked
down the driveway quickly. Lieutenant Borgnine was behind
me and seemed to be taking his time.

My heart dropped when he hesitated by the former garage.
"This was converted into a guest house, wasn't it?" He stopped
by the door. "I've been thinking of converting my garage into
living space. Maybe I could get some ideas from your place.
Mind if I look around?"

I knew I had every right to say no, but also knew that was
tantamount to saying I had something to hide, which I actually
did. Sammy. The lieutenant had quickly lost interest in looking
around the house when I'd said it was fine. I was hoping that
giving him carte blanche would work again. I was wishing
Julius had come with us and given the lieutenant more of the
hostile staring with the tail thumps as insurance.

"Great, sure, have a look inside," I said, trying to pump
up the enthusiasm like I meant it. I waited, expecting a
similar reaction to what I'd gotten in the house.

"Okay," he said, nodding toward the door, "unlock the
door."

I froze. It wasn't supposed to go like this. He was supposed to not want to look around now.

"On second thought," I said. It was no act to sound dis-
mayed because I was. "My retreat people are waiting for

me. How about I give you a rain check on that?" To punctu-
ate it, I took a step down the driveway.

"I'm here now. It'll just take a few minutes," he said, not
moving away from the door.

"It's probably kind of messy. I was making up the tote
bags in there."

"No problem."

"It's just kind of embarrassing," I said.

"I won't pass judgment on your housekeeping," he said.
"Go on, open the door. We're wasting time discussing it."

There was just a hint of it being an order. I knew I could
refuse, but I also knew that he could come back alone and
claim he thought he heard someone scream inside, which
gave him probable cause to break down the door.

Saying a silent "I'm sorry" to Sammy, I put the key in the
lock.

I wondered if the cop could hear my heartbeat. I could
certainly feel it thudding against my chest. I glanced around,
hoping a meteor might drop out of the sky and distract him,
but there was nothing.

I finally opened the door to the dark interior. I took my time
in the doorway, but Lieutenant Borgnine pushed past me and
walked inside. "Hey, how about we get some lights," he said.

I reached for the light by the door, but when I turned it
on, I was actually relieved when nothing happened. "It must
be burned out," I said.

Now that he was inside, the lieutenant seemed to have
forgotten his ruse for why he wanted to look. No more casual
"I want to get some ideas for my place."

"There must be some other light." He sounded impatient.

"There's an overhead fixture."

"Well," he said when I continued to just stand there. "Go
ahead and turn it on." I felt my way along the wall until my

hand touched the plastic plate. I couldn't stall anymore and reached over for the light switch. As my finger pushed it up, I looked away, wanting to avoid the confrontation. I waited to hear something, but after a few moments, the cop was silent. I turned my gaze into the center of the room and I was shocked. The bed had been folded into the wall and the doors with the shelves slid over it. Everything looked orderly as if no one had been there.

"Well, there you have it," I said, trying to keep the relief out of my voice. The cop grunted with displeasure and started to tour the room.

As I expected, he eyed the shelves against the wall suspiciously. "That's one of those wall beds, isn't it?" He stepped closer. "You don't mind if I see how it works?"

Was there a chance that Sammy had crushed his tall hulky frame against the bed and was folded up with it? At the very least, the bed would probably look slept in, but I gave him the okay.

He slid the two bookcases back and then pulled down the bed. No Sammy came popping out and surprisingly the bed was not only made, but so tightly, I was sure you could bounce a quarter on it. It certainly didn't look like anybody had slept in it recently.

The cop didn't look happy. I saw him glancing at the two doors in the place. I rushed ahead and opened the door to the bathroom. It felt warm and moist, like someone had showered recently. Before Borgnine could step inside the small room, I whipped back the shower curtain and turned on the water to cover it up. "See, a full-functioning bathroom," I said. I turned the faucet on and off and flushed the toilet.

"I see that it all works," he said, taking a step backward to get out of the close damp space. Good, my efforts had worked.

Back in the main room, he stared at the other door in the

place. "It's just a closet," I said, trying to keep my voice light. It was the most likely hiding place and I felt my heart thud as the lieutenant's mouth curved in an expectant smile. He stepped up to the door.

"Let's just see what's in there," he said, putting his hand on the doorknob.

I have to admit, I held my breath as he turned the handle and pulled the door open. Then I waited, expecting something to happen, like Sammy to pop out. But there was only silence as the bulldog-shaped cop stepped inside. A few clothing items were still hanging on the rod and he batted them aside impatiently. I don't think he meant to let out the groan when all he saw was the back wall of the small enclosure. He shut the door with an annoyed swat.

After that he moved to the kitchen area and opened every cabinet as if he thought he'd find Sammy folded up in one of them. Did he really think that six-foot-one Sammy could fit in that small a space? I started breathing again and wondered where Sammy was.

"I hope you've found what you were looking for," I said, doing my best to keep the relief out of my voice.

He just glowered at me. I guess not.

14

IT WAS A RELIEF TO GET TO THE BLUE DOOR.
Baking the desserts and the muffins for the coffee spots was
my last to-do task of the day. I was glad the restaurant was
empty and there were no diners lingering over their coffee. Tag
was precise about most things, but somehow he relented when
it came to the restaurant and would let people sit as long as they
wanted, sometimes well after the restaurant had closed.

But even the cook had left when I got there. Tag was
doing the last-minute setup so that the tables would be ready
for the morning.

I was still recovering from the run-in with Lieutenant
Borgnine. It was amazing how he seemed to have forgotten
his gallant offer to escort me back across the street once he'd
had his look around the guest house. I'd barely put the key
in the lock and he was gone. Not that I minded at all. Though
I knew it wasn't over. I was sure he thought I knew where
Sammy was—which was funny because for the moment I

didn't. I tried calling Sammy's cell phone and it went to voice mail right away. Either he had shut it off or it was dead.

I had made a quick stop back at Vista Del Mar. Everything seemed fine and it seemed most everyone was heading toward Hummingbird Hall to see the movie. Madeleine had returned. I saw her walking with Lucinda. Good, she wasn't alone.

Tag looked up from folding the cloth napkins. For a man in his late fifties, he had a lot of hair. When I'd first met him, I'd thought all that thick brown hair had to be a wig or a toupee. But it was all his—he'd certainly lucked out in the hair genes. When he saw I was alone, he looked disappointed. "Lucinda didn't come with you, huh," he said.

The possibility of her coming with me was only in his imagination. She was having a wonderful time being away from all this, and even him.

"I'm glad that Lucinda likes your retreats so much, but I miss her." I went on into the kitchen to drop off the bags of supplies for the muffins and he came in behind me. "You know that we knew each other in high school." I nodded. Not only did I know the story, but it was on the menu back written in fairy-tale fashion—how they'd known each other in high school and then reconnected all these years later and found their happily ever after. There were a few flies in the ointment that the flowery story didn't mention. Mainly that Tag had gotten more and more fussy as he'd gotten older and bordered on OCD. Mostly Lucinda dealt with it with good humor, but I think that was partly because she got these yarn weekends off, even if it was just a five-minute drive away.

"When I heard that someone died on the grounds, I wanted to go over to Vista Del Mar and talk her into coming home. Are you sure she's okay? There are rumors flying around town. You don't think I should go over there and check on her?"

"There's no need for you to worry. The person who died wasn't part of our retreat and Cadbury's finest Lieutenant Borgnine is telling everyone that he believes it was personal to the woman who died and that there's no need to worry about a crazed killer on the loose."

He seemed slightly reassured about that anyway. "Lucinda told me you have some information about the Delacorte secret heir. I wish you'd leave that alone. You really should think twice before you stir things up."

"What have you heard?" I asked. Tag was not the kind of person to say something like that without a reason.

"The Delacorte sisters were in here for dinner a few nights ago. That Cora's voice carries more than she realizes. I think she was trying to whisper, but I heard it all. She told Madeleine she believes their brother had a love child. That he 'got about,' as she put it. Then she told Madeleine she was glad nobody knew who it was and that the whole thing had been dropped." Tag swallowed as if what he was going to say next made him uncomfortable. "Then she said that they might have to take measures if somebody brought it up again. It seemed like she was thinking of someone in particular when she said 'somebody.'" He left it at that, but I knew Tag thought Cora meant me.

I had a dark thought. I'd gotten the impression that Madeleine might be okay with me finding her brother's heir, but maybe she was just trying to get information to pass it to her sister. And "take measures"? What did that mean?

I started to lay out the ingredients for the desserts and Tag finally bade me a good night.

I turned on some soft jazz and put all thoughts on the back burner. Baking was like meditation for me. I got lost in the flow of wonderful smells, sifting, mixing, pouring— lost in the process of turning a bunch of ingredients into something delicious.

A noise interfered with my concentration. Was it a knock on the door? I was ready to chalk it up to my imagination, but I heard it again and this time I was sure it was real. I went to check the door and all I saw was a fist aimed at the glass portion of the entrance. Even when I got closer, it looked like a fist floating in space before it connected with the glass again and made a knocking sound.

"Hello, is someone there?" I asked, trying to sound tough. I was all alone in the place.

"Open the door," a whispery voice commanded.

"Not until you identify yourself." I considered grabbing something to use as a weapon. What? The best I could do was to pull an umbrella out of the holder by the door. It had been left by someone months ago and it looked like the ribs were broken. I held it out and waited.

"Case, it's me." There was only one person who called me that.

"Sammy?" I lowered the umbrella and opened the door. He was crouched on the ground with only one arm sticking up. Because of the dark clothing, the fist he'd used to knock with had appeared to be floating in space. He began to unfold himself and, when he got to standing, looked around quickly.

"Can I come in?" he asked.

I stepped aside and waved him in. He was still wearing the tuxedo, but it looked the worse for wear. The cummerbund was long gone, the white shirt was wrinkled and open at the collar, and the satiny lapels of the jacket looked scuffed. He looked haggard, but partly because he needed a shave. Stubble was sexy on some men, but not on Sammy.

"What's—" Before I could finish the sentence, he had slipped to the floor and was crawling past the windows.

"I don't know who's out there watching," he said as I followed him across the former living room floor. He crawled into the bathroom off the second small dining room. Like the other rooms, the restroom's window faced Grand Street, but the glass was frosted so no one could see in. He stood up and leaned against the flowery wallpaper. Then he let out a heavy sigh, and I got to finish my sentence.

"What's going on?"

"I'm sorry, Case, but I'm not cut out to be a bad boy. I thought all this running and hiding would be exciting, but it's really just tiring. I was going to try to sneak into my room and get some clean clothes, but when I got to the B and B, I saw that Lieutenant Borgnine was in the parlor."

Sammy was still renting a room in a bed-and-breakfast just down the street from the Blue Door restaurant. Part of the charm of the place for travelers was they had a gathering in the parlor every night. Sammy's room was on the first floor in the back, and the only way in was going past the front room and the lieutenant.

"He figured out the silk piece was my streamer, didn't he?" Sammy said, and I nodded. "That's what I figured when I saw him come to your place."

"So you were there? But where? The place looked so neat. And the way the bed was made, it looked like nobody had slept in it."

Sammy's face brightened. "Case, I'm not the kind of guy who throws his socks on the floor. And I'm used to precision. You forget that I'm not just any old doctor of urology. I'm a surgeon, too. I don't just make rabbits appear out of hats. I can create a bladder out of other body parts. You have to be precise when you do that. I just used the same logic and applied it to making the bed and cleaning up the place."

Sammy almost never talked about his medical knowledge, and other than occasionally seeing him in his white coat, I mostly forgot about it.

"Okay, but how was it we didn't see you?" I said.

He let out a tired laugh. "I'm not sure I should divulge that. You know, it's like the magician code—you don't reveal how you do a trick."

"C'mon, Sammy," I said, rolling my eyes.

"I was just teasing. What I did hardly counts as anything much." He stopped and laughed to himself. "It's a funny thing about human nature. We tend to follow patterns, so a slight deviation from an initial impulse is all you need." I didn't understand exactly what he meant and he gave me an example.

"Say you're walking under a fire escape that starts to fall. Your impulse would be to run forward. And you'd probably get smacked in the head before you were clear of it. But all you'd have to do is to take a few steps to the side and you'd miss getting hit by it completely. I like to think that's what I did. I heard the lieutenant and figured it was only a matter of time before he would want to look inside the guest house. I loosened the bulb on the lamp by the door so it wouldn't go on. I knew it would make you both walk farther inside before you turned the lights on, and I figured you'd leave the door open until you got them on. Instead of trying to hide somewhere, I stepped behind the door. Then when you opened it, I simply slipped out while you were both distracted."

"Then what?"

"I went around to the side of your place. There's that bathroom that has the door to the outside. I know you leave a spare set of keys in the potted plant next to the door."

He was right about that. I started doing it after I locked myself out once when I took the litter box outside to clean it.

"I was pretty sure the lieutenant wouldn't want to look in the house again, but just in case, I hid in the closet full of yarn." He pulled out a ball of blue yarn that had gotten stuck in his jacket and handed it to me. "Your aunt sure left you a lot of it."

"Why don't you go back to the guest house? Lieutenant Borgnine isn't going to be looking for you there now."

"Case, I knew I could depend on you." He hugged me and another ball of yarn fell out of his jacket.

It was the least I could do. Here he was so grateful to me and I don't think it occurred to him for one second that he would have been thousands of miles away from this mess if I hadn't moved here. I told him about the dinner in the fridge and said I'd bring him some muffins.

"I've been thinking it over a lot and I know I can't remember what happened, but these are healing hands," he said, holding them out to me. "Not hands that would strangle someone. I just want you to know that." A car went by on the street making a loud noise and Sammy jumped, then he shook his head wearily. "Please find out who killed that woman as quickly as possible. I'm not cut out for life as a fugitive." He pressed a key into my hand. "And Case, maybe you can sneak into my room and get me some clean clothes." He hugged me again before slipping back to the floor and crawling across the restaurant to the door, and then he slipped out into the night.

A little while later my cell phone rang and Sammy let me know he was safely ensconced in the guest house. He had parked his car blocks away and he'd made sure that no light was coming from the guest house windows. The only problem he'd had was with Julius. The cat tried to keep him from coming into the house to retrieve the food from the refrigerator.

"But it's okay now. We're good buddies," Sammy said. "It's amazing what a little stink fish will do." Leave it to Sammy to win over my cat.

It was a relief to get back to baking. I had the batter for

the carrot cakes whipped up in no time. As they baked, the kitchen filled with a sweet fragrance of cinnamon and I began on the muffins. Banana nut this time, or as I called them, Gone Bananas. I heard a knock at the door. It wasn't tentative like before and I recognized the sound right away. Had Sammy gotten into more trouble?

I wiped my hands on my apron and went into the main room. No floating hand this time, I could just make out a bouquet of sunflowers but not who was holding them in the darkness of the porch.

Anybody bringing flowers had to be all right, so I just opened the door. "Dane?" I said when the light hit his face. He was wearing his midnight blue uniform under a canvas cop jacket.

"In the flesh," he said. "These are for you. To make up for the embarrassing end of our date." He held out the yellow flowers and looked away as he did it as if he was somehow uncomfortable, which was odd. Dane was a look-you-in-the-eye kind of guy.

He followed me into the kitchen while I searched for something to put them in. "You didn't have to," I said. I found an old coffee can and filled it with water. "Where'd you get flowers on a Thursday night at this hour?" They practically rolled the streets of Cadbury up at ten o'clock and it was close to midnight.

"It doesn't matter. I'd go to the ends of the earth for you. I wanted to get you something."

What? That was a line if I'd ever heard one. Dane didn't seem like a "line" sort of guy. He leaned against the counter and looked at me with a tilted head. "You look really nice." He touched my forearm and ran his finger up it in a seductive manner. I looked down at the black jeans that had spatters of flour; flecks of grated carrots were stuck to my arm and probably on my face as well. I'd pulled my hair back to get it out of the way and tucked it under a knitted kerchief. I had done it by feel instead of looking in a mirror and I was sure it was cockeyed. In short, I didn't look really nice and he knew it. The flowers, the fake compliment, the wandering finger, it all seemed odd and not him. I could believe him showing up with a pan of lasagna a lot more than a bunch of sunflowers.

"Here, let me help with that." The timer had gone off. He pulled on the oven mitts and started to take out the cakes.

"That's okay," I said, pulling on another set of oven mitts and going for the other cakes. We bumped into each other and the tube pan in his mitts dropped to the floor and rolled. The cake didn't hit the floor, but it broke apart in the pan.

He apologized profusely. "This isn't going right."

"What isn't going right?" I looked at his uniform. "Aren't you supposed to be out guarding the streets of Cadbury?"

"Yes," he said finally. Then he mumbled something under his breath about not caring if he got the midnight shift forever, he couldn't do this. "Lieutenant Borgnine suggested I stop by and—"

"Oh, my goodness," I squealed. Now I got it. The flowers, the line about going to the ends of the earth and telling me I look nice. "He told you to come here and flirt with me to try and get information."

"So you saw through it," he said.

"You could say that." I laughed and he wanted to know what was so funny. "It's just that my old boss Frank's usual suggestion is for me to try to get information by flirting with you." I left off the rest, that Frank was convinced if I kept just flirting and no nookie as he called it followed, I'd lose the information opportunity after a while. To show him, I did a few bats of my eyes and did my best impression of a sexy look. He responded by cracking up completely. "I didn't say I was good at it."

"So that's where it came from?" he said, referring to several times when I'd come over to his place. "I thought it was your own idea, but you just weren't very good at flirting." He shook his head with dismay. "It was kind of cute the way you were so bad at it." He suddenly seemed wary. "I wasn't that bad, was I?" he asked.

"Everybody isn't as naturally flirty as you are," I said. "Though even you aren't so good at it when you're trying too hard. It seemed pretty off. I mean flowers, and telling me I look good when I'm wearing food. And the uniform is a dead giveaway that you're working."

"Geez, I didn't realize I was so transparent." He looked at the cake on the floor. "Sorry about that. Can I at least help you make another one?" I studied his face to see if the sentiment was genuine or he was trying the fake flirty stuff again. He picked up on it. "I'm really sorry for making more work for you and I'm honestly offering to help."

"So what did Lieutenant Borgnine want you to find out?" I pushed aside the muffin things and went for another round of carrot cake ingredients. Dane volunteered for carrot-grating duty and I handed him a bunch of carrots. He scrubbed them and put the shredding blade on the food processor.

"He thinks you know where Sammy is." He didn't seem to want to look at me as he spoke and loaded some carrots in the chute, getting ready to turn the machine on. Still with his eyes on his work, he continued, "I shouldn't do this, but don't say anything."

The food processor made a racket for a few minutes and it was impossible to talk. When he finally shut it off, I couldn't help myself. "It's ridiculous that Lieutenant Borgnine is wasting time looking for Sammy. How about trying to find the real killer? He must have some other suspects in mind," I said.

Dane seemed to be fighting with himself. "I knew you were going to say something like that. And I was going to answer it by saying that the best thing is that neither of us say anything about the case." He shook his head. "But I'm with you. I think it's ridiculous that he's wasting time looking for Sammy. The trouble is that his streamer is what strangled her. Any ideas?"

"Do you know the time of death?" I asked.

"I thought you were supposed to flirt with me when you wanted information," he teased.

I did some hair flipping and eye bats, thankful that he would realize I was vamping. I have just never mastered all the girly stuff. It came off as comedy even when I tried to be serious about it.

"How can I resist a show like that?" he said. "This isn't the way this is supposed to be going. It's bad enough I didn't get him any information, but giving it out—If the lieutenant finds out, I'll be working the worst shift every holiday from now to eternity." He leaned close as if the lieutenant were hanging out someplace within earshot. "The best guess is that it was between eleven and midnight."

"I wish I knew who had the streamer at that hour."

"Well, yeah," Dane said. "If you knew that, you'd know who the killer was." He rolled his head back and looked skyward. "I'm going to pay for this. I just know it."

I thought back to the incident when Diana had pulled it from Sammy's sleeve and I tried to remember what happened next. "He tried to smooth things over and said she was his assistant, but it seemed to set her off. I'm trying to think what happened to the streamer after that. Normally, Sammy puts the chain of silk squares in his pocket." I made a discouraging noise. "Forget I said that."

"So you don't know what happened to the streamer after that," he said.

I shook my head. "I left and Sammy doesn't remember anything. It seems there was a martini bar set up and he was upset and took a shaker of the cocktails to the beach."

Dane put his hand up to stop me. "I think we should leave it at that. I don't want to know how you came by that information."

He stayed until the replacement cake was in the oven. "I better go. Lieutenant Borgnine is waiting to hear from me."

"What are you going to tell him?"

"That I messed up your cake and had to help you make another one and that I meant it when I said you look nice." He plucked a shred of carrot off my arm. "Baking becomes you," he said with a grin. "Okay, just joking. Really, what I'm going to tell him is the truth. You said nothing about where Sammy was."

"He's probably not going to like that," I said.

"Nope." He leaned against the counter. "About last night. I really think we should give it another chance." He glanced around the empty kitchen. "We're all alone. No chance for someone to make a juvenile comment." His eyes were shining as he leaned toward me, and just as we were about to make contact, the timer went off. Saved by the bell.

15

I WAS DRAGGING BY THE TIME I DISTRIBUTED THE last of the muffins around town, and I was just about ready to head for my car when I noticed the imposing yellow Queen Anne–style bed-and-breakfast that Sammy called home on the corner up ahead. Should I seize the moment, slip in and get his things? At this hour of the night the front door would be locked, but he had given me his after-hours key to the front door along with the key to his room. Though the lights were on in the parlor, I imagined everyone had gone to sleep.

It wasn't breaking and entering. I had a key and Sammy's permission, but I still hesitated when I reached the walkway leading to the inn. I didn't want to run into the owners. I'd have to do way too much explaining and I didn't know what they knew about the situation with Sammy. The house took up the whole corner with a garden on one side. The owners clearly hadn't gone along with the idea of native plants, and even in the dark I could make out beautifully shaped bushes. And I could smell the heady fragrance of gardenias.

I could see into the front windows now and the room was empty. Sammy seemed so demoralized wearing that soiled shirt and messy tuxedo. It would be nice to deliver him some clean clothes. Figuring I could be in and out quickly, I made the snap decision to go in. I climbed the short staircase that led to the small curved front porch feeling more apprehensive with each step.

If I hadn't felt really guilty about the situation Sammy was in, I would have turned back. I had had bad dreams about doing stuff like this. I let out a sigh and put the key in the front door. It turned with no effort and the front door opened. I found myself in a small entryway with another door at the end that led into the house. The inner door was unlocked and beyond that was a large entrance hall. A small reception desk had been built in next to the stairway and made it obvious that this residence had been turned into a hotel. The parlor or living room was to my right. I glanced in, relieved to see it was as I'd thought, deserted.

Sammy had started staying here when he first got to Cadbury and had taken one of the bedrooms on the second floor. He outgrew the room quickly and they'd moved him to the first floor and a room that had been a library at one time. The owners were in the process of making a storage area into a small apartment, which he was considering taking—if he couldn't talk me into renting him my guest house.

Sammy hadn't really settled in Cadbury. It was more like he'd taken a leave of absence from his practice and life in Chicago, or that's what I kept telling myself.

He had insisted that he wasn't there because of me. That he'd wanted a change and liked the area and it was a chance for him to perform his magic away from the frowning stares of his family. I didn't buy it since it seemed like our paths were always crossing and he kept telling me how I was the only one who "got" him. But whether I was there or not, I suspected when this whole mess with Diana Rathman got settled, he'd pack up his stuff and move back to Chicago.

Despite his many invitations, I had never actually seen Sammy's room. The house was huge with halls on either side of the staircase. I knew Sammy had a view of the side garden, which meant his room was off the left hall, but I quickly discovered there were two doors.

As I was trying to decide which one to try, I heard noise coming from the back of the house and then some voices. I imagined there was a big kitchen and a butler's pantry in the back. Maybe the owners were getting things ready for breakfast before they went to bed.

I panicked, worrying about running into them and all the questions to follow. Sammy could survive without clean clothes for another day. I retraced my steps and was about to open the door to the small entryway when I heard voices getting louder.

"You better check the front door," a woman said. I froze for a moment and then I thought of what Sammy had done with the guest house. I only had to make a small adjustment. There was no way I could hide behind the door, but there was a coat tree next to it. It seemed more for decoration and the coats hanging on it were all vintage. I could practically hear my mother's voice saying, "Is this what your life has come to, sneaking around and hiding under coats?" I barely made it under an old trench coat when I felt the couple walk by.

They were distracted and certainly didn't expect someone to be hiding in their coat tree, so they didn't notice my legs showing below the beige raincoat. The man went out to the front door and shook the door to make sure it was locked.

He joined the woman in the area near the reception desk and they lowered the lights. I watched as they went back toward where Sammy's room was. The woman opened one of the two doors and I got a glimpse inside. It was their private area.

I said a silent prayer that I hadn't gone opening doors. Just imagine if I'd opened the door to their room and gone inside, thinking it was Sammy's. I shivered with horror thinking about what would have happened if they'd walked in and found me.

Well, at least I knew which room was his now. I waited a few moments to make sure they weren't coming out again, and then I slipped out from under the coats. I considered going to his room now, but I was too shaken thinking about what could have happened, and I just wanted to get out of there.

My mother's voice haunted me as I retraced my steps down the deserted street in downtown Cadbury. I could hear her fussing at me for burning the candle at both ends. Then she'd move on to Sammy.

"Poor Sammy," she'd say. "What have you done to get him out of this mess? You better fix it fast before the police arrest him." She would definitely give me an opinion on Dane. "Casey, your instincts are right. Don't get involved." Even in my imagination I was shocked to hear her admit that I was right about something. Would that happen in real life? Probably not. She'd be more likely to say, "Stay away from the cop. You'll only make a mess."

I argued with myself the whole way back to my car about whether I needed her approval too much. I didn't pass one car as I drove home. It was so quiet at night here that all the stoplights became just blinking red lights. I pulled into my driveway. The guest house looked dark. Not even a sliver of light showed under the door. I slipped a note under the door even though I didn't think anyone was watching. But who knew for sure. It explained the lack of his clothes along with telling him I'd left the muffins outside the door. There was carrot cake as a bonus. I didn't explain why.

With that taken care of, I took the plastic container across the street with the muffins for Vista Del Mar. It was just habit to look both ways before I crossed. The whole length of the street was empty of traffic. The grounds looked dark and mysterious, and I avoided shining my flashlight anyplace but directly ahead of myself. As always, the lights in the Lodge shone through the windows like a beacon in the darkness.

After all the activity I'd seen in there earlier, it seemed even emptier now somehow. Though not completely. The desk clerk was talking to a man in sweats. I held up my hand in greeting as I crossed to the café.

"Hey, Casey, maybe you can help," the clerk said. I dropped off the container in front of the Cora and Madeleine Delacorte Café and came back to the massive counter. "He's looking for some aspirin. He's got a headache." The clerk explained that I lived across the street from Vista Del Mar.

The man looked familiar as he turned toward me, but something seemed off.

"Bobbie Listorie," he said. "We met earlier. You were with Madeleine Delacorte." He put enough emphasis on her last name to make it clear he knew who she was and how important her family was to the area. "You wouldn't have a couple of aspirin. I've got a monster of a headache. I thought I had some, but all I have are these." I could see the pain in his bloodshot blue eyes as he held out a small yellow tin. "This light isn't helping." He put on a pair of tinted glasses and massaged his temple.

"It's the sweats," I said half to myself. "That's why I didn't recognize you."

"I've been dressing the part this weekend. I probably should have gotten some sharkskin sweats," he joked.

I said I had aspirin and he offered to come across the street for it, but the last thing I wanted was the chance for anybody to notice Sammy's presence, so I insisted I'd bring them to him.

While I was picking up the bottle, it occurred to me that he might know something about what happened to Diana Rathman or at least what Sammy did with his evening.

Bobbie was lounging on one of the sofas in the Lodge when I came back. I brought him some of the carrot cake along with the aspirin and joked that it was an old baker's cure for a headache.

"Thank you, babe. You saved my life," the singer said as he took the pills with some water provided by the desk clerk. "I didn't realize what the accommodations were like at this place when I accepted this gig." He looked around the large room, which was comfortable but hardly plush.

"Vista Del Mar has a unique charm," I said. I mentioned that one of my helpers for the retreat, Wanda Krug, had said he did some kind of work at the same posh Pebble Beach resort she worked at.

"You know Wanda," he said with a smile. "She doesn't look it, but she's one heck of a good golfer. I know she's annoyed that I get all the glory—and a lot better pay. But it's a proven fact that people like to hang out with celebrities and play golf with them. My hanging out there gives the place a certain aura, if you will. And I do an occasional show in the bar to liven things up." He chuckled. "The shows only look like the guests talked me into performing; actually they're all planned. I always act like I'm not going to do 'It's All in the Eyes,' and they go crazy until I do. I guess it is pretty amazing that after all these years, they still want to hear it."

I was surprised at how talkative he was and I let him go

on while I tried to figure out how to steer the conversation toward what I wanted to know. "The only reason I'm here is they didn't need me this weekend at my usual spot. The resort was taken over by a charity tournament and they brought their own entertainment. That's why Wanda was available, too." He stopped long enough to take a bite of the carrot cake.

"Whew, the aspirin is taking effect," he said. "And your carrot cake is helping, too. You're some baker. I guess I can go back to my 'cell' now." His expression showed distaste. "The beds are like cots, no TV or fluffy towels."

I rushed to stop him before he got up. It wasn't hard. He didn't seem to be in a hurry to go back to his room. "Before you go, I wonder if I could ask you about something."

"Sure, sweetheart, you brought the pills that saved the old Bobberino from having to spend the night with a thudding headache. Ask away."

I figured he'd been around the Lodge most of the evening that first night. Maybe he could help with an alibi for Sammy. Not for me. I was sure he was innocent, but I wanted something to throw in front of Lieutenant Borgnine.

"You must have seen what was going on in the Lodge the night of the mixer," I began.

At first he seemed puzzled, but then he nodded with recognition. "You mean because of that woman getting whacked, er, killed? Who'd have expected something like that to happen here."

I mentioned being a friend of the magician's and his face lit with understanding. "Rumor has it the cops think he's the one who killed that woman."

"I'm sure he didn't. He isn't that kind of person. The trouble is he doesn't remember what happened."

"I get it now, you're looking for a way to get him off the

hook. A very admirable quality." Bobbie slumped against the back of the sofa and took another bite of the carrot cake. "Let me see. I hung around here all evening." He looked around the room as if it would stir his memory. "I was mingling and signing some of the CD cases." He gestured toward the cases of merchandise up near the registration counter. "The hotel people were handling the sales. It's much classier that way. They're a regular item in the gift shop of the other resort. Jimmie Phelps, Dotty Night and I kind of divided the room up and then hung out in our section. Jimmie had quite a crowd." Bobbie stopped for a moment. "I think that woman was hanging around him. I don't know why, but I got the feeling they might have known each other from before."

He went on about the martini bar being a hit except with him. "I just nursed one drink. You have to be careful around the fans. I wouldn't want anything to mess up what I have."

I was close to nodding off by now. Bobbie sure liked to talk. I got it. He was very lucky to have the gig with the other resort. And he was going to hang on to it, but he was particularly excited about a tour he had coming up. "The last stop is a lounge in Vegas." He looked at me and I did my best to look impressed.

"You were saying about last night . . ." I said, trying to get him back on track.

"Yeah, yeah," Bobbie said. "There was some kind of program around ten o'clock, and most of the people left. I figured my work for the evening was almost done so I—"

I interrupted. "It's really Sammy I want to know about. What did he do?"

"Right, the magician. He seemed pretty upset. Nobody likes it when your act gets ruined. I suppose it's even worse for a magician. With me, it's more a problem of people wanting me to sing their favorite hit of mine. They don't seem to understand that shouting it out ruins the mood. The magician was muttering about something else, or someone else. Lacey or Casey." His face lit up with recognition. "That must be you."

"Yeah, that's me," I said, feeling uncomfortable.

"There was a fuss about setting up the martini bar. The manager of the place wasn't happy about it, but Norman Rathman pushed it through. He had somebody who would make the drinks and had brought all the supplies. I think the magician was their first customer. He took the whole shaker and went off toward the beach." He saw my disappointed look. "Sorry I couldn't give you what you wanted, but all I can do is tell you what I saw."

"There's one other thing," I said. "Did you see what happened to the silk streamer?"

"You mean the bright-colored thing that woman pulled out of his sleeve?"

I nodded.

"When she left," he continued, "I saw it hanging out of her pocket."

I felt a temporary sense of relief. If Diana had the streamer, then it was available to anybody. But then it occurred to me that telling that to Lieutenant Borgnine wouldn't do any good. Because being available to anybody included being available to Sammy.

16

WHEN I FINALLY WENT HOME, I WAS WIRED FROM
the seemingly endless day, and I was frustrated that I hadn't
managed to find out anything to get Sammy off the top of
the lieutenant's suspect list. I hadn't even managed to get
him some clean clothes. Did I really hide in a coatrack?
And then leave rather than complete the job? My old boss,
Frank, would surely not be proud. I went over the events of
the day again, hoping there was something useful I might
have missed. A ray of hope popped out when I remembered
that Bobbie Listorie had said Diana had more than a casual
conversation with the baseball player, Jimmie Phelps. Was
that who Scarlett had seen her with outside?

I tried going to bed, knowing I had another long day
ahead of me. The workshop was a little behind. I had hoped
the group would have started their projects already. It
wouldn't matter for some of the experienced knitters. They
worked fast and would be able to finish their project or be

close to it. But for the others, the people like me and Madeleine, it was another story. We needed as much time during the weekend as possible.

I tried chamomile tea and a warm bath, hoping to slow my mind down, but I had a restless night, which certainly didn't make Julius happy. He'd taken to sleeping wrapped in my arms, and every time I turned over and readjusted my position, he got pushed out of his comfy spot. But leave it to the cat to solve the problem. When I awoke, he was cuddled next to my head.

Before I even made coffee, I punched in Frank's number.

"Hey, Feldstein," he said when he answered.

"How'd you know it was me?" I asked. Frank chortled.

"I finally figured out how to get the caller ID thing to work. So now before I even pick up the phone, some robotic woman mangles the name." He sounded like he took a sip of something and I heard the squeak of his recliner chair. Frank always pushed it to its limit of recline. I had this fantasy that one day the chair would revolt and send him catapulting into the air. "So what's the problem now?" he asked.

"It's more like still," I began. I ran down the whole thing with Sammy and the guest house and the lieutenant thinking I knew where he was.

"And you do," Frank said. "Be careful, Feldstein, they could get you for withholding evidence. The obvious answer to your next question is that you should find out who killed the woman and get some evidence to wave in front of the cop."

"How'd you know what I was going to ask you?"

"I'm a PI, and besides it was pretty obvious. And I even know what you're going to ask me next. You're going to want to know how to do what I just told you. My best advice would be to find out as much as you can about the victim."

"I'm trying to do that," I said. "I already found out that

she showed up here at the last minute. Even her husband didn't seem to know she was coming."

Frank let out an *ahhh* sort of sound. "Yes, Feldstein, that's the kind of thing I meant. Find out why she decided to come."

"There's something else," I said.

"There always is. Okay, shoot."

I told him about the contents of the envelope and the secret heir. "I tried checking the records using the woman's name on the sheet from the safety-deposit box sign-in, but it's a fake name. And yes, I know you've always said that when people use fake names, they often use the same initials." I told him about Lucinda's idea of talking to people who were in the right age group. He made some grunts to show he was listening. "The thing is, if I uncover the heir, it's going to cause trouble." I repeated what I'd heard Cora say that sounded almost like a threat.

"What's in it for you, Feldstein?"

"Nothing, really," I said.

"So maybe you should just let it be, though from what you said about Cora Delacorte, it sounds like her concept of taking measures might be smacking you with her purse."

"It's just that Edmund Delacorte said he wanted Vista Del Mar to go to his child or children. He sounds like he was a good guy and I'd like to see his wishes honored. Besides, the other sister seems to be curious about finding a relative. I think she's lonely for family."

Frank groaned. "So you're one of those idealists now. Good luck and watch your back."

I'd barely hung up the phone when it rang. It was my mother wanting an update on Sammy.

"You're hiding him in your guest house?" my mother said. "I hope you're feeding him. Does he have clean clothes?"

"I'm working on it," I said.

"I'm not going to say a word to his parents. They'd have a fit if they knew."

"And they'd blame me," I said, and my mother didn't object. "I notice you aren't mentioning anything about the cooking school in Paris." My mother had enrolled me at a fancy school and even found a place for me to stay. It was all on hold, but she was so sure that I wasn't going to stay in Cadbury, since in the past I'd developed a bit of a reputation for moving on from things, that almost every time she called, she asked if she should push the button on it.

"Please don't tell me that you want to go now," my mother said. "You can't abandon Sammy."

"I don't intend to. And you can really just cancel the whole cooking school thing. I've made a life here in Cadbury. I'm staying here. I really am."

"Sweetheart, you've said that before and something always happens. Just wait until Sammy is free."

Did she really think there was any chance I'd take off and leave Sammy in the lurch? It was useless to argue with her. She was convinced she knew me better than I knew myself. But I really believed I had changed. I noticed she didn't end the call with her usual "When I was your age, I was a wife, a mother and a doctor and you're what?" I almost wished she had.

Julius watched while I made a fast breakfast, although it wasn't for me. It was for Sammy. It is amazing what a motivator guilt is. Everyone knows that I might be a great baker, but when it comes to actual meals, I'm a washout. It's not that I can't cook regular food, I just have no interest—most of the time. I would have felt rotten taking Sammy the kind of stuff I usually eat for breakfast, like instant oatmeal and instant orange drink.

Julius glanced up at me with shock as I went back and forth to the refrigerator and turned on the stove burner. He jumped up on the kitchen table for a better view. I noticed he sniffed the air, maybe hoping there was something for him in it.

The smell of melting butter was certainly a lot better than stink fish. I mixed up a couple of eggs and added a little half-and-half. When the butter was sizzling, I poured in the eggs. With a few maneuvers of the pan and a spatula, I turned out a perfect omelette. I added some slices of strawberries and two pieces of buttered toast, not burned this time. I found a tray my aunt had left and filled a thermal carafe with freshly brewed coffee. I even added a cloth napkin.

Julius looked so disappointed when I headed to the door with the food, I stopped and cut off a little piece of the omelette and offered it to him. He ate it with the same gusto he had for stink fish. Then he followed me outside, licking his whiskers. Oh, no, had I just created a new food obsession for him? With stink fish I just had to open the can and then wrap it in endless layers of plastic to contain the smell. Eggs required actual cooking. I looked down at him at my feet. "This is a special occasion. Remember, eggs are only for special occasions."

Julius blinked a few times like he was thinking over what I said, or maybe he was planning how he could change my mind.

I checked the street in front of my house and the driveway. It appeared completely dead. I felt pretty comfortable that nobody was watching, that is, unless Lieutenant Borgnine was hiding behind a tree on the Vista Del Mar grounds with high-powered binoculars trained on me. To be on the safe side, I went to a window that couldn't be seen from the street.

I knocked softly on the glass, and Sammy opened the shutters and pulled up the window.

His eyes bugged out when he saw the food. "Wow, Case, did you make this?" he asked, taking the tray.

"It's no big deal. I figured you were used to a hot break-fast after living where you do." As I was talking, I noticed Julius watching from outside the kitchen door. "I'll work on getting you some clean clothes." I handed him my laptop, which I'd been holding under the tray. "So you won't die of boredom."

"When you get my clothes, could you get my phone char-ger? My cell's dead."

"I'm not sure you should be using it anyway," I said, reminding him how the cops could track people by following pings from the phone. "Though they can only track you within a radius of a couple hundred yards, and by the time Lieutenant Borgnine gets around to doing that, this whole thing should be settled. In the meantime, there's a cordless connected to my landline."

I wanted to know who he needed to call. It turned out no one really. He had no appointments booked until after the weekend. He didn't want to talk to his parents. "The only one I need to contact is you," he said.

Sammy looked like he was wearing the tuxedo shirt and not much else. Typical Sammy, he'd bounced back from the previous night and seemed in a better humor. "I'm sorry for all this," I said. "I know that you wouldn't be here if it wasn't for me. You'd still be in Chicago going about your regular day, seeing patients, wearing clean clothes, and not having to exist off handouts from me."

"Case, I was looking for a change," he said. "Like I've told you all along, I didn't move here to follow you. I'm not some kind of stalker."

He wasn't somebody who would blame me, either. Some-times I wished that Sammy could be a jerk once in a while, but he was always so nice to me. No matter what he said, I knew he'd moved here because he still hoped we'd end up together. Maybe he thought persistence would pay off.

"Thanks, Case, for everything. I know you'll get it all straightened out." His eyes were shining with optimism, but I wasn't sure if it was because he thought that I'd get him off or he hoped that all this time spent with him was going to lead to something.

I dressed quickly and left Julius some crunchies to snack on. He'd finally broadened his food taste to include some of the dry cat food, but it was emphasis on including rather than in place of. The cat definitely knew something was up, and it had made him uneasy. He followed me to the door, rubbing against my ankles. Then just before I opened the kitchen door to leave, he sat down in front of me, blocking my path. He looked up at me with a puzzled expression in his yellow eyes, or at least that was what it seemed like to me. Was he worried about losing my affection?

"Sammy isn't staying," I said. Did the cat understand? He got up after I said it and did a few figure eights around my ankles and with a final affectionate butt of his head walked away with his tail held high.

Breakfast was already in session when I crossed the street to Vista Del Mar, and the grounds were quiet as they always were during meals. The air had its usual damp chill, and the sky was a flat white as if the clouds had been spread like frosting across the sky.

As I neared the Sea Foam dining hall, I could already smell the coffee and buttery fragrance of hot breakfast food. And now I could enjoy it guilt-free because I had provided Sammy with a real meal.

Lucinda was acting as host and circling the tables of my people with a coffeepot. It was nice to see them all talking and appearing to be enjoying the retreat. It was also easy to pick out the table of my people. They were wearing contemporary clothes.

There were always some people who brought their knitting to meals and I noticed some balls of yarn and needles on the tables. They could knit almost as automatically as they breathed. I wondered if I would ever get close to that ease with the craft.

I went around the tables with my people and greeted them all, then I headed for the food line. I could barely remember when I'd last eaten a meal. I'd brought my dinner the night before for Sammy, and after the whole run-in with Lieutenant Borgnine, I'd lost my appetite. But it was back with a vengeance now.

Breakfast was my favorite meal at Vista Del Mar anyway. I came back to the table balancing several plates loaded with blueberry pancakes, baked French toast, one egg Florentine, cut-up fruit and a bowl filled with fresh-cooked oatmeal drizzled with butter and sprinkled with brown sugar, walnuts and raisins. I set everything down on the table and pulled out the chair next to Lucinda's. Even though she was moving around with the coffeepot, there was no question which seat was hers. The one with the Prada bag.

I was ready to dig in and was almost drunk with all the delicious fragrances when I saw Lieutenant Borgnine come in the dining hall. I could never tell if he'd been working all night or if he always looked that rumpled.

It appeared like he was headed for me, and I felt my appetite instantly disappear. Some people ate when they were tense. I was the opposite. But then miraculously, he veered off and stopped next to Norman Rathman. I let out a sigh of relief as my appetite reappeared.

For a few minutes I concentrated on eating. I might have

seemed a little like a bear who'd just come out of hibernation. Lucinda came by and filled my coffee cup and I stopped hovering over my plate. For the first time I noticed that Scarlett was sitting across the table from me. Even though she'd joined our retreat, she was still dressing as part of the 1963 retreat, probably because that was all she'd brought to wear. The capri pants and flats didn't look all that strange. It was only the blouse with a big tie done into a bow that seemed from another time. She was my inside person and main source for information about Diana Rathman. If anyone knew who would want her out of the way, it was Scarlett.

"It looks like the lieutenant is grilling Norman," I said as a way of steering the conversation. "He probably wants to know if Norman really didn't know she was coming to the retreat," I said.

Scarlett put down her coffee cup and took the bait. "I am sure that Norman had no idea she was coming." We both watched as the cop talked to the handsome retreat leader and then Scarlett began to speak again. "Please don't tell anyone, but the reason I know that Diana made a last-minute decision to come was because I'm the one who told her about it. Or gave her the details. She didn't know the venue had been changed or about the program additions the manager of Vista Del Mar made."

"I thought you said she was a co-owner of the business with him. It seems odd she wouldn't know all the details," I said.

"She still owned half of it, but it was really in name only. He and Sally were really in charge of everything, at least usually." Again she mentioned how it had been very different at their usual venue. "They just provided the space and Norman arranged the program. My husband said that the only way Norman could get this place was if he let the manager make a lot of the arrangements. That's why they're here," she said as Dotty Night, Bobbie Listorie and Jimmie Phelps came into the dining hall.

Kevin St. John came in right after and arranged for each of them to sit at a different table. I was surprised when Lieutenant Borgnine looked away from Norman and seemed entranced by Jimmie Phelps. A moment later the cop was pulling out a chair next to the baseball player. It was clear it had nothing to do with Diana Rathman's death and everything to do with the lieutenant's hero worship of the athlete. I had to hand it to Kevin St. John. He'd been right about bringing in the three notable people from 1963.

"Diana seemed very interested in this retreat after I told her about it, though she didn't say why. She certainly didn't tell me she was planning to come, either. That's why I was surprised to see her. Everybody was. But then she's the kind who has always gone her own way. As I told you before, I'd heard that Diana was pretty wild when she was young. I remember her telling me that she had a strange life growing up. She spent a lot of time with her father. He traveled a lot and she went along." Scarlett stopped and seemed to be thinking. "I can't remember the rest of it."

"So did you have some kind of falling-out with her?" I asked.

Scarlett made a funny sort of laugh. "It was really more that out paths stopped crossing. When I told her about this retreat, it was the first time I'd seen her in probably a year. She stopped going to faculty events." Scarlett made a face. "Not that I could blame her." From here Scarlett stopped talking about Diana and instead went on about how boring it was to play the part of the polite spouse.

While Scarlett talked, I finished my breakfast. Having some food and coffee made me feel much better. So much better that when I passed the rumpled cop as I was leaving, all I really wanted to do with him was to make peace, so I went out of my way to smile and offer him a friendly hello and a bit of information.

"I suppose you know that the victim was carrying the streamer in her pocket," I said, maintaining my friendly demeanor.

Lieutenant Borgnine glared at me. "If you want to help in this investigation, tell your friend Dr. Glickner to give me a call."

Like that was going to happen.

17

KEVIN ST. JOHN HAD HEARD THE INTERCHANGE
between me and Lieutenant Borgnine, and as soon as the cop
walked away, the Vista Del Mar manager joined me. In his
usual dark suit, white shirt and conservative tie, he looked
more like a funeral director than the manager of a rustic
resort. "I'm sorry I ever hired the Amazing Dr. Sammy,"
the manager said in a voice full of reproach. With the way
he was glaring at me, he seemed to think it was all my fault.
The truth was that he had hired Sammy to do table magic
on the weekends on his own. It certainly wasn't because
Sammy and I were friends. It seemed more in spite of it.
And I certainly had nothing to do with his having Sammy
do the show for the 1963 mixer.

I don't know if he was expecting a comment from me or
not, but after a beat he continued talking as the dining hall
cleared out. "Do you have any idea what I have riding on
the success of this retreat?"

I think he meant that as a rhetorical question because he went right on talking. "Vista Del Mar is perfect for the retreats they put on. I was sure that once Norman Rathman saw what a blank canvas Vista Del Mar is, we'd get their future business, too. With these historic buildings and original details, we can look like any year, whether they choose 1932 or 1982."

"But not 2012," I said, and he gave me a sour look.

"That's a ridiculous comment. They only pick years from the distant past." Kevin St. John glared directly at me.

"All the work I did putting this together. I arranged for the celebrities to be here. I put together the screening, the softball game and the Saturday night dance. We need to get this unfortunate incident with Norman Rathman's wife settled quickly."

Unfortunate incident? That sounded like somebody had sprained their ankle, not like somebody died in a wild part of the grounds. I was still processing his choice of words as he went on. "If you are in any way helping Dr. Glickner avoid the law, you could be in big trouble." He jutted his moon-shaped face a little closer to me. "I see how you've cozied up to Madeleine Delacorte, but Cora is the one who calls the shots, and if she thinks we have missed out on a big account because of something you did or didn't do, I think you can kiss your special deal with them good-bye. And then you'll have to deal directly with me." He let out a malevolent chuckle. "I wonder how you'd feel if the room rates for your people suddenly tripled?" He let it sink in for a moment. "So be smart and tell the lieutenant where Dr. Glickner is now."

I thought he was done, but as he was about to walk away, he reminded me of the deal we'd made about including the guests in our knitting sessions. "Of course, nothing I just said changes that, now does it?"

I ignored his latest rhetorical question. "There are other people who are much more likely suspects," I said. "What about her husband? You must have heard them arguing. I heard they were getting a divorce and that Diana and Norman owned the Favorite Year Club together. It sounds to me that he has a number of reasons he'd want her out of the way."

Kevin St. John looked horrified by my comment. "Would you please keep it down? It isn't going to help me keep their business if Lieutenant Borgnine starts treating Mr. Rathman like a suspect." He glanced around to see if anyone was listening. For the moment we had the area to ourselves, but even so, he seemed exasperated by what I'd said.

"Calm down, Ms. Feldstein. He has an alibi. You don't know this because you weren't here when it happened, but after the martini bar, there was a screening of newsreels from 1963, from ten o'clock until half past midnight. I saw Norman Rathman go into the Cypress meeting room, where the viewing was held. And when I came in, as the screening was ending, he was still in there."

"And the time of death was between eleven and midnight," I said. "Except, did it occur to you that seeing Norman at the beginning and end didn't mean he'd been in the room during the time in between?"

"Ms. Feldstein," he said, gritting his teeth. "Remember what I said." Then he walked away in a huff.

Lucinda was waiting outside when I finally exited the building. She glanced toward the receding figure of Kevin St. John as he marched angrily toward the Lodge. "What's up with him?"

"He's jumped on the Sammy-is-guilty bandwagon and he wants me to turn him in."

"He said that?" She was incredulous.

"Not in those exact words. He's worried about losing the

future business of the 1963 retreat people. You should have seen his reaction when I said the dead woman's husband should be a suspect. He even tried to claim he was Norman's alibi." I saw people walking toward the assorted meeting rooms. "I don't care what he threatens me with, I would never turn Sammy in." I said it in a whisper, but even so, looked around to make sure no one was listening. "But I have to push all of that under the table for now." My voice had returned to normal as we began to walk up the pathway. "It's workshop time for us!"

18

THE MEETING ROOM WAS ALREADY FILLING WITH people when Lucinda and I walked in. I was glad I'd chosen the Pines meeting room. The fireplace added a warm glow, and the wall of windows looked toward the dunes and showed a sliver of the ocean. Several people were helping themselves to the coffee and tea service set up on the counter. There was an empty place next to the cups and tea bags. I had forgotten all about bringing cookies again.

I was glad that Crystal and Wanda were there hanging around the two long tables. The two women appeared as mismatched as a pair of Crystal's earrings. It was pretty clear that, for Wanda, clothes were purely functional. The loose-fitting white polo shirt and medium blue pants didn't have the slightest hint of style. If she wore makeup, it was so subtle as to be invisible. The vibe she gave off was straightforward and brusque. Crystal had the heavy eye makeup, the wild ringlets of black hair and a colorful layering of different patterned shirts. Of course, the socks that showed through her shoes didn't match. I still had a hard time realizing they were both about my age.

"Casey," Scarlett said, putting her hand on my arm to stop me. "This is Alys Chin, and when she heard about this group, she asked if she could join." I had an extra mystery bag and the group hadn't really started, so it seemed okay. Alys beamed a big smile and pushed a check on me on the spot. Scarlett took Alys with her and arranged for them to sit together.

I was glad to see the early birds had spread themselves between the tables and were acting as assistants. When it seemed like everyone had settled, I stepped to the front of the room. "I'm sorry about the interruptions yesterday," I said without mentioning they were connected to Diana's death. "We're a little behind, but I'm sure we'll make up for lost time now." I repeated that Wanda's group would be making a scarf and Crystal's group would make the worry doll or something else. They each went to the head of one of their tables.

"I changed my mind. I'm with her now," a woman with her hair in a topknot said, pointing at Wanda. "I need structure, direction and knowing the road I'm on." I saw Bree Meyers flinch. That's how she'd been at the first retreat. She tried to tell the woman what she'd learned about doing something unique, but it fell on deaf ears. The woman with the topknot seemed to have started something, and a number of the others, including Scarlett and Alys, who had been sitting at Crystal's table relocated to Wanda's,

Crystal had several samples of the worry dolls in the middle of the table, along with some other toys and purses that had been made from the mystery kits the yarn store sold. She assured everyone she had patterns and would help them, but the women who had moved over wouldn't reconsider.

Scott and Olivia joined Bree and the cluster of brave souls who had stuck with Crystal. Lucinda hung with me for a moment and then joined Crystal's table as well, but not before reminding me that this was a chance for us to see what we could find out about Crystal and Wanda's families. I knew Lucinda meant well, but at the moment I wasn't that concerned about tracking down the mystery heir.

"Am I late?" Madeleine said as she came in. All eyes turned toward her and I heard some grumbling that she was here. None of the women knew who Madeleine was and that, as a Delacorte, she was used to a certain kind of treatment. She seemed to have forgotten she wanted to make the scarf, and the only thing she was concerned with was that she wanted to sit with me.

Crystal sized up the situation and helped Madeleine find her bag and got her situated at the doll table.

"Before you start," Crystal said, "I want to make sure you all understand about working with beads." Wanda seemed miffed that Crystal had spoken first and interjected that then she would talk about planning how they were going to use the yarn.

The group was at all different skill levels, and I'm sure that, for some, working with beads was nothing new, but they all listened attentively as Crystal demonstrated that the beads needed to be put on the yarn first and then were slid in place as they knitted. It was new to me and I watched as she showed how to overcome the problem of getting the yarn through the small bead hole with a piece of thin wire folded over the yarn. Then Wanda jumped in and explained how to figure out what order to use the different yarns in and reminded them to add the beads to each new strand of yarn before they attached it to their work.

I was too keyed up and didn't think I could concentrate

enough to start working on the doll until Madeleine asked for my help.

As soon as I started thinking about helping her, I forgot how tense I was and emptied my bag on the table. Madeleine had knitted a long time ago, so for her it was mostly about refreshing her memory. I was still learning. I knew the basics, like the knit and purl stitches, and casting on and off, but I still had to pay close attention to my work. Madeleine and I worked together to figure out what yarn we'd use for the doll's body and hair. We both decided to keep the beads for her dress, which it turned out wasn't knitted at all. It was crocheted. Crystal said her mother was bringing over crochet hooks, stuffing and some odds and ends of supplies that weren't in the bags for the doll. I noticed Wanda's group was already ahead of us. They had cast on their stitches and done a few rows.

Once the doll makers at our table got started, it turned out that the beginning of the doll was very easy. Just row after row of knitted stitches. As everyone settled into their work, they began to talk.

"I'm relatively new to this area, but both Crystal and Wanda are Cadbury natives," Lucinda said with a wink at me.

"Don't forget me," Madeleine said, sounding a little miffed. "My family practically built Cadbury. And Vista Del Mar wouldn't be here if it weren't for my brother, Edmund."

I knew what Lucinda was doing. Her idea was to eliminate people in the age group of the secret heir with the hopes that eventually we'd be left with the right person. Honestly I thought it was a bad plan except that we might gather some useful information along the way so I went along with it. "How interesting." I looked at the three Cadbury natives. "Did your families know each other?"

It came out pretty quickly that everybody in town knew the

Delacortes, but the Delacortes knew almost nobody. "I thought it was too bad," Madeleine said. "My brother and I both wanted to mix with everybody, but our mother was a snob."

I persisted. "Of course, Madeleine would have been more likely to know your mothers and grandmothers," I said. "What were their names?"

Wanda was helping the woman with the topknot cast on. "That seems pretty irrelevant to what's going on." Wanda gestured toward the knitters. Then she shrugged and turned to Madeleine. "My mother's name is Edwina Howe Thompson, and her mother's name was Marisa Jenkins Howe." She started to talk about her grandfather and said that he hadn't been from Cadbury and had come to work at the cannery the Delacortes had owned.

"The cannery has been turned into a shopping center," I explained to the group. "What about you, Crystal?" Crystal was demonstrating how to put a marker at the end of the doll's head.

"My family goes way back here. My mother owns the local yarn shop, but it was started by her mother. I barely knew my granny. She died when I was just starting kindergarten."

"What was her name?" I coached, supposedly for Madeleine's benefit.

"She had a funny name," Crystal said. "Marigold Jerkowski. But then when she married my grandfather, her name became Marigold Wardlow."

Madeleine looked up at the name. "I remember Marigold. How could you forget a name like that when everyone was named Mary or Elizabeth? She was in my class at school. For a year anyway until Mother sent Cora and me to private school."

Wanda seemed a little miffed that Madeleine hadn't made a comment about her family. "I suppose I should have expected as much," she said. "You don't remember my grandmother, do you? She worked for your family."

I was curious about the information we were getting, but it was starting to interfere with the workshop session. Wanda's whole body language had changed. She seemed to carry a lot of pent-up anger. She seemed to think she'd gotten the shaft on everything. And in a way she had. It was pretty clear that she was a great golfer and yet the resort made more fuss over Bobbie Listorie. And then I had seen her sister. She had the same features as Wanda but in a different arrangement and without the stout body. Her sister had been the prom queen.

Madeleine had blinders on. No matter what she said about herself and her brother wanting to know all the different kinds of people, I don't think she'd ever really thought about how the other half lived. Or how arrogant her comment about mixing with everybody sounded. The air was getting a little tense and it wasn't good for the group. I quickly changed the subject to other events going on at Vista Del Mar over the weekend and how our group was being included in the 1963 events.

I was glad when the tension went out of Wanda's face. I was surprised when she was interested in coming to the dance on Saturday night. Crystal said she was in for sure. Madeleine got dreamy eyed. "Bobbie Listorie is going to sing."

Everyone seemed satisfied with their progress when the session ended. We decided to leave everything as is for the afternoon workshop. They'd been sitting a long time and I heard Scott suggesting a walk through the dunes before lunch. A group left with him. Several others, who wanted more knitting time, went with Olivia to work on squares. The group that was having a hard time not having their cell phones or tablets went with Bree to the phone booths and message board. Crystal and Wanda headed off in separate directions.

Lucinda and I hung back until everyone had left. Lucinda stayed calm until we were alone and then her eyes lit up. "Did you hear them? Wanda's mother's name is Edwina. Get it—Edmond Edwina. And her grandmother's initials were M.J. and she worked for the family."

"Yes, but Crystal's grandmother's initials were also M.J. and Madeleine remembered her." I agreed that it seemed that we couldn't rule out either of their mothers as being the secret heir. "I need your help with something more immediate," I said. When I brought her up to speed on Sammy's clothing situation and other stuff he needed, she understood.

"Poor Sammy. He's not the kind of guy who would be happy wearing yesterday's clothes," she said before offering her help.

I felt bad asking her to leave Vista Del Mar with me. The whole point of the weekend for her was to stay there and pretend she was far away from her regular life.

"It's fine. The only thing is I'm not going into the Blue Door. If I do, Tag will be wanting me to stay to help with the lunch crowd and it will go on from there." When we went outside, we ran into Scarlett and her friend.

"Thanks for letting Alys join. She's in the same boat I am. Her husband is really the one here for the 1963 retreat. Both of our husbands do the work, while Norman gets all the glory."

I asked her what she meant. "Jason does a lot of the research and puts together the program. Alys's husband, Ryan, does research as well and is a presenter." She seemed like she was going to walk away, but then stopped. "I almost said something before when you were talking to those ladies about their family history in this town. I think I know why Diana Rathman decided to come to this retreat. When I told her where the new venue for the retreat was, she said she'd grown up in Cadbury. I wonder if she knew either Wanda's or Crystal's mother."

When they'd gone, I looked at Lucinda. "Are you thinking what I'm thinking?"

Lucinda nodded. "She could be Edmund's child."

We talked back and forth about who we could get more information from. There was one person in town who seemed to have her finger on the pulse of Cadbury.

"Maggie," we said in unison.

19

"SAMMY'S NEEDS COME FIRST," I SAID AS I PULLED my car into one of the angled parking spots on Grand Street in downtown Cadbury. Lucinda had instructed me not to park close to the Blue Door so she wouldn't be tempted to drop in. We just had to go down the block to reach The Butterfly Bed-and-Breakfast. While Lucinda didn't go into the restaurant, we hadn't considered that her husband might look out. We had barely started walking toward the bed-and-breakfast when Tag came running across the street and caught up with us.

With his practically obsessive-compulsive nature, you wouldn't expect him to be a romantic, but he certainly was as far as Lucinda was concerned. He greeted her with such gusto you'd think she'd been gone for months instead of one night.

"Why'd you park on the other side of the street? There's a spot almost in front of the Blue Door." He looped his arm in hers. Lucinda seemed uncomfortable as she broke the news that she wasn't there to come to the restaurant. "I'm helping Casey with something," she said. Was there any chance he would leave it at that?

Tag wanted to know not only what she was helping me with, but the exact details. Lucinda tried to dance around the truth, but he kept prodding. Finally she threw me a helpless look. I had not wanted anyone else to know that I knew where Sammy was and, even more important, to divulge his actual location. It put them in an awkward position where they might have to lie. It would be even worse if they told the truth. Tag, with all his knife straightening and things having to be just so, didn't seem like a good candidate for keeping the secret. But it seemed that I wouldn't have the chance to get Sammy's stuff unless Tag knew what was going on.

"It's okay," I said to Lucinda. I turned to Tag. "I need to get something out of Sammy's room, and Lucinda is going to act as a distraction."

I quickly added that I had Sammy's permission and the key to the room so it was all perfectly legal.

"Then you should be able to just go in there and get his things. I don't see why you should have to sneak in," Tag said. "If you don't want to do it, I will."

"You don't understand." I looked to Lucinda for assistance in dealing with him.

"Honey, Casey is worried about having to answer questions about Sammy. It's easier this way."

"Oh," Tag said. "Is that because the police are looking for him?" A breeze came through and ruffled Tag's thick hair. Without even thinking, he took out a comb and straightened the flyaway strands. He seemed to think things over for a moment, and I was betting that he was going to insist that Lucinda not get involved, but he surprised me. "I think they're wrong. I know Dr. Glickner's character and he's not a killer."

I so wanted to say "duh," but I contained myself and let Tag continue. "I'm surprised to be saying this, but I don't want any details, and I hope you haven't given too many to Lucinda. I'd like to help. I'm sure you realize two people would make a better distraction than one."

Lucinda was so pleased, she squeezed his hand and hugged him. "I knew living with me would change you. You're finally loosening up."

Or maybe not. In the next breath Tag wanted to know exactly how they were going to distract the owners of the Butterfly Bed-and-Breakfast.

"I thought I'd just go in there and ask about their business," Lucinda said. Tag didn't think that would do. I just wanted them to hurry up. Finally they agreed to talk to them about somehow working together. They discussed it and practically made up a script.

We walked the rest of the way to the imposing structure on the corner. The plan was they would go in first and I would stay outside where I could see in the window. Lucinda was going to wave her hand behind her when the coast was clear.

They'd barely gotten in there when Lucinda did the hand wave.

I went up the stairs quickly. No need to unlock the outer door at this hour. I was in the entrance hall in a flash. There was a different vibe in the place at this time of day. A housekeeper went up the stairs carrying linens while some guests came down. I veered to the left and the hall that led to Sammy's room, glad that I knew which door was his.

As soon as I was in the room, I let out a sigh of relief and took a moment to look around. The room was large and had soft green wallpaper. It was arranged so there was a seating area separated from the bed. His magic props were in a small metal trunk that was open. Sammy had been living there long enough to have added a few personal touches, but it was hardly homey.

I reminded myself I was there on a mission and unfolded the large brown trash bag I'd brought to put his things in. I quickly went to the dresser and closet and grabbed several sets of clothes and underwear. His underwear drawer was a lot neater than mine.

I collected his shaving stuff and lastly the pajamas he'd requested. I was a little surprised to find they were black silk. That was something new.

I quickly packed everything into the bag I'd brought. I didn't trust walking out with it, so I opened the window and tossed it outside into the side garden and hoped no one was walking by. Then I locked up and began to retrace my steps toward the front door, but of course there was a problem. I heard voices coming from the living room. A woman was saying she wanted to check something in the kitchen, which meant she would be crossing my path.

She came out of the parlor and I made a snap decision. Instead of trying to elude her, I walked toward her as if it was my intention all along. She looked puzzled when she saw me, but I didn't wait for her to say something and spoke first. Thankfully I had never come there with Sammy so there was a chance she didn't know the connection.

"I'm looking for the Thornkills," I said. "They own the Blue Door restaurant. Are they here?" The frantic sound to my voice was genuine and the woman perceived there was some kind of problem. She didn't take the time to question who I was, but instead led me into the parlor.

"There you are," I said with feigned relief. "You have to come right away. The cook burned himself."

"Burned himself! How did he do it?" Tag asked. Lucinda's eyes were rolling. I was pretty sure she was thinking what I was, that Tag had forgotten they were there to divert the people's attention and believed what I said was real. This was the problem with including him in anything. What is that saying—wherever you go, you take yourself with. He started to ask more questions, but Lucinda used her arm like a hook and dragged him toward the door with me close behind.

As soon as we were outside, I started to reassure him that I'd just made up the whole thing about the cook. To my surprise, the worried look left his face and he laughed.

"I know," he said. "I was just pretending. I think I did pretty well."

I let out a big sigh of relief. "You definitely fooled me."

Tag seemed immensely pleased with himself. "Who says I can't be spontaneous?"

Reluctantly he went back to the restaurant alone, but before he went in, he looked at me and smiled. "You know, I could be part of your investigations, too."

"That man is bonkers for you," I said, and Lucinda's face lit up in a happy smile.

"You're right, he is. Isn't that nice." She was smiling brightly and then her expression faded. "No matter what he just said, having him along was a definite challenge. I know our plan was to talk to the proprietors about doing something jointly during the Monarch Butterfly Parade week. And we are actually going to work something out between us, but most of the time they were talking about Sammy."

I must have looked worried because she instantly reassured me that they loved Sammy and had no doubt about his innocence. "But Lieutenant Borgnine has been by the inn a number of times. He asked a lot of questions about when they'd last seen him. He even did a number on them about having relatives coming in from out of town and maybe they would stay there. Could he have a look at the accommodations and then conveniently suggested the room Sammy's renting."

"Did they show the room to him?" I asked.

"No, but he threw around that he'd be getting a warrant soon." She let out a sigh. "It's lucky that Tag didn't know anything because I'm afraid he would have said too much. By the way, the proprietors think he should turn himself in. But that's because they think once he talks to the cops, the cops will just believe that he didn't do it because he's such a nice guy."

"If only that was true. Sammy can't even defend himself since he doesn't remember what happened after he started on the martinis."

Lucinda looked at my hands. "Speaking of Sammy, where's his stuff?"

My eyes flew skyward as I ran back toward the B and B. The bag had landed on a gardenia bush, and as I retrieved it, some of the fragrant white petals fluttered to the ground. We put it in the back of my car and we moved on to our next order of business.

"Hey," Maggie said in greeting when Lucinda and I walked into the Coffee Shop. She was just finishing up making an espresso drink and handed it to the customer. Then she turned all her attention to us. She pointed at the empty basket with a sign reading CASEY'S MUFFINS above it. "We've branded you. People come in asking for your muffins now. Anytime you want to double the order, I'm willing," she said.

The top, made out of red bandannas, was Maggie's red item of the day. She wore the bright color to keep herself cheerful, but it cheered everyone who saw her as well. The warmth of her personality had something to do with it, too. She honestly seemed to love her customers. "The usual?" she said, going to get a couple of cups. We both nodded and she started building our coffee drinks.

"I heard what happened at Vista Del Mar. It can't be true that Dr. Glickner is the main suspect?" She looked over her shoulder from the espresso machine. I didn't say anything, but I guess my expression did.

"Lieutenant Borgnine is totally focused on Sammy. Kevin St. John is on the Sammy-is-guilty bandwagon, too. Of course, he's blaming it all on me." Maggie finished with the drinks and carried them to a table. We sat down together.

"Actually I thought you might be able to help." Maggie's eyes lit up.

"Glad to be of assistance. Kevin can be difficult," she said and I realized she thought I wanted help with the manager.

"He's such a weird guy. I don't really know anything about him. Does he have a wife, a girlfriend, a boyfriend?" I took a sip of the drink. As usual, it was perfect. "I suppose you know all about him."

"You have to cut him some slack. I'm sure you've realized by now that Vista Del Mar is his life. He had a very messy family situation. His mother was sixteen when he was born. It raised a lot of eyebrows around here. No one seemed to know who his father was. Kevin's mother took off a couple of years later and never looked back, leaving her mother to care for him." Maggie stopped and gave her head a little shake. "She was young and beautiful and hated the title of grandmother. She seemed to go through husbands. The first one was kind of a mystery and I think I'm not the only one who doesn't know if he was real or imaginary, though the second one created quite a stir. It didn't mean anything to me because I don't know the difference between a basketball and a soccer ball. They're all just round to me. But he was an announcer for the San Francisco Giants. He was long gone when Muriel took over Kevin's care."

"Who's Muriel?" I asked, confused by the family saga.

"Sorry," Maggie said. "That's Kevin's grandmother, the one who brought him up. From the time he was a kid, Kevin loved Vista Del Mar. He started working there as desk clerk when he was in high school. That place is his whole world. I'm sure that's why he acts so strange to you."

I didn't mean to, but I suddenly felt sympathetic to the moonfaced manager. If the hotel and conference center meant that much to him, it was no wonder he wanted to control everything.

"Thanks for the Kevin story, but I'd really like some info on something else. Really someone else," I said. Maggie checked the front of the store for any customers that might have just come in and, seeing none, turned back to us.

"Fire away, though I don't really know everything that goes on here."

"I just found out the woman who died was from Cadbury originally. I thought you might know something about her."

"What's her name?" Maggie asked.

"I don't have her maiden name, but her married name was Diana Rathman."

The computer in Maggie's brain began to whir and her eyes darted around as she mentally scrolled through her mind. "How old?" Maggie asked.

"I think she was somewhere in her fifties?"

Maggie seemed to have come to something. Her eyes stopped darting. "There's only one Diana I can think of. This is almost too coincidental to be true." She looked directly at me and Lucinda. "Remember I said Kevin was brought up by his grandmother. She had a daughter with her second husband. I'm sure her name was Diana."

Maggie stopped for a minute to collect her thoughts. "Now it's coming back to me. Diana didn't stay around here long. She went off to live with her father. He had some kind of interesting job in sports and traveled a lot. Kevin was just a small kid when Diana left. I suppose she probably came back to visit. I don't know *everything* that goes on in town."

I was processing what she'd said and thought she was done, but then she added the kicker. "There's something else about Kevin St. John," she said. "Kevin's grandmother died when he was in high school. The story is that when he came home from school, he found her lying at the bottom of the stairs. Her cause of death was listed as a blow to the head as a result of the fall, but there was no way to tell if she'd fallen or was pushed. It was listed as inconclusive."

None of us said anything, but I am pretty sure we were all thinking the same thing. Did Kevin find her or did he push her?

20

"DID EVERYONE IN TOWN GIVE THEIR DAUGHTERS a name that started with an *M*?" Lucinda said, trying to lighten the mood as we pulled into my driveway. Then I heard her suck in her breath. "Her name was Muriel St. John. Don't you get it? It's not exactly M.J., but it's pretty close. And that could make Kevin's mother Edmund's love child?"

"Don't even say that," I said.

"Look, I can see my shadow," Lucinda said as she got out of the Mini Cooper. With all the flat light and white skies around here, seeing your shadow was a big deal. I looked up at the sky, which had an apricot cast to it, as if the sun was burning through the clouds.

The lunch bell had just begun to ring as I unloaded Sammy's belongings from my car while Lucinda stood at the front of the driveway acting as my lookout. I went back to the window I'd used before to pass things to Sammy. I knocked softly, and a moment later, the shutters opened a crack. Once he saw it was me, he pulled them back and opened the window.

I handed in the trash bag full of his belongings. He was still wearing the tuxedo shirt with the sleeves rolled up. He'd gone from stubble to the beginning of a beard. "Case, thank you," he said as he pulled it inside. Afterward I handed him a shopping bag.

"Wow, more food," Sammy said, checking the contents of the bag. He was licking his lips as he opened the containers and looked at their contents. One held a grilled sandwich with four kinds of cheese and tomato on thick-cut rustic bread that smelled of browned butter. The others had mixed green salad, cold sliced garlic potatoes and sliced mixed fruit. Then suddenly he looked worried. "Where'd this come from?"

I explained that Tag had intercepted Lucinda and me as we'd headed back to the car after our stop at Maggie's. He'd handed me the shopping bag without a word. "Tag knows, but he doesn't know," I said, but Sammy still seemed worried. "As long as he doesn't know for sure, he's okay."

"How's it going with your investigation?" His soulful eyes looked hopeful.

I told him what I'd found out. "Wow, Kevin St. John was related to the victim." He thought for a moment. "That's it. He was probably angry at her about something and killed her."

"I'm not sure that Kevin St. John realized who she was." Then I told him the rest of what I'd heard from Maggie. "Diana went to live with her father. His lifestyle appealed to her a lot more than staying in a small town. The point is that Kevin was a small kid when she left and Maggie didn't know if Diana ever came back."

"What about Kevin's grandmother? That would be Diana's mother, right? You could talk to her," Sammy said.

"No. She's dead." Then I told Sammy about her "accident."

Sammy was listening intently. "That could be it. Maybe Diana knew that Kevin St. John really pushed his grandmother down the stairs. Maybe she came looking for hush money from him and he killed her instead."

I wasn't a big fan of Kevin St. John's so I could certainly believe that was possible, but when Sammy wanted me to take the information to Lieutenant Borgnine, I had to explain that the cop would ignore my conjecture. "If I'm going to get his attention, I need proof."

I heard Lucinda start whistling, which was our agreed signal that someone was coming. I backed out quickly and Sammy pulled the window shut.

As we walked down the driveway, Dane's red Ford 150 pulled to a stop.

"Hey," he said in greeting.

I swallowed hard. "Hey," I said, hoping I didn't look guilty.

"What have you two been up to?" he asked, looking from Lucinda to me. "I'm surprised you're not across the street." He left it hanging like he was expecting some kind of explanation.

Lucinda mumbled something about us coming over because she needed to use her cell phone. "All done now," Lucinda said, holding up her phone and then dropping it into the pocket of her Ralph Lauren jacket. "I'm going to head back. No rush—I'll act as the host at lunch until you get there."

Dane's truck was blocking my driveway and he cut the motor. "You want to tell me what's going on? I saw you two coming out of Maggie's."

I brightened. He'd just made it easy. I simply left out the

first part of our trip to town and told him about Diana's identity.

"Hmm, she was Kevin St. John's half aunt," he said thoughtfully.

"Do you think Lieutenant Borgnine knows who she really was?" Hoping he'd pass along the info without mentioning where he'd heard it.

"I'd rather talk about something more pleasant. Like how about we give dinner another try?"

"Haven't we been over that and decided that it was a bad idea?"

"You decided that on your own. It was a mistake to do it in Cadbury. And who says it has to be dinner?" He reminded me how he was willing to take the night shift forever rather than do what the lieutenant had demanded. Dane didn't have to try to flirt. It was second nature to him.

"C'mon, Casey, you know you want to go," he said, touching my arm. "It'll be fun."

The best I could do was say I'd think about it. I hoped Sammy hadn't heard the whole conversation through the door.

I caught up with Lucinda as she headed to the dining hall.

"It doesn't look like Dane is giving up," she said. I heard the motor of his truck as he drove down the street to his place.

"He really should. It's the best for everyone. If it didn't work out, it would make it so awkward for both of us."

"But did you ever consider that it might work out?"

"Actually, no," I said.

Our retreat people had automatically gone to the same tables and we joined them. Lucinda grabbed the pitcher of ice tea and we made the rounds, talking to everyone. The early birds had spread themselves out into the group and were acting like sub hosts. I wanted to hug Bree, Scott and Olivia for all they were doing.

Finally I got plates of food for Lucinda and me and we sat down. I was having a hard time joining in the conversations. I kept looking over at the tables of people from the other retreat. Norman Rathman was talking to his whole table. His assistant, Sally Winston, was seated at another table, but she kept her eyes on him.

Dotty Night was holding court at a table near the windows. She had the attention of all the people as she performed. I say performed because she seemed very animated. Her hands and arms moved as she talked, and her blond hair bounced.

Jimmie Phelps was the center of attention at his table. He still had the ease of an athlete even though I was sure he was well into his sixties. He was holding up a can of the energy drink. I remembered overhearing that the company was paying him to push the drinks at the retreat. As I watched him, I began to make all these connections to Diana. Her father had been the announcer for the Giants, and Jimmie played for the Giants. Diana had traveled with her father, so chances were good that she had met the baseball player. And hadn't somebody said they saw Jimmie and Diana talking and it seemed like they knew each other from before? Yes, I definitely wanted to talk to him.

Bobbie Listorie was hosting a table by the window. He seemed to have gotten rid of the headache and the sweats. He was back in the sharkskin suit. It appeared he was quite the storyteller. The whole table was hanging on to his every word.

"Ridiculous, isn't it," Wanda said, pulling out the chair next to me. "It's the same at the resort. He's always got an entourage of guests around him. He's not even that good a golfer, but the guests don't care. They go home saying they hung out with him."

Crystal took the chair on the other side of Wanda. I was glad that my two leaders had decided to join us for lunch. It was too bad they didn't mix in with the group, but I remembered from before that Wanda had a thing about not letting the retreaters see behind the curtain. Like she was the Great Oz or something. Crystal heard what we were talking about.

"He's lucky to still have a career. My ex is barely hanging on. Or at least that's what I hear when he's supposed to pay child support." In case Wanda didn't know, Crystal explained that she'd been married to a self-proclaimed rock god.

"I could understand it more if the resort hired him," Wanda said, indicating Jimmie Phelps. "He's at least an athlete."

The three of us turned our attention to the table the retreat leader was hosting. "It's amazing how they're all going on like it's business as usual," Crystal said, shaking her head. "I mean, that guy's wife died a couple of nights ago."

Lucinda joined in. "Maybe Norman Rathman is just going through the motions."

I wondered what the truth was and knew the only way to find out was to talk to him directly.

Lunch ended and the dining hall cleared out. Lucinda and I walked outside together. People from the 1963 group were going in different directions for their afternoon activities. Our people stayed together and headed up the slope toward our meeting room. Lucinda excused herself and went on ahead because she wanted to pick up something from her room. As I passed the deck outside the Lodge, Kevin St. John and Lieutenant Borgnine came outside and stopped on the wooden expanse. The cop appeared more agitated than usual. The two men looked in my direction and I felt their stares settle on me.

It is such a weird feeling to know people are talking about you and know for sure they're not saying anything good. After a moment the lieutenant came down the stairs and stopped in front of me.

"I don't suppose you know anything about an anonymous tip that Dr. Glickner is hiding out in Castorville."

"What?" My surprise was honest.

"Yeah, some no-name called it in. I wasted the morning checking it out." I noticed his hand had started to massage one of his temples. "You wouldn't have any aspirin on you, would you?"

Here was my chance to redeem myself with him. "As a matter of fact I do." I pulled out the bottle I'd put in my purse when I brought it over for Bobbie Listorie's middle-of-the-night headache. I poured a pair of white pills into his cupped hand.

He seemed almost disappointed that I'd met his request and grumbled a thank-you. "If I find out who made that false tip, there are going to be consequences," he said in a threatening voice.

I put up my hands. "It wasn't me." The rumble of his sigh sounded like he didn't believe it. Naturally, I immediately wondered who had done it and ran through the possibilities. Sammy could have done it himself. Tag seemed to be loosening up, but would he actually call in a false tip? There was Lucinda, but I thought she would tell me. What about Madeleine? She really liked Sammy and she seemed entranced with the idea of playing detective. Dane? No way, he was a cop.

There was still some time before the activities were to begin, and when I saw Norman Rathman come out of the

Lodge, I realized this was an opportunity to talk to him. I tried to appear casual as I went up to him.

"I'm sorry I didn't say anything before," I began, "but I'm very sorry about your wife." This time it was different talking to him. The first time had only been for a moment when he thought I was one of his retreaters. This time I was studying him as we spoke.

He certainly knew how to relate to people and make them feel comfortable. He looked at me directly and he touched my arm as he spoke. Not in a graspy sort of way, more like he was making a connection with me. Between his manner and the good looks, I figured he must be a killer on campus.

If I started asking questions about his wife, it would seem odd or worse—like I was investigating. Instead I started talking about the retreat business. "I don't know how you're managing so well. I have much less to deal with and I'm a wreck."

He smiled warmly. "I'm sure you're doing better than you think. You've already spirited away a couple of my people and the knitting sessions are the talk of my group." He leaned a little closer as if he was going to impart a secret. "The way I'm getting through this weekend is by thinking of my people and wanting to let them down." He paused for a beat. "It helps that the police have a suspect, though I'd feel better if they just arrested him." He let out his breath and then continued. "I regret that I handled things so poorly during the mixer. Diana caught me by surprise and I over-reacted."

"So you weren't expecting to see her?" I said, feigning ignorance.

"Diana used to be very active in the retreats. We actually developed the idea together. But she hadn't come to one for years." Several of his people passed by us and waved as they did. "Here's a little hint for your retreat business. Be very careful who you go in business with and definitely have an exit strategy in case it doesn't go well."

I seized the moment. "Then I'm guessing that it wasn't working out and breaking up the partnership was hard."

He didn't answer and I had the feeling he might have regretted what he'd just said, considering the problem was solved by her death. He seemed like he was about to walk away. I quickly continued the conversation. "If your wife wasn't coming to the retreats, why did she decide to come to this one?"

"I have no idea. I didn't even know how she knew the details until Scarlett Miller told me that she'd run into Diana last week and told her about it."

"They must be good friends."

"Hardly. I think Scarlett hoped Diana would come and do what she did—make a scene. I don't know if you have any people putting on workshops for you, but be careful if you do. They can think they deserve a piece of the business."

It didn't take much reading between the lines that he meant Scarlett's husband. I could tell he was really going to leave this time so I quickly threw out another comment. "I understand your wife was from Cadbury."

My comment caught him off guard. "I'd forgotten about that. She told everybody she came from San Francisco because that's where she and her father lived."

"Does she have any family in Cadbury?"

He looked at me oddly as if he suddenly noticed I was asking too many questions. "The magician is a friend of yours, isn't he?" I noticed the friendliness had drained from his face. "Well, have a good afternoon." He left before I could wish him the same.

By now I was on mental overload. There was too much swirling in my mind. Someone had called in a false sighting of Sammy. Was Scarlett more than an innocent bystander? What about Kevin St. John and the mysterious death of his grandmother, who also happened to be Diana's mother?

21

IT WAS TIME TO FOCUS ON *MY* RETREAT. I TOOK THE
long way to get to our meeting room, hoping I could clear
my head. I had hoped my people would be much further
along on their projects by now, but the first session had gotten interrupted by Scarlett finding Diana Rathman's earring
in her bag and all that ensued afterward. I hadn't anticipated
how long it would take everyone to decide what they wanted
to make. And who knew they would start swapping their
yarn and supplies? If there was one thing I had learned, it
was that things never seemed to go as planned.

All I really wanted was for everyone to have a satisfying
time. Not that anyone had complained. If anything, they
seemed to like all the excitement.

Whatever else Norman Rathman might have done, he
certainly knew how to organize their retreat. I had seen their
schedule, and his people had a number of choices. They
could take dancing lessons for the popular dances of 1963.

It was interesting how they all had names, such as the Hully Gully, the Mashed Potato and the Monkey. Not that I danced much, but I didn't think the current ones were called anything more than slow or fast.

There was a hike along the beach to the lighthouse. That activity worked for almost any year they were celebrating since it was built in 1855. And for the more sedentary, there was a discussion and screening of episodes of the *Dick Van Dyke Show* and a bridge tournament in the lobby of one of the guest room buildings.

The brief hint of sun had disappeared and now fingers of fog were blowing in, making it feel like I was walking through gossamer. Up ahead the small white building that housed our meeting room seemed to be disappearing in the mist.

The walk there had done the trick and I felt refreshed when I went inside The Pines. Thanks to the fire glowing in the brick fireplace, the meeting room seemed cozy and bright after the gray sky outside. Some women were already sitting at the long tables. They were working on projects they'd brought with them and talking.

When I saw the coffee and tea service set up on a counter, I realized I still hadn't brought over any cookies. I also noticed Madeleine staring at the tea bags and urn of hot water.

"You do know how to make a cup of tea," I said, noting her confused expression.

"Of course. Cora and I don't have the staff my mother had. I just can't remember if you put the hot water in the cup first or the tea bag?"

"Let me," I said. "Which kind do you want?" There was a selection of different kinds of tea bags in a wicker basket.

"I didn't realize there were so many kinds. We always just had Lipton's tea. What do you recommend?"

I picked the aged Earl Grey and showed her how to put

the bag in first and then the hot water. The fragrance drifted up from the cup immediately, and her face lit up. "That smells wonderful," she said with a delighted smile. I explained the lovely scent came from the oil of bergamot that the tea was sprayed with. The Delacorte sister's eyes were bright. "Casey, I can't thank you enough. I never would have thought that at this time of my life, the world would be opening up for me." She glanced around the room and out the window. "And it was right here all along." She suddenly turned wistful. "If Edmund hadn't died, everything would have been different. I would have done more brave things than just that one time."

I didn't know what she was talking about, and I guess it must have showed on my face. Her eyes flashed and she made an impatient *tsk* sound. "I told you about it before. Bobbie Listorie did a show after a Giants game at Candlestick Park. I thought it would be the same as when I saw him with my brother."

Now I remembered she had said something about seeing the singer a second time, but I hadn't really been listening. "You mean you went on your own?"

She nodded, but when she gave me the details, I realized she wasn't quite on her own. She and Cora had been in San Francisco with the Cadbury Women's Club. "Our orders were to stay with the group but there was another woman with us who was a big fan of Bobbie's." Madeleine giggled when she called him by his first name. "We got the concierge of the Mark Hopkins Hotel to get us tickets and arrange for transportation. We got there too late for the baseball game, but in time to see Bobbie and the fireworks."

She shook her head with regret. "I was about your age. What a silly timid mouse I was. Look at you. You've done all kinds of things. Moved to a new town and started a new life and now you're even sort of a detective."

I loved her perspective on my life and wondered if there was any way I could get her to talk to my mother.

In the meantime everyone else had arrived for the afternoon workshop. Crystal and Wanda had taken their spots at the front of the two tables and there was someone else. I waved a greeting at Gwen Selwyn, Crystal's mother and the owner of Cadbury Yarn. She had a bin on wheels with her and had started putting out yarn on the end of Crystal's table.

"I hope it's okay, but Crystal realized that the people making the dolls might want different yarn for the hair. She was concerned they might not have crochet hooks for the doll's dress, too." She gestured toward the array of small balls of brown, black and yellow yarn and a handful of crochet hooks. "And as long as I was coming, I brought along some small balls of novelty yarn, packets of beads and some other things for the dolls' faces."

Before I could say yes or no, a crowd was at the front of the table poking through the supplies. Wanda had stepped close to me and watched as her group joined in, looking through what Gwen had brought. "I tried to tell you the mystery bag idea wouldn't work. People like to pick their own supplies." Wanda moved away and Lucinda took her spot.

"So much for the mystery bags," I muttered.

"As long as they're happy, so what?" Lucinda said, and I realized she had a point. And as long as Gwen was there, I decided to grab some black yarn for my doll's hair.

"Crystal said you were asking a bunch of questions about the family trees of people in Cadbury."

I didn't want to tell her why, so instead said I found it fascinating how all their lives intertwined in the small town. "Growing up in Chicago and living in a tall building downtown was a much different experience," I said. "You know how people always fantasize about how friendly life in a small town is."

"Nothing is ever as perfect as people imagine, but all in all, Cadbury is a good place to live," Gwen said. It was funny, but if I were picking whose mother she was by looking at her clothes, I would have thought that she was Wanda's. She was a plain dresser and her socks matched, unlike her daughter's. But in temperament she probably was more like her daughters, both of whom had milder personalities than Wanda.

I mentioned to her who Maggie thought Diana could be and Gwen's eyes opened wider. "Oh my goodness, that's who the dead woman is." She let it all sink in for a moment. "We were in Girl Scouts together. Her parents had broken up and I thought we might be friends since we now both had single mothers, but Diana wanted no part of it." Gwen looked down at her plain attire. "I was too dull for her. She was kind of wild, and the next thing I heard, she'd gone off to live with her father. If she came back to town, I didn't see her. I don't know if she even came for her grandmother's funeral." Gwen stopped again. "You were interested in our intertwined lives. How about this—she was Kevin St. John's half aunt."

I feigned surprise and then asked about their relationship. "Diana was much younger than his mother so she hardly would have seemed like an aunt. And she wasn't around long after he was born. Neither was his own mother." I got the details again that Kevin's mother was very young and unmarried and only stayed around until she turned eighteen before she left, too. "I have to tell you, he was an odd kid. The kind who seemed old already. I suppose it was hard being brought up by his grandmother. She worked at Vista Del Mar in the gift shop and she brought him with her and let him wander on the grounds. I guess it is no wonder he thinks of it as being his place."

I saw Gwen do a double take when she noticed Madeleine thumbing through the yarn for the doll's hair. "So now she's trying to pretend she's one of us," Gwen said. I was surprised by the yarn store owner's harsh tone. I had thought of her as one of those people who accepted what the world delivered to her and got along with everybody. When I said something, Gwen rushed to smooth it over. "Everybody puts the Delacortes on a level above the rest of us, and they have always seemed to think they deserve it. I was just a little surprised to see one of the sisters acting like a normal person."

I wondered if there was more to it than that. I noticed that Gwen let Crystal take care of Madeleine's sale. I was relieved when no one seemed to mind buying what they needed instead of expecting me to pick up the tab.

As it was, putting on these retreats was closer to a hobby than a moneymaking business. I regretted not getting more information from Norman Rathman about the business end of things as he seemed to be turning a nice profit.

I could hear my aunt saying she'd put them on out of the love of doing it. I could also hear my mother's response to the whole thing. "You're really turning down cooking school in Paris for this?"

Then my mother would remind me that my father's sister had been in a different place in her life when she started the yarn retreat business. I couldn't dispute that. My aunt Joan had had a long acting career in L.A. She wasn't the kind of actress where people recognized her name, but they did recognize her face, particularly after she was the Tidy Soft toilet paper lady. That commercial had left her with a nice nest egg, so she didn't have to worry about the yarn retreat business making a profit.

If anybody needed a worry doll, it was me. I was worried about Sammy, worried about making a decision with Dane, worried that my mother might be right and I was wasting my time. I joined the others and picked out some bulky black yarn to use for hair on my doll. Then I picked up my needles and got to work. I was pleased that I'd gotten a lot of rows done by the time Wanda announced the session was ending. She and Crystal discussed it and then told both their groups that it was okay to take their projects with them to work on during their free time as long as they didn't need any help with them. A lot of the people took theirs. I didn't feel confident that I wouldn't need help and left mine on the table.

I was deep in thought as I did a little cleanup and pulled the door shut.

The mist was gone when I went outside. Not that I noticed. I was so busy thinking about all the information on Kevin St. John and his family that I paid no attention to my surroundings until I bumped into Jimmie Phelps. When I say bumped into him, I mean I literally smacked into him. He reached out to steady me so I wouldn't fall.

"I'm sorry," he said. "I should look where I'm going."

I laughed. "I think I'm the one who should do that. I knocked into you." He wouldn't let me take the blame, and all I could think was what a gentleman. He then insisted on making sure I wasn't hurt in any way. "It's been years since I played pro, but I've still got the arms." He made a muscle and showed off his biceps and mentioned I could see him in action the next day when he took part in the softball game.

Up close I could see his tanned skin was a little leathery from all those games in the sun. His hair was silver with just a hint that it was once black. He had more going than just his biceps, though; he moved with the grace of someone for whom keeping in shape was second nature.

"I think I could use one of those energy drinks I saw you offering your people," I said, thinking how much I needed a boost to get through the rest of the afternoon and evening ahead of me.

He flashed the smile straight off his baseball card and

led me by the hand. "I think this is your lucky day." A red cooler was sitting next to one of the Monterey pines and he flipped up the lid. The interior was filled with the red cans and some ice. He grabbed a can and handed it to me.

"Are you going to join me?" I said, popping open the top.

"It's a great drink and believe me I do use them a lot, but moderation is my watchword." I took a sip and he regarded me with interest. "What do you think?" he said.

It tasted like sweet raspberries and I did feel an immediate boost of energy. "It's good. What's in it?" I looked over the ingredients.

"It's nothing too secret. Caffeine is what provides the 'energy,'" he said. "There is a display in the gift shop. With all the vitamins and minerals, this drink is a lot better than the packets of caffeine tablets they sell."

Maybe it was the boost of the drink, but my mind seemed very clear and things I'd heard earlier slipped back into my thoughts. It had been brought up that Diana's father had been an announcer for the Giants. Jimmie Phelps had played for the team. Of course he must have known her father. I wondered if he'd known her then as well.

"It was terrible about that woman," I said. Jimmie's good humor faded in an instant.

"Yes," he said with anger in his voice. I took a chance and seized on his response.

"It sounds personal. Did you know her?" I asked. He seemed uncomfortable with my question.

"I told the cop the whole story." He paused and I thought that was going to be the end of it, but after a brief hesitation he explained her father's connection with the team. "It's useless to try to act indifferent. I watched Diana grow up. Her father always brought her along. She was literally at every game we played."

"Do you think she came to the retreat because she knew you were going to be here?" I asked.

"We lost touch a long time ago." He suddenly seemed nervous. "Nothing ever happened between us when she was underage," he said quickly.

Right after he said it, he seemed regretful about what he'd said and I had the feeling if I pursued it, he'd simply stop talking. So I glossed right over it and continued on.

"Did you spend much time with her here?" I said.

"No. She came up to me at the mixer and we talked about old times. She told me she was getting a divorce and wanted to start a new chapter in her life." He stopped and seemed to consider his words. "Okay, I thought she might mean she wanted something romantic with me. I kind of ended the conversation and said we'd talk more over the weekend. Then she made that scene with her husband and the magician. I thought she might have been upset because I gave her the brush-off."

What I was really looking for was an alibi for Sammy. "Did you see what happened to the magician's silk after she grabbed it?'

"She took it, like it was some kind of prize, and stuffed it in the pocket of her sweater." He suddenly looked wary. "Why all the questions? Are you the one Kevin St. John warned us about? The amateur sleuth?"

"I'm more than an amateur. I'll have you know I was an assistant detective at a very large firm in Chicago." The title I gave myself was questionable. I think Frank would have been more likely to refer to me as a detective's assistant. But I figured my version put me ahead of the Miss Marple wannabes of the world.

"Whatever you are, I assure you I had nothing to do with her death. Why would I want to kill her?"

I offered a reassuring smile and nodded in agreement, but all the while I was thinking that he'd offered a possible motive when he brought up the underage thing. At the very least it implied they'd had some kind of relationship. Suppose what he'd said about nothing underage wasn't true and she'd decided to bring it out into the open? Even if it was too late to make a criminal charge, it would kill his squeaky clean image and end his lucrative business with the energy drink.

I wanted to ask him more about their relationship, although I was pretty sure he wouldn't answer. But maybe if I told him what I was after, I'd catch him off guard. "Sorry for all the questions," I said. "This is really about the magician. He's a friend of mine. I'm hoping I can find out an alibi for him."

"Oh," Jimmie said, his demeanor changing. "Now I understand what you're doing. But I'm afraid I can't help you there." I wasn't expecting such a short answer and was trying to figure how to steer the conversation back to Jimmie's relationship with Diana, but we were interrupted as Bree Meyers caught up with us. Her blond fluff of curls bounced as she waved her hands. She had baseballs in each and wanted Jimmie to sign them for her boys.

"If you think of anything, please let me know," I said.

"How?" he said, bringing up the difficulty of communicating at Vista Del Mar.

"There's always the message board," I said.

"Right. Just like the old days."

22

I HAD TO TAKE NUMEROUS PHOTOS OF BREE WITH Jimmie before I could extricate myself. My early bird retreater's cell phone might not work to make calls, but the camera function was still fine. She was all aflutter about how impressed her husband would be that she'd met a real baseball star. Even when I walked away, I could hear her excited voice. The grounds were busy with people now that the afternoon activities had all ended and both groups had free time.

A number of the 1963 people were heading to the boardwalk that cut through the dunes. It looked like some kind of impromptu nature walk.

A breeze ruffled past, making me want to zip up my fleece jacket. Today's was a dark olive green and I'd added a pale blue lacy mohair scarf my aunt had made. I had to remind myself again that it was August and summer. I realized this was a good area for knitters to live. It was scarf weather year-round.

My group had spread out. I recognized Lucinda's Ralph Lauren jacket up ahead with several other people. They turned off at the Sea and Sand building. Her room was in there, but I guessed she and the others were heading to the living room–like lobby. With soft easy chairs and the glowing fire, it was a perfect spot to hold a knitting session, and it was certainly an appealing one on a cool afternoon like this.

When I got to the bottom of the small hill, I saw Olivia walking with a bunch of the others toward the Lodge. They were no doubt going to have a square-making session. It was such a relief not to have to worry about everyone. I pictured them in the Cora and Madeleine Delacorte Café sitting around a table full of steaming mugs. It was definitely coffee weather.

Gwen and her daughter were headed the other way. Crystal pulled her mother's plastic bin toward a small parking area near the main building. Since the hotel and conference center was over a hundred years old, when it was designed where to put cars was hardly an issue. Parking spots had been added in small spaces around the grounds. Wanda was already shutting the door to her blue Smart Car. A moment later, she zipped out of the parking lot and headed up the driveway.

I watched the dynamic of the mother and daughter for a moment. Because of my up-and-down relationship with my mother, I was always curious to see how other mother-daughter combos reacted. It was clear from the body language that there was no contention going on. I found that so surprising, considering the difference between the plain utilitarian look of Gwen and the unmatched and colorful vibe of her daughter. The fact that they were able to live together with Crystal's kids in that small house amazed me.

I shuddered to think what life would be like if I showed up on my mother's doorstep with a couple of kids.

They stopped when they got next to Gwen's boxy Volvo wagon with the Cadbury Yarn decal on the door. Neither of them seemed to notice that just beyond the small parking lot, yellow tape still marked off the area where Diana Rathman had been found.

I didn't want to have to answer any questions about where I was going or, worse, have Madeleine show up and want to join me. I held back until Gwen had gotten in her car and Crystal walked down to her dusty Ford Explorer. I was relieved to see Madeleine rush up to her golf cart. She had a lead foot with the small vehicle and was already turning out of the driveway before the other two cars had backed out.

When they were all gone, I walked up toward the street. I wanted to check on Sammy, and I wanted to call Frank. Maybe my ex-boss could help me make some sense of all that I knew. Everything seemed quiet as I headed up my driveway. I looked at the guest house and it was so silent I wondered if Sammy was still in there. I was about to knock on the window that was only visible from my small backyard in what had become our signal.

I glanced around wondering if Lieutenant Borgnine had someone watching. I knew a little about surveillance. I'd done it once when I was working for Frank. One of his associates had a toothache and I took over for him so he could go to the dentist. I always told Frank it would have turned out differently if I'd known I was going to be doing surveillance when I came to work. I certainly wouldn't have worn a bloodred shirt. Of course, with that shirt I was noticed and the whole thing went bust.

But I'd learned from the experience. If somebody was

watching my place, they'd have to do it from the street. I
retraced my steps and looked down the expanse of the black
asphalt in both directions. The only vehicle parked was an
old blue van with some kind of writing on the side. Could
it be a cover?

I walked down to it and looked in the windows. It appeared
empty, but there was something blocking the view of the rear
area. I went around to check the back. I leaned against the doors
to see if I could hear anything.

"What are you doing?" a voice said, startling me, and
instinctively I jumped back.

"Hey, that's my foot," the voice complained as arms grabbed
me. My instinct was to push away, but then my surroundings
came into focus and I saw that the red truck had pulled to
the curb in front of the van. When I looked over my shoulder,
Dane's face was inches from mine.

"So what exactly are you up to?" he said, releasing me.
"You're not planning on stealing that van." His grin made
it clear he was teasing.

I went with the truth. "I thought your lieutenant might
have someone watching my place."

Dane shook his head. "Cadbury PD isn't that sophisti-
cated. When we watch people, it's more direct." He made a
V out of his fingers and pointed at his eyes. "Besides, Borgnine doesn't think Sammy is here. He's gotten it into his
head that the doctor/magician has left the area, but he thinks
you know where Sammy is. By the way, he's saying that
he's not looking to arrest Sammy, that he just wants to talk
to him."

"Yeah, right," I said. "How about he's telling you that so
you'll tell me and then I'll give up Sammy's location."

"Probably true," Dane said with a shrug. There was a silence after that. Was Dane expecting me to say something, like actually give up Sammy's location?

"You said Lieutenant Borgnine thinks Sammy has left the area. Where does he think he is?" I asked, choosing to try to get information rather than give it.

"He got a tip that he was at the San Jose Airport waiting to board a plane for Chicago, but when Borgnine got there, he wasn't on the passenger list."

"Who said it?" I asked.

Dane shrugged. "Don't know. It was an anonymous tip."

Just then a man carrying a toolbox approached the van and gave us a suspicious stare. "Are you trying to steal my van?" I looked horrified and Dane started to laugh. He pulled me away and let the guy open the back. Even so, I stole a look inside. There was no setup of cameras and people with headphones. Just a bunch of pipes and rotors.

The man shut the back with a slam and got into the front, giving us a dirty look. A moment later, he drove away.

"You're out and about a lot today," I said, noting that his truck was pointed in the opposite direction of his house as if he was on the way somewhere.

"I've got the karate kids coming over later," he said. "I'm on the way to the grocery store to load up on spaghetti noodles."

"I don't think they'd want you to call them kids." I'd seen some of his students in his garage studio and could just picture how they would react if they heard him. I wondered if they had any idea how lucky they were that Dane gave them lessons, a place to hang out and even cooked for them. It was his way to hopefully keep them out of trouble. Just thinking about his homemade tomato sauce made my mouth water.

"Right, young people. There'll be eats for you tonight," he said. He always left me a plate of whatever he cooked. He reminded me of what a great team we made. He made dinner and I made dessert.

"I'll be eating at Vista Del Mar with my group. Then when I'm sure all is well, I'll be baking."

"So you're going home for a break now?" he said, glancing toward my place.

"I found out some stuff and I was going to call Frank and talk it over. Try to make sense of it all."

"Frank, huh. How about you talk to me? I might not be a PI, but I am a cop." He looked down at his jeans. "Even if I'm not in uniform."

I thought it over for a moment. I couldn't tell him anything about where Sammy was, but other than that, why not? It might even be better because he knew the players. With Frank it would take half an hour just to explain who everyone was.

"Okay," I said finally.

"Your place or mine?" he asked as he got a satisfied smile.

"How about the beach?" I offered. For so many reasons it seemed to be a better alternative.

"So I'm listening," he prompted when we'd walked back across the grounds of Vista Del Mar, taken the boardwalk through the dunes and crossed the street that wound between the edge of the Vista Del Mar grounds and the beach.

We had the place to ourselves. There was a constant breeze coming off the water and it ruffled my hair and blew a strand across my face. Dane, ever the gentleman, brushed it out of my eyes. We struggled through the silky sand to the darker damp area near the water's edge where it was easier to walk. A wave rolled onto the shore and away, for a moment leaving a mirror that reflected back our images before it became damp sand again.

"I've found out quite a bit about the victim," I began. "Like she's originally from Cadbury and is probably Kevin St. John's half aunt."

Dane stopped walking. "Wow, that's a piece of news Lieutenant Borgnine doesn't have. Kevin St. John's step-aunt, huh."

"There's more. I think there was something going on with her and Jimmie Phelps."

"The old baseball player who's pushing the energy drinks now?" he asked, and I nodded.

"And she and her husband are splitting up and she owns half the My Favorite Year business."

Dane's eyes widened. "You have been a busy little detective." He caught himself and he winced. "I'm sorry, that sounded demeaning." His eyes twinkled as he said, "I am just truly amazed that while you are in the process of putting on your yarn retreat, you managed to find out all that information."

With the sameness of the sand and plantings along the edge of the beach, it was hard to tell how far we'd walked. The air had brought color to his face and I guessed mine as well. "Maybe we should turn back," I said. As we did, he took my hand as if to steady me. He didn't let go when we started walking again.

"See, I told you that you could talk to me," he said as, hand in hand, we walked back.

"Except that Frank gives me advice about what to do."

"I can do that, too. Sort of. You seem to have a number of possibilities, but if you want Lieutenant Borgnine to get off of Sammy as a suspect, you need to give him some evidence, something he can build a case on. Or better yet. Get someone to confess."

He walked me all the way home, only letting go of my hand when we got to my driveway. As he walked to his truck, he turned back and glanced at the guest house for a split second. "I'll leave the plate of food anyway."

23

DANE STOOD BY HIS TRUCK AS I WENT UP MY driveway. My guess was that he suspected Sammy was in my guest house. Even so, I didn't want to confirm it. So I walked to my kitchen door and went inside.

I waited until I heard Dane's truck drive off and then I slipped back outside. I knocked at the guest house window and there was just silence in response. For a moment I wondered if the story about Sammy being sighted at the San Jose Airport might be true, but then the shutters opened and Sammy pulled up the window.

Being clean shaven and wearing fresh clothes seemed to have given him a lift, but his dark eyes looked tense. "I'm going nuts, being stuck in here. Thanks for the movies, the food, the clothes and your computer, but I need my life back." It came out like a cranky roar, which was unusual for Sammy. I felt bad for him and reached in and gave him a semblance of a hug.

"I'm sorry for all this," I said with a sigh. "I'm working on it. I really am."

"Please hurry," he said.

"I have to go back across the street, but Dane is going to leave a plate of food later."

Sammy looked stricken. "He knows I'm here?"

"He doesn't know, but he might suspect. But don't worry, I don't think he will say anything."

"Case, don't you see the food is a trap. He wants to get rid of me because I'm his competition." Sammy suddenly looked horrified. "Strike that. I'm not here because of you. No, it's all about a change and doing my magic."

"Okay, don't take the food. I'll bring you some frozen stuff." The guest house was still fully functional and had a refrigerator and a microwave. I slipped into my kitchen and brought him back a selection of entrées. "I gotta go," I said. I reminded him that I was in the middle of a retreat along with everything else. He pulled himself back inside and closed the shutter tight up.

What Sammy said couldn't be true about Dane wanting to get Sammy out of the way. That was crazy. Sammy's being here had nothing to do with my resistance against getting involved with Dane, or did it?

Julius was waiting by the door when I came in. He seemed a little perturbed, maybe because I hadn't acknowledged him when I came in before. He jumped on the counter and rubbed against my arm. I picked him up and considered nuzzling him. The cuddling always seemed to be on his terms and I wasn't sure how he'd react to me taking the initiative.

"What a mess. Sammy's stuck in the guest house and a killer is on the loose," I said, going for it and rubbing my face against his head. I waited for a second to see if he would jump out of my arms or, worse, hiss at me, but he butted my cheek softly with his head and started to purr. "Julius, you're full of surprises. Who would have thought independent you would turn out to be a snuggle bunny?"

A temporary snuggle bunny. In typical cat fashion, after a few minutes he'd had enough and squirmed out of my arms. Julius was definitely his own cat, but I was beginning to believe that he felt a connection to me. I certainly did to him. It was so nice to come home to somebody.

The cat followed me as I took care of a few chores, mostly related to him. I ended by pouring some crunchies in his bowl and adding a scoop of stink fish on top. I spruced myself up a bit for the evening and was headed for the door when the phone rang.

"Frank," I said in surprise when I picked up. I already knew it was him courtesy of the mechanical voice that phonetically announced who was calling. "Is something wrong?"

He made some kind of a noise. I'd heard it before when I worked for him. He did it when he was annoyed with himself. "Feldstein, I thought you were going to keep me informed."

"Frank, you called *me*," I said with a happy laugh. "I knew all your grumbling about helping me wasn't real. You like to help me. You really like to help me."

"Don't go getting all crazy, Feldstein, over a simple call. You sounded distraught before and it's really personal for you being that it's the Amazing Dr. Sammy Glickner who is the main suspect."

"Thanks for reminding me," I said with just a touch of sarcasm.

"So?" he said. "Are you just going to waste all the time fussing about my calling you or are you going to bring me up to speed?"

"Okay, you asked for it." All the names tumbled out and

I started mixing up the two things I was concerned about—getting it so Sammy could go home and finding out the real identity of Edmund Delacorte's heir.

"Feldstein, stop," Frank ordered. "I'm going on overload here. All those names. I know who Dotty Night and Bobbie Listorie are. And what baseball fan doesn't know who Jimmie Phelps is, but all the rest are in a knot in my mind. I have one piece of advice on the murder investigation. You've got a lot of eyes and ears that were around after you left who probably know something. You just need to figure out the right questions to ask. About the heir thing—I still don't know why you're bothering with something that is only going to be trouble for you. You must realize that in the mishmash of information you gave me, it came through that Kevin St. John's mother might have been the secret heir."

"I know, and he could try to claim that he should inherit Vista Del Mar. But his mother would really be the heir. All I know about her is that she left town a long time ago."

"I don't know how the will was worded and if he could reopen things, but from everything you've said about that guy, I think if there was a way he could claim that place, he would." He heard me gulp. "Maybe you want to just forget about pursuing that for now. I'm sure you didn't miss that his grandmother's death is suspicious and now another person he's related to was killed."

I held my head as I listened. "Oh, no, Frank, that overload you were talking about just hit me." There was more to add, but instead I said nothing and there was a moment of silence.

Frank, the detective, picked up on it. "Feldstein, there's more, isn't there?"

"There might be one more thing," I said.

"Okay, shoot," he said, and I could picture him leaning back in his recliner, shaking his head in dismay that he'd made the call.

I brought up my doubts about Dane. I told him about the walk and everything Dane had said and the plate of food. "Do you think he's setting me up to get information?"

Frank chortled. "Feldstein, I told you there'd be a problem if you were all flirt and no nookie when you were trying to get information from him."

"It's not like that, Frank," I protested. "We're friends, neighbors."

"And he's a man and a cop. No matter what you think, he'd probably like to make the Amazing Dr. Sammy appear for Lieutenant Borgnine and disappear for you. How about he could get in trouble if they think he's withholding information or at the least get a horrible schedule, like working Christmas and the graveyard shift for the rest of his career. That's the cop part, and as for the man part—Feldstein, he doesn't want another rooster hanging around the henhouse. The hen being you. Turning in the magician takes care of everything. So, no, you can't trust him."

AFTER THE LONG SPIEL HE SUDDENLY GOT impatient and said he'd already talked too long. "You will let me know what happens, right?" He was deliberately trying to make his voice sound gruffer.

I told him I would and clicked off the phone. Go figure. Frank always made it sound like he was doing me a favor to take my call, and here he was basically telling me to keep in touch. Once before I'd looked out the window to see if pigs were flying and I now did it again.

*   *   *

AFTER TALKING TO FRANK, I WAS ANXIOUS TO GET back to Vista Del Mar. Now I had a plan.

I was so deep in thought I barely noticed crossing the street and entering the grounds. I only came into focus as I went into the Lodge. It was lively with activity and there seemed to be groups of people everywhere. The pool table and table tennis table were occupied. The nature hike people had come back there afterward, and they were gathered around Dotty Night. Her platinum blond hair stood out like a beacon as she told them about something.

Kevin St. John was standing near the massive registration desk in his usual black suit. He glanced at me and then away as if he hoped I would disappear.

Did he even know that Diana was his half aunt? I had been saying *could* be his half aunt all along, but there was no doubt that she was. What were the chances that two women named Diana from Cadbury would have fathers who were baseball announcers?

Frank was right. I did have eyes and ears who had been there that night. I saw Olivia, Bree and Scott sitting with a group of knitters. Just like they were that first night when I left. I wanted to kick myself for not thinking about it before. But Frank was right about something else as well. I had to ask the right questions.

Joining the group was no problem. I took out a square I had started and sat down. Olivia had taken charge of the gathering and she introduced me to the two women from the 1963 group just as they got up to leave. Three women from our group took their place. I looked around the large room and realized what a perfect spot it was to see everything that was going on. I could see both doors to the outside, the entrance to the café and at the other end to the gift shop.

I moved next to Bree. "This is the same spot you were all in the night of the mixer, right?"

Bree nodded. "We had a front row seat to everything. It was embarrassing when that woman and her husband started arguing. I cringed when she ruined the Amazing Dr. Sammy's trick. It's no wonder he was the first customer at the martini bar."

"I suppose she went over there, too. She seemed pretty upset and probably thought a drink would take the edge off."

"Take the edge off?" Scott said. "She went way past that. She went over to Jimmie Phelps and interrupted while he was offering someone one of his energy drinks. He tried to smooth things over and walked her to the corner of the room. She didn't seem happy with what he said and pulled away."

"And then she started in on her husband's assistant," Olivia said. I wasn't surprised Olivia had noticed that. My early bird could relate since she had been dumped by her husband for someone who worked for him. "It got pretty heated and Scarlett, the woman from their group who joined us, had to step in. It looked to me like she was on Sally Winston's side," Olivia added.

"Where was Sammy in all this?" I asked. The early birds looked at each other and shrugged. "I kind of remember him going out on the deck side of the building. I thought he was going to take his drink to the beach."

"A lot of people left. There was a screening of newsreels from 1963 in that meeting room over by the parking lot that started at ten," Scott said. "I went over to have a look. They call it the Cabin and it was one of the first buildings constructed

when this was a camp. I was curious about seeing the inside
and the event was open to everybody."

"Then what?" I said.

"I checked out the outside of the building before I went
in. It looked really old and weathered like the other buildings that were part of the original camp. The inside was
paneled in dark wood like some of the guest rooms and the
carpeting looked vintage." He started to describe the design
on the carpeting. I didn't want to interrupt, but I was more
interested in who was there and what happened than the
floor covering. As soon as there was a break, I stepped in.

"Did you notice who was there?" I asked. I wanted to see
what he would say before I asked about anyone in particular.

"Let me see," he said. "The furniture had been pushed to
the side and a bunch of folding chairs brought in. I took a seat
on the end of a row because I wasn't sure how long I was
going to stay. There was some fussing between Norman Rathman and Kevin St. John over the video equipment. I think
the 1963 retreat leader was hoping for an old-fashioned movie
screen and a projector instead of the flat screen and DVD
player."

"Did you see who else was in there? Like maybe Sammy?"
I asked.

Scott shook his head in response. He seemed so conservative with his close-cut dark blond hair and preppie clothes,
yet being an out-in-the-open knitter made him a renegade.
"No. He wasn't there for sure. Madeleine Delacorte took a
seat in the front row. Scarlett, the woman from their group
who joined ours, was in the front row, too. She was with a
man I suppose was her husband. Some more people came
to the front of the room. Then there was another disagree-
ment between Rathman and St. John about introductions, I
think. I heard Kevin St. John say that since he invited them,

he ought to be able to introduce them. Rathman's point was that he was the head of the retreat. St. John seemed to bristle when Rathman said that. I got the feeling that Kevin St. John thought he was the head of their retreat. The Rathman guy won out. He introduced Dotty Night before they showed some trailers of movies she'd made that year." Scotte went off on describing how silly they seemed and how different taste was in those days.

"Rathman brought Bobbie Listorie up next. They played a clip of him on the *Ed Sullivan Show* and a newsreel of him arriving at the airport." Scott laughed and rolled his eyes. "He was a lot thinner in those days, though the suit and the hairstyle were the same. Those women were frantic, and one of them fainted when he reached out and touched her hand. That guy sure loves the spotlight. At the end of the segment, he re-created the moment and reached out to touch Scarlett's hand. Only she didn't faint. Personally, I liked watching the old sports shorts that featured Jimmie Phelps the best. It's amazing how much he looks the same."

"Anything else?" I asked. Scott thought it over.

"I saw Rathman's wife had come in. She was standing on the side of the room near where I was sitting. Then she said something."

I suggested that Scott close his eyes and see if he could remember what she had said. "It's important."

He did as I asked. By now, the whole group had fallen silent. After a few moments his expression got troubled and he shrugged his shoulders as if he was confused. Then he opened his eyes and looked at me. "She said, 'You're not going to get away with that. I know how to ruin you.'"

The whole group seemed to suck in their breaths at once. I looked around and was relieved nobody outside our group seemed to be listening to us.

Scott couldn't say who she was looking at when she spoke and said she wasn't there at the end of the program, but he didn't notice when she left. The only good news was that Sammy definitely wasn't there.

Lucinda slipped in and plopped down next to me. "What's going on? Did I miss something important?" I quickly filled her in on what Scott had said. "What about after that?" Lucinda asked.

"That's what I want to find out." When I looked up, one of the 1963 people had snagged Scott for a knitting lesson. He took teaching very seriously, and even though I was impatient to hear the rest of the story, I waited until he had the woman knitting rows on her own before I pulled him aside.

"As you were saying about that first night," I said, trying to prod him to continue, "what about after the celebrity stuff?"

Scott launched into talking about some tapes of old TV news shows they played. He couldn't get over how boring they seemed. The newscasters didn't joke with each other or throw in their own opinions. "They just read the news," he said with distaste. It was all very interesting, but not what I was after. With some effort I guided him back on topic and he said he'd stayed the whole time, but had noticed that people seemed to be going in and out.

"You didn't happen to notice who came and went, did you?" I asked hopefully.

He seemed to be struggling to answer. "Here's the problem. I was watching the news films, not really what was going on in the room." He had been knitting the whole time we were talking. I have to admit, I had stopped in the middle of a row to give him my full attention. He looked up at the stone fireplace but his fingers kept moving. I could tell by his expression he was thinking. "The celebrities left as soon as their pieces were done. I think Norman Rathman was there the whole time. I saw him in the beginning and at the end when he came to the front and thanked everyone for coming." It seemed like Scott was finished, but then his long face became animated.

"I remember another detail," he said as he automatically reached the end of a row and started on a new one by switching his needles. "Rathman's wife never sat down. She hung back by me. She was a still a little loose from the martinis and she knocked into my chair as she turned to go. Her pocket was close to my eye level and I remember seeing something stuffed in it that was brightly colored. I didn't think about it at the time, but now I bet it was the Amazing Dr. Sammy's trail of scarves."

"She had Sammy's silks," Lucinda said. "That must prove something."

"I wish," I said. "I already knew that. Unfortunately it doesn't exclude Sammy; it just means everyone had access to the string of scarves, including him. I think the thing to focus on is that she was planning to ruin someone."

"That sounds like a motive if I've ever heard one," Lucinda said. "The big question is who." She turned to me. "Any ideas?" Scott seemed to be relieved to be out of the spotlight and moved closer to the rest of the group.

"I have one possibility. Diana's father was the announcer for the Giants and she hung around the team." I told Lucinda about my conversation with Jimmie Phelps earlier. "He said something really odd. He said that nothing went on between them when she was underage."

Lucinda's eyes were as round as the Swarovski faceted

jet-black buttons on her tunic. "Wow. So you think something did happen between them and she was going to expose him?"

"Even if it was too late to bring any criminal charges against him, that energy drink company would drop him in a second if anything tarnished his squeaky clean reputation."

"And he seems like such a nice guy."

"That's what I thought, too, but who knows? It could just be an act. And he's not the only one she might have something on," I said. "Just because Kevin St. John is acting like he doesn't know that Diana Rathman was his half aunt doesn't mean it's true. Remember, Maggie said his grandmother died under suspicious circumstances. She was the one who was found at the bottom of a stairway. Suppose Kevin pushed her and somehow Diana knew." Lucinda automatically looked toward the front of the big room where Kevin St. John usually hung out. For once he wasn't there.

"We've always thought there was something sinister about him. If he killed his grandmother, it probably wouldn't be that hard to kill someone else."

"That's pretty much what my ex-boss said," I said, along with reminding me that Kevin's mother could be the secret heir and that, if Kevin found out, he'd try to claim the place as his.

"Oh dear, heaven help us if Kevin St. John manages to get hold of this place."

"Back to who else Diana could have wanted to ruin. What about her husband? I don't know exactly what she might have on him, but she is half owner of the My Favorite Year business. They make a lot more profit on their retreats than I do," I said. "I got the feeling they were battling over how to split it up. He seemed to think he was the business. Maybe she wanted to ruin him out of spite." I noticed that the knitting group seemed to be putting away their work and the others in the room started to head toward the doors as the dinner bell began to ring.

I put my hand on Lucinda's arm to hold her back a second. "That's just what I know about. Who knows who else Diana had a grudge against?"

24

I HAD A MISSION WHEN I WENT TO THE DINING hall. Frank's advice had been right on and I wanted to continue checking with other eyes and ears from that first night. And I had someone in mind who had a different perspective than Scott's. As soon as I got inside, I took up a position next to the group of tables our retreat had been using and watched as people came in. I greeted my people as they arrived, though by now they'd made friends with each other and knew the ropes about getting their food. As soon as Lucinda joined me, she picked up the pitcher of ice tea and started making the rounds.

I kept my eye toward the door until Scarlett came in. She had been at the newsreel event, too, and might have noticed things Scott had missed. She had been going back and forth eating with our group and the 1963 people. I wanted to make sure she chose to eat this meal with us. I started across the room, hoping to direct her our way, but then I saw she'd walked in with Dotty Night and Bobbie Listorie. All of them were headed toward the table with Norman Rathman, Sally Winston, and Scarlett's husband. I quickened my pace, hoping to grab her before she sat down.

I was too late and got behind her chair just as she'd sat in it. "Scarlett, I was hoping you'd sit with our group," I said, touching the shoulder of her shirt, which was in a color that matched her name. Maggie would have loved the shade of red.

She looked from Dotty Night on one side of her to Bobbie Listorie on the other. "I kind of want to stay here," she said.

Bobbie Listorie looked up at me and beamed a big smile. "This lady is the one who saved the old Bobberino the other night." He told everyone how I'd given him the aspirin. He looked at an empty seat. "Why don't you sit with us. Dotty was just going to give us the inside scoop about her co-star Stone Garner."

He got up, gallantly telling Dotty he'd get her food. "I hope you'll be here when I get back," he said to me with a wink. I found myself blushing from all his attention. I could see why the Pebble Beach resort paid him to hang out there even if, as Wanda insisted, he wasn't the best golfer. He knew how to charm the crowd.

Close-up, Dotty Night's platinum blond hair was practically blinding. It suited her sparkling personality. She repeated Bobbie's offer and pointed to a chair next to Norman Rathman. No surprise, Sally Winston immediately stepped in and said they were saving the seat for someone.

It was pretty much now or I'd have to wait and try to talk to her the next morning. After dinner I was just going to spend a few minutes making sure my group all got to the screening of Dotty's movie before I left to start baking. How was I going to get her to leave that table and come to ours?

I thought back through my multitude of jobs for something

that could help now. There was nothing from when I'd worked as a teacher, but maybe something from the time I'd spent spritzing samples of perfume on customers coming into a department store, not one of my more stellar positions. The point was to get them to go to the perfume counter so the clerks could try to sell them. When all else failed, I'd gone with the truth. As I gave out a sample of the perfume, I told the shopper that I was going to lose my job if I didn't get a certain number of people to go to the counter. They didn't have to buy anything, just make an appearance and look at the perfume for me to get credit. I was amazed at how many people agreed to do it to help me out. Maybe the same thing would work with Scarlett.

"I really need your help with something at our table," I said. Just like with the perfume people, Scarlett's attitude changed and she popped out of her chair, telling them she'd be back in a few minutes.

As soon as we were out of earshot, I brought up the newsreel event. "You were there, weren't you?" I asked.

She fluttered her eyes in surprise at my question. I suppose it did seem a little out of the blue, but I didn't have a lot of time to segue into it. "Yes, but I was a little loopy. The martini had gone right to my head," she said, using her finger to point to her temple. Frank had said it was all about phrasing the questions right. I zeroed in on what I really wanted to know. I knew that Norman Rathman was there at the beginning and someone had told me they saw him there at the end, but I wanted to know if he'd been there the whole time.

"I know that Diana Rathman left during the program. Did you notice if Norman left, too?"

Scarlett understood what I was after. "You mean, did he follow her out?" She shuddered. "It's so much more comfortable to think it was the magician who strangled her. I don't know him. But the idea that someone I know did it." She shook her head, trying to get rid of the thought.

"Do you know if Diana had a reason to want to ruin Norman?"

Scarlett's eyes looked at me as if it was an absurd question. "Are you kidding? Their marriage was breaking up and I'm sure they were fussing about the property settlement. I can only guess, but I bet Norman was claiming he was entitled to a bigger share of the retreat business."

"Why? I thought they were partners?" I asked.

"Professors are like rock stars to their students. And you've seen him. He's got looks and charisma. The whole business took off because of him. People joined the club because of him. Diana started out as one of his students and she was like a groupie." We'd stopped near a window by then, and people brushed past us on their way to the food line. Scarlett seemed to have forgotten her rush to get back to her table as she continued. "I have an opinion about people like Diana. I think people like her can't quite become somebody important themselves, so the next best thing is to latch on to somebody who is." Scarlett was on a roll now and I just nodded to show I was listening. It was becoming increasingly apparent that while she thought Norman Rathman was charismatic, she didn't really like him.

"Norman was the one who wanted the divorce and told her not to come to the retreats anymore. She cramped his style and made a fuss every time she saw people hanging all over him. Sally Winston doesn't have that problem. So, yes, I'm sure Diana would have loved to ruin him and the business even if it ended up costing her. She was a vindictive person."

I really wanted to ask Scarlett more about who else Diana's comment about ruining someone could have been referring to, but Scarlett suddenly seemed to remember where she was and started walking to our group of tables. "I'm sorry I got off track. You said you needed my help with something."

For a moment I got that deer in the headlights feeling and froze. *Think fast,* I told myself. By the time we'd reached the first table with our people, I'd come up with something.

I pointed to all the balls of yarn on the table. "They are still fussing around with swapping yarns. I thought if you could show them the scarf you're making with what came in your bag, they might realize the whole point of the retreat was the serendipity effect."

"You should have said something before. My tote bag is back at the table." She rushed back to get it and happily showed off her work in progress while explaining that half the fun was being surprised how it came out instead of planning too much. As an example, she picked up one of the worry dolls in progress off the table. Instead of trying to do the body in one color of yarn that seemed vaguely skin colored, the woman had mixed the yarns so that the doll's body was done in shades of blue and lavender.

Since the yarn swapping hadn't really been a problem at the table, the group seemed puzzled by Scarlett's rant. I stepped in before anyone said anything and pulled her aside, thanking her profusely and letting her go back to her table.

"What was that about?" Lucinda asked as we headed to the back to get our food. I explained all as we picked up our lasagna and salad. "I really wish I could have asked her more. She added to the motive that Norman might have had, but she didn't say if he'd left and come back during the program. Scott said it ended at midnight, so judging by the time of death that Dane told me, it seems like she was killed while the program was going on. Norman could have slipped out and followed her. The 1963 people were all in there, our people had gone to bed or were inside knitting somewhere, so even if there was a struggle, who would have heard it?"

We clammed up when we got back to our table. The lasagna didn't come close to Dane's version.

I hung with my people after dinner. A few of them were skipping the movie, more anxious to spend the time together working on their projects, but I walked with most of them to Hummingbird Hall. The auditorium was built into a slope on the grounds. Like the Lodge, it was designed in the Arts and Crafts style and one of the original buildings. The inside seemed bright and inviting after the darkness outside.

Kevin St. John had outdone himself. He had turned the large space into a movie theater. The first thing I noticed was the scent of fresh popcorn along with the sound of popping coming from a red cart. As fast as it came down into the glass case, one of the kitchen help scooped it up and put it in a cardboard container and handed it to the next person in line. A glass counter had been set up with candy that was available in 1963. There were boxes of Good and Plenty, Dots, Tootsie Rolls and Milk Duds.

Rows of plush seats had been set up. There were no drink holders and they didn't recline like the modern movie theater seats did. I watched as the crowd filed in and, after getting their treats, found their seats. I saw that Madeleine had returned and had her sister, Cora, with her. Madeleine carried popcorn and candy and looked around in awe. Cora appeared more critical of her surroundings, but I saw her smile in spite of herself.

Kevin St. John came in and stopped next to me. There was so much more going on in my mind about him now. Before I had just been concerned with how difficult he tried to make it for me and how he wanted to push me out of the retreat business. His personal life had been a mystery to me.

Now I knew that he had a teenage mother who had abandoned him and a grandmother who died under suspicious circumstances. The dead woman at the retreat was his relative, and there was a possibility, which I was doing my best to deny, that Edmund Delacorte might have been his grandfather. I tried to act as if nothing had changed.

Certainly he wasn't acting any different. "This is how you put on a retreat," he said, gloating as he gazed over the treat setup and the seats. "The movie screen and projector are vintage, the movie is from the correct year, and we even have the star to talk about it." He looked around the open framework of the wood building, and I could feel the love he had for the place. And the pride he felt in a job well done for this event. We'd had our differences and he might be a double murderer, but I just couldn't bust his moment.

"You really did re-create an old theater," I said.

He had the best smile I'd ever seen. "Wait until you see the dance tomorrow night." He turned and looked at my black jeans and matching turtleneck under my toast-colored fleece jacket. "But if you want to come, you'll have to wear something from that year." I waited to see if he was going to add a snippy remark, but all he said was, "Casey, you have no idea what I'm capable of when it comes to Vista Del Mar." Then he went to the front and introduced Dotty Night.

Like Bobbie Listorie, she had kept the same hairstyle she'd worn all those years ago. The bubble of blond hair made her look the same as she did on the movie poster displayed in the Lodge and now in Hummingbird Hall. She was perky and upbeat as she greeted the audience. "I'm going to tell you all the inside dope about making *Bridget and the Bachelor*, but before I start, I want to show off my pride and joy, the Dotty Night Inn. As she said it, a slide of the place showed on the screen. I thought she was just going to start doing a sales pitch, but it turned out the cottagelike inn was connected to the movie.

"We filmed the movie in Carmel and I fell in love with this area. When the movie wrapped, I kept coming back up here. I rented a place in Cadbury until I found the inn." She went on about how she had lovingly fixed it up before segueing into her real point. She was offering a discount to all the attendees. She showed some more slides and then got down to telling some stories about the making of the film. Finally the lights dimmed and the movie came on. I started to leave, but I got caught up in how differently movies started in 1963. I was used to jumping right into the story. No credits or even the title. *Bridget and the Bachelor* began with the title splashed across the screen and then a cartoon image of the character played in the background as extensive credits rolled. The music was all upbeat and bubbly. One thing that did seem ahead of its time was that it started off with Bridget addressing the audience.

I would have liked to stay, but the Blue Door needed their desserts and the town their muffins. The night air felt fresh and chilly as I headed up the path, thinking about what I was going to bake. I was surprised to hear footsteps behind me and turned to see who was following. Even in the dark I recognized Dotty's superbright hair as she caught up with me.

"You're not staying," I said, gesturing back toward the auditorium.

She laughed. "I've already seen the movie. And it's been a long day, a very long day. I just want to go to my room and put my feet up." There was no perkiness in her voice now.

Maybe because she saw me as a fellow worker rather than a guest of Vista Del Mar, she began to let her hair down.

"Having a celebrity name on the inn helps, but I've got to keep getting it out there to people. Everybody thinks performers are loaded, but take it from me, we're not. Or I'm not. Luckily my name still means something even though I haven't starred in a movie for years. The same goes for Bobbie Listorie and Jimmie Phelps. They're both still celebrities. That's why the resort pays Bobbie to hang out and the energy drink company pays Jimmie Phelps to be a spokesperson." She massaged her cheeks. "All this smiling has worn me out. I felt like I had to do double duty keeping things cheerful around here. Who'd have thought there'd be a murder?"

We had reached the deck side of the Lodge. Here the walkway was lower than the building, and I could see the glow of light from the windows, but not see inside.

I took the opportunity to see if she had any information to offer. "I noticed you mentioned spending a lot of time in the area. You know the woman who died was originally from Cadbury. Did you know her?"

"I never laid eyes on her until that first night. I was appalled at the way she acted to that magician. We performers have to stick together, and I wanted to say something reassuring to him when I saw him outside on the deck. But he was talking to her, and I didn't want to interrupt."

My ears had perked up. "What time was it? Did you hear what they were saying?" I attempted to keep the urgency out of my voice.

"I don't remember the time, just that it was dark. I didn't hear anything intelligible, but we actors are students of body language. He was weaving from side to side as he talked to her, which to me meant he was drunk. I noticed the light from the window reflecting off the martini shaker in his hand, which kind of confirmed it. He seemed to lean toward her, and I had the feeling he was giving her a rough time about messing up his show. Then she gave him a shove and walked away. No, not walked. I'd call it more of a march, an angry march. I didn't think about it at the time, but I should have gone up to him then. Maybe then he wouldn't have strangled her."

"What?" I squeaked in surprise. "How do you know he's the one who killed her?"

"That's what that police lieutenant who looks like a bulldog playing Columbo told me after he questioned me." She let out a tired sigh and wished me a good night before walking toward the buildings with the guest rooms.

For the first time, I had a doubt about Sammy. Maybe the alcohol had brought out a dark side in him that I had never seen.

I went up the stairs to the deck and was going to cut through the Lodge, but luckily I looked through the window first. Lieutenant Borgnine had come in the other door and was approaching Kevin St. John. I couldn't hear what was being said, but I thought of Dotty Night and how she read body language.

It looked like they made small talk at first and then Lieutenant Borgnine seemed to ask Kevin St. John something. The placid face of the manager changed abruptly to shock and dismay, and he fell back against the registration desk. I was only guessing, but the cop with no neck and a rumpled jacket might have just dropped the bomb about Diana Rathman's relationship to the manager. I tried to evaluate Kevin's reaction. Was it real or not? It was so over the top, it made me wonder.

Did the lieutenant's presence mean he was still looking for suspects or just clearing up loose ends while he tried to find Sammy? Having the cop so close to my place made me nervous. I backtracked and walked around the Lodge and out the driveway. When I got across the street, I walked right past my guest house without even a glance. I could hear the music coming from Dane's place down the street. The karate group was probably just finishing up. I looked at the stoop outside my back door. There was no plate of food. What did that mean?

25

I STOPPED IN MY PLACE JUST LONG ENOUGH TO greet Julius and pick up the bag of supplies for the night's muffins.

In case there were eyes out there watching, I didn't check on Sammy, but got into my Mini Cooper and drove to downtown Cadbury. Since it was Friday night, there were still people on the streets walking around the main part of town. People were headed toward the movies and coming out of restaurants. The stores were all closed. I slowed as I passed by the site of the long-closed Cadbury Bank. The store that had taken over the space was gone now, too, and it looked lonely and dark. When I'd first found the envelope with the safety-deposit sheet from the Cadbury Bank, I had tried to track down some old employees who might have noticed the woman signing in on Fridays after Edmund had left. I'd only found one woman who'd worked there, but she hadn't been any help. Not really a surprise when you considered that it had happened over fifty years ago.

With all the dead ends, I was ready to give up on the whole thing. The possibility that Kevin St. John might turn out to be a Delacorte factored into that, too. Maybe some things were best left alone. On Monday after the retreat was over, I was going to throw all the stuff away.

The Blue Door was still open and several tables of customers were finishing their meals. Tag always introduced me if there were still diners when I came in. It was my ego boost for the day. Invariably they raved about my desserts.

I dropped off my bag of muffin-making supplies in the kitchen. The cook gave me a wary glance, letting me know the space still belonged to him. I went out to remind Tag about the plans for the desserts. I was making a double batch of the cheesecakes so he would have them for two nights, and I would have Saturday night free to spend with my group. The muffins weren't his concern, but I'd just be baking for Saturday, and Cadbury would have to deal with a muffinless Sunday again.

He was fine with any dessert I made because the menu simply said "homemade desserts," so as long as I made something, it was accurate. "How's Lucinda?" he asked.

I told him about the screening and he sighed. "I could have taken her to the movies." He nodded toward the window and the view of the theater down the street. "Do you think she'd mind if I showed up at Vista Del Mar and slipped into the seat next to her?"

Before I could answer that the seat next to her was probably already taken and the movie half over, he rethought the whole thing. "Of course I can't do that. I'm not signed up for any of the retreats. I would be trespassing."

It seemed like he was being a little extreme about the

trespassing. I was pretty sure that Lucinda would find his thought of showing up as a sweet gesture, but would be glad that he didn't come. Tag wouldn't be able to help himself and would start straightening the candy stand and freaking out about popcorn that had landed on the ground.

I waited until the cook finished up and had left the building before I took over the kitchen. When the last of the diners were gone and everything cleaned up, Tag and the rest of the staff left and I had the place to myself.

I let out a tired sigh of relief and turned on some soft jazz. It was amazing how someone like me who had trouble sticking with things never got bored with baking. The sifting, mixing and pouring batter into a pan made me happy. I loved the wonderful scent as something baked, and seeing the finished product was a beautiful finale.

It was a relief that for now I could forget about everything and everyone except for the ingredients that were on the counter before me. Or so I thought. I'd barely unwrapped the blocks of cream cheese when I heard a soft knocking at the door. This time I wasn't startled when I saw the floating fist and I opened the door right away. Sammy crawled in. "I'm sorry, Case, but I had cabin fever. I was going to go nuts if I didn't get out. It's dark. I'm sure nobody saw me." He let out a happy sigh. "Oh, to be out in the world." He sniffed. "What are you baking?"

He followed me into the kitchen, but we didn't exactly walk together. He crawled to avoid the windows and I walked. The kitchen window was covered over, so he felt safe enough to stand.

"I can help you. I'll be your sous chef," he said. He seemed amazingly cheerful, all things considered. "And you can fill me in on what's going on with your investigation."

I kept thinking about what Dotty Night had said about

Sammy talking to Diana. It was useless to ask him about it because he didn't remember. Dotty had to be wrong. Just because Sammy and Diana had had some kind of confrontation didn't mean he had killed her.

Here he was acting cheerful and happy to see me without a word of reproach or a complaint about his situation. He was a big teddy bear, more likely to snuggle someone than attack them. I told him about the anonymous tip that he was seen at the airport in San Jose. "Did you call that in?"

"No, but that's a good idea. Maybe we could keep Lieutenant Borgnine running all over the place while you find out who really killed that woman."

"I'm afraid he's not going to fall for it anymore." Sammy looked disappointed. "If you really want to help, you can cut the cream cheese into cubes and put them in a bowl." Sammy wanted to know why, and I told him they would get to room temperature faster and mix better. He insisted on scrubbing his hands before he began and then started cutting the cream cheese with the precision of a surgeon.

He was about to turn on the mixer when I heard a knock at the glass door. Sammy froze. "Nobody can see me here." He looked around frantically for a door. The problem was the back door led onto the same porch as the front door. There was a large pantry in the kitchen and Sammy pulled open the double doors and crouched inside.

I went to the door not sure who to expect. I could just make out Dane in his uniform. I immediately thought of what Frank had said about not trusting him.

"What are you doing here?" I said when I opened the door. It made me nervous to realize that he was on duty and I was afraid I'd sounded a little sharp. He looked wounded by my manner.

"You don't sound glad to see me," he said. I didn't make

a move to ask him to come in. Had he followed Sammy, or did he just think that he was likely to show up here? Dane glanced toward the street as a car drove by. "Can I come in?" He seemed a little nervous. "Lieutenant Borgnine wasn't happy with my report the other night, and I'm stuck on night duty. He better not see me here unless the place is in the midst of a robbery.

"Well," Dane said when I still didn't move. "If he drives by and sees me standing here, he'll find a worse shift to give me, if that's possible."

"Okay," I said, finally stepping aside and letting him in. He shut the door behind him. I planned on keeping him corralled in the main dining room and figured I'd get rid of him quickly.

"I don't mean to keep you from your work." He looked toward the kitchen, no doubt expecting us to go in there as we had before but I didn't move.

"What exactly are you here for?" I said, wondering how well Sammy could hear. I really didn't want him to hear Dane say anything about the other night and our supposed date.

"I wanted to tell you that when I talked to Lieutenant Borgnine, I dropped that I'd heard Diana Rathman was from Cadbury and that she was Kevin St. John's aunt."

So I had been right about what was going on between Lieutenant Borgnine and Kevin St. John before I'd left Vista Del Mar. "Thank you. Hopefully it will get him to go in another direction."

"Maybe, but he's still fixated on wanting to talk to Sammy and he's not going to let up until he finds him," Dane said.

I didn't want to add what I really thought, that the lieutenant wouldn't let up until he arrested Sammy.

I thanked Dane and was going to ease him back out the door before he could say anything embarrassing, but his head shot up as he glanced out the window. Then he seemed agitated. "I should have figured he'd come by." A dark car had pulled to the curb and the driver's door opened. "He doesn't have a warrant. He'll just do that number asking if he can look around. Just say no."

Dane looked around and seemed concerned. "I've got to hide someplace." Before I could stop him, he ran into the kitchen. I heard doors opening and closing, and I cringed. A moment later, he ran back into the room, stopped and surveyed the surroundings. "The bathroom," he said, rushing in and closing the door.

Nothing happened for a few minutes, and I thought the coast was clear. Then there was sharp knocking on the glass. When I looked out, it was the lieutenant and he wasn't alone. Tag was with him. "Casey, let us in," Tag said.

Lieutenant Borgnine seemed pleased at my uncomfortable expression. "He called me and said he thought somebody was trying to kidnap you," Tag said, looking around for evidence of trouble. The holes in that line were as big as the ones in Swiss cheese, but I didn't argue.

Tag pointed at my apron with a residue of sugar on it and turned to the cop. "She looks all right to me. You must have been mistaken."

Lieutenant Borgnine ran his hand through his bristly salt-and-pepper hair. "I'm sure I saw someone else in here just a moment ago," the cop said, staring at me. I stumbled, trying to come up with an excuse. Meanwhile Tag gave him carte blanche to look around and satisfy himself that no one was there.

This was worse than the guest house. There was nothing I could do to stop him. Mentally I was already apologizing to Sammy for ruining his life. His parents would never speak to my parents and they'd spread the word that it was all my fault that their son was a doctor in prison. I pictured him in one of those striped suits trying to entertain the inmates with card tricks. Without realizing it, I'd plastered myself in front of the kitchen doorway. Lieutenant Borgnine's eyes glistened with triumph as he took a step toward me.

Just as I said "no," the bathroom door opened and Dane stepped out nonchalantly as if he'd just been using the facilities. "What's going on?" I quickly brought him up to speed, though I was sure Dane had heard everything.

"Somebody kidnapping Casey?" he said with a laugh. "No way. It was me you saw." He touched his superior on the shoulder in a friendly way. "C'mon, you were young once. Didn't you ever want to stop by and grab a moment with someone? If anyone saw someone holding Casey, it was me." As if to demonstrate, he pulled me in his arms and kissed me. It was even more embarrassing than when his fellow officer had sung the stupid ditty. But I wasn't about to object. Anything to stall Lieutenant Borgnine.

It was no wonder the lieutenant made a bunch of grumbling sounds. The cop couldn't exactly ask Tag if he could look around now. He glared at Dane and mumbled something about having to look into the schedule.

If Dane heard him, he ignored it and was all smiles. "C'mon, we better all get out of here, so Casey can do her work." He put his arms around the two men and walked them to the door. Just before they all went out, he looked back and our eyes met and he blew me a kiss.

I watched them through the window as they went to their respective cars and drove away. I waited another five minutes to make sure no one turned around and came back and then I went and let Sammy out of the pantry.

"Whew, Case, that was close," he said, trying to get the kinks out after being huddled in the small space. Sammy had no idea how close and I didn't tell him.

"Maybe I shouldn't go back to your guest house," Sammy said.

"No, that's the best place, just be careful that nobody sees you when you go back."

"I'll leave my car parked blocks away and I'll make sure the street is clear before I go in." He came over to me. "Case, I'm sorry for all the trouble." He hung his head, and his usual cheerful demeanor was gone. I gave him a reassuring hug and saw him to the door.

So much time had passed I had to hustle with the cheesecakes, and then instead of making all the trays of muffins, I put the cinnamon nut muffin batter in square pans. I hoped the muffin lovers of Cadbury wouldn't freak out at seeing square muffins instead of round ones.

This time when I made my delivery to Vista Del Mar, the Lodge was empty and the grounds were silent except for the sounds of the waves.

I gave Julius a late-night snack of stink fish. Then the two of us went to bed and at least I fell into a dead sleep.

26

"THERE YOU ARE," LUCINDA SAID AS I RUSHED UP
to the table. The dining hall was full and the conversations
loud because most people had finished eating their breakfast
and were lingering over their coffee.

"I'm sorry I'm late," I said to her and to the table of
retreaters. I think Lucinda was the only one who paid attention to my apology; everyone else seemed to be involved
with their knitting or talking.

Lucinda had gotten my breakfast and had covered the
plate with a metal dome to keep it warm. A to-go box sat in
front of it, and when I lifted it, I realized it was already filled.
"I told them you were very, very hungry and got you an extra
portion," she said with a knowing smile.

I slid into my chair, still in the process of waking up.
After the long day I'd had, it wasn't really a surprise that I
had slept through the alarm and Julius sitting on my chest.
It was only when he began to lick my cheek with his rough

tongue that I finally woke up. I had showered and thrown on clothes in record time.

"I'll get you a fresh cup," Lucinda said, reaching for the full cup in front of me. But I shook my head and picked it up despite her protests that it was lukewarm. The temperature was actually a benefit. I was able to drink it down in a few mouthfuls and the caffeine hit my brain. Like magic, my eyes opened wider and I was alert and present. The group at the table came into focus and I noticed that they all had their projects with them.

"Look at mine," Bree said. She held up her worry doll. "I'm making it into a worry bear." It was amazing how much knitters could accomplish when they had blocks of time to work. Bree had finished the basic body and stuffed it. The head of the doll was squarish and she had shaped the top corners into ears. Some of the others showed off their projects. It was exciting to see how different each scarf was even though they'd been using the same pattern. There were more worry dolls and they all looked different, too.

"I'm making mine into a worry cat," the woman with sayings on her T-shirts said as if she'd just invented sliced bread.

"That's silly," the woman next to her said. "Everybody knows cats don't worry."

"Worry dolls, bears and cats. They were all okay with me," I said brightly. Then I turned to Lucinda. "And I would like to gather them all up and hand them my troubles. I think it would take a whole gang of them to handle my worries." My friend looked concerned as I continued. "I have to figure out this thing with Sammy soon." I told her about the previous night and all my visitors while I was baking. "No worries for the restaurant, though; the cheesecake turned out great." I threw in Tag's desire to sneak into the movie at Vista Del Mar.

"That's sweet," she said. "But I'm glad he didn't. He needs

to understand that absence makes the heart grow fonder—and makes it easier to deal with his idiosyncrasies. Of course, if he had come, Lieutenant Borgnine wouldn't have reached him with that ridiculous story." She went over what I'd said. "And why is it Dane stopped by?"

"I'm not sure. Frank said I shouldn't trust Dane. But then he didn't blow the whistle on Sammy."

"Are you sure Dane saw him?" Lucinda asked.

"I didn't consider that, but now that you mention it, he probably didn't," I said, thinking back over the situation. "Sammy would have said something if Dane had opened the pantry door." I looked at my friend, feeling confused. "But if you went into the kitchen of the Blue Door and you were looking for a place to hide, wouldn't you check out the pantry?"

Lucinda nodded. "I see what you mean. It does seem odd that he didn't look in there. Still, I see Frank's point about not trusting him. Dane is a cop and they are looking for Sammy."

"I suppose all that stuff about giving him another chance for a date is just to cover why he really keeps showing up."

Lucinda laughed at my disappointed expression. "From everything you've been saying, that should be a relief for you. You keep saying it isn't a good idea for the two of you to get involved."

"True, but I guess I wanted it to be my decision." I leaned closer to her and dropped my voice even lower. "The worst is, I was beginning to think maybe he was right and we should try another dinner."

Our conversation abruptly ended with the arrival of Kevin St. John. He had his usual placid expression on his moon-shaped face, and I wondered what was really going on in his mind. Was he reeling from the information I was pretty sure Lieutenant Borgnine had given him the previous night, or was his calm exterior genuine because he had known all along who she was and dealt with the information? By "dealt with," I meant that he was the one who'd strangled her.

He directed his comments to me and my tablemates. "I wanted to remind you that you are all welcome to attend the dance that I arranged as part of the My Favorite Year retreat. There is one caveat. They would appreciate it if you would wear something from no later than 1963." He paused as someone passed by. "And as a bonus, you can come and watch the softball game Jimmie Phelps and I have arranged for the 1963 group this afternoon at the park by the light-house." He started to leave and turned back. "You can wear whatever you want to the game," he said, cracking a smile.

By the time he'd spread the news to all of our tables, the dining hall was beginning to clear out. Our group didn't want any free time after breakfast and they headed en masse to our meeting room. Lucinda went on with them, but I made a detour to my place with Sammy's breakfast. Fog had begun to drift in, softening the edges of everything. I hoped it would act as a veil, making it harder for anyone watching to see me head across the street.

I went around to the window that was only visible from my yard. Sammy answered almost before I'd finished knock-ing and threw open the window. He took the food container and looked at me with his eyes drawn in worry. "Case, I've been thinking about it. I think I'm going to have to make a run for it. Lieutenant Borgnine is just like Javert, the cop in *Les Misérables*. He's not to give up hunting me down."

"Just give me a little more time," I said.

Sammy sighed. "I hate the thought of leaving. But just remember, we'll always have Paris."

"Huh?" I said. I looked past him and saw that the TV was on. "You do realize you're using the cop from *Les Misérables* as a reference but spouting lines from *Casablanca*."

Sammy blinked a few times as if to clear his head. "Geez. You're right. That's what comes from being stuck in here with nothing to do but watch movie marathons."

"I'm just curious about last night," I said, thinking back to my conversation with Lucinda. "Did Dane open the pantry door?"

Sammy shrugged. "No. I saw the handle begin to turn, and I was trying not to make any noise, but my elbow hit a can of baking powder and it hit the floor. I was kind of surprised when I heard all the other cabinets being opened after that, but not the pantry." Sammy set the food down and straightened. "I mean it about leaving. How about if you haven't found the real killer by midnight, I'll be gone by dawn."

I tried to argue, but he was insistent. He reached out of the window to hug me. "So then this could be good-bye." He let go, and as I stepped away, he said, "Here's looking at you, Case," in his best Humphrey Bogart voice. Impressions were definitely not his thing.

The fog was getting thicker as I crossed back to Vista Del Mar. Sammy couldn't really be serious about going on the lam. I couldn't let it happen.

I thought of my aunt Joan and her acting ability. I hoped there was some of it in my genes as I pushed all of what Sammy had said onto the far back burner of my mind and tried to become the confident retreat leader as I walked into our meeting room.

The group was already in full knitting mode. Wanda and Crystal walked in together and seemed surprised to see everyone already there. Madeleine was close behind.

"Nobody told me we were starting early," the Delacorte sister said as she went to her seat.

Unlike the rest of them, Madeleine and I had left our projects in the room. Their worry dolls and scarves were all well on the way; mine was still just a flat rectangle. Her work was about the same. I picked mine up and began to knit quickly as if there was a chance I could catch up. I had to laugh when she did the same.

"I've brought more things for the worry dolls, er, and animals," Crystal said, seeing Bree's creation. She laid out some additional lengths of bulky black yarn and explained she'd show them how to use them to attach the "hair," along with how to do the face. She held up another handful of crochet hooks and said she'd brought them in case anyone still needed one to make the doll's dress.

Wanda made a few harumph sounds and said she hadn't brought any more supplies because her group had everything they needed in their bags.

"We're all invited to the dance tonight," the woman who wore the T-shirts with the clever sayings said.

"Yes, but we have to dress up in old stuff," the woman with the topknot added.

There was a rumble of grumbles and I stepped in, still trying to keep to the part of confident retreat leader. "I was thinking we could take what Kevin St. John said literally. He said *something* and we could take it as some thing, like one thing from 1963 or before."

"And I can help," Madeleine interjected in an excited voice. "Cora and I have all kinds of old stuff."

The group brightened at the prospect. We agreed that Lucinda and I would go with Madeleine to the Delacorte house and bring back a box of things the retreaters could use.

The workshop session time ended, Wanda and Crystal left, but the group didn't move. They happily knitted on and talked about the softball game. They planned to work on squares for Olivia during the game.

After a few minutes, I stood up. "I hate to leave you without a leader, but if we're going to get the things for the dance, now's a good time."

Madeleine and Lucinda got their things and went to the door.

"We're grown women—I mean people," the woman with the topknot said, glancing at Scott. "We can find our way to lunch and to the softball game if we have directions."

She'd barely finished when Scott stood up and addressed the group. "I know where the park is. How about we meet outside the Lodge after lunch." Bree and Olivia volunteered their services as well and I promised we'd meet them at the park.

It felt like a whole new day when we walked outside. The fog had melted and the sun was making an appearance. It was like someone had turned on the lights. Our group was the only one prolonging their workshop. The 1963 people all had free time and we had to thread through groups of them as Lucinda, Madeleine and I went down the sloping narrow road toward what I called the heart of Vista Del Mar.

I saw there was a crowd of people on the deck outside the Lodge. As we got closer, I saw Jimmie Phelps in the group. When he looked up and saw me, he waved me over.

"I'll be back in a minute," I said, leaving the two women on the path. I got a better view of what was going on when I went up the stairs to the large deck and realized they were getting things ready for the softball game. Dotty Night was gathering up pom-poms for a cheering squad, Bobbie Listorie was putting catcher's mitts in a canvas bag. Sally Winston hovered over a large red cooler, adding cans of the energy drink. She picked up one and popped open the lid before handing it to Norman Rathman. He wiped his brow and took a drink and went back to attending to the bats.

I was surprised to see Scarlett helping her husband with boxes of T-shirts for the players and realized she'd skipped our morning workshop. Jimmie Phelps was in the middle of it all.

I'd barely gotten out a greeting, when Jimmie's face clouded. "About the other day. You said if I thought of anything else—I'd like to explain something." I nodded in recognition and stepped closer in anticipation, but Kevin St. John showed up carrying a box of baseball caps and literally stepped between Jimmie and me.

"Ms. Feldstein, I don't think you want to keep Madeleine Delacorte waiting, do you?"

Jimmie apparently recognized the last name and understood the power that was connected to it. "I don't want to hold you up. We can talk later. Better yet, I'll leave you a message." He gestured toward the inside of the building in the direction where the corkboard stood.

It didn't seem like I had a choice.

27

"I CAN'T WAIT TO SEE WHAT MADELEINE'S HOUSE is like," Lucinda said. We were in my Mini Cooper following Madeleine's golf cart as it slowly maneuvered through the streets of Cadbury. When I say slowly, I mean almost creeping. I was basically driving with my foot hovering over the brake. I didn't realize how slowly the golf cart really went, as when I'd ridden in it with Madeleine, it seemed like she was a fast driver. It had been Madeleine's suggestion that we follow her instead of driving with her because there would be no room for us and the box of vintage pieces.

Madeleine pulled the golf cart into the driveway and I parked at the curb. I'd seen the Delacorte place before, but never gone inside. The imposing Victorian-style house was painted lavender and had fish scale siding. I was sure you could see out into the ocean from the second-floor balcony. They had a lawn and a border of flowers that wrapped around the front of the house.

She led us up to the small porch and inside. The first thing I noticed was that the entrance hall was so big it had its own fireplace. I only got a glimpse of the living room and saw that it had a bay window and ornate furniture.

Madeleine took us up the grand staircase. There was a window on the landing before it turned and went up the rest of the way to the second floor.

Once upstairs, she took us directly to her room. "This is so much fun, like having girlfriends over," she said. "Mother would never let us have company in our rooms or have sleepovers." She turned back to us. "Maybe we could do that sometime." Then she apologized for her silliness, saying she'd gotten carried away with the idea of doing all the things she'd missed.

"What about Cora?" I said, glancing around apprehensively. "I hope she won't mind that you're lending us things for the dance."

"Don't worry about her. She's gone to a meeting all day." She directed us to the seating area in the bay window before excusing herself to get the goods. She came back a few minutes later pulling a box heaped with clothing items. I noticed the box had *1963* written on the side. She set it down and began to go through it. We quickly separated scarves, hats and some tops to bring to our group, while Madeleine left to get another box. Leave it to Lucinda to find an Oleg Cassini beige silk dress to wear.

"Look what I have," Madeleine said when she came back. She picked up an old cigar box from the pile of clothes. She opened it and started taking out the contents. She had the ticket stub from the concert her brother had taken her to, the menu from their dinner and stubs from other attractions they'd gone to. All of it reminded me of Edmund's heir.

"Remember that hunt I was on," I said to Lucinda. It took

her a moment and then she understood. "I've officially given it up."

Madeleine was too engrossed in the contents of the box to pay attention to what I'd said. "It's still here," she said with delight as she pulled out a champagne flute with a residue of the drink dried in the bottom. "Did I tell you we drank champagne backstage with Bobbie? I took Bobbie's glass as a souvenir. Do you suppose I should bring it and offer it to him?"

Lucinda looked horrified and urged her to put it back in the box before she turned to me.

"Sometimes you have to protect people from themselves," she said.

It was getting late, and as we packed what we were taking back into the boxes, Madeleine held up an apricot-colored dress. "It's a copy of one Jackie Kennedy wore. Why don't you wear it?"

It was beautiful and like nothing I'd ever worn. I accepted and she added a pair of long white gloves and sling-back heels.

As we drove back, I took the opportunity to tell Lucinda about Sammy's plan. "I feel terribly guilty spending time picking out dress-up clothes when he's ready to do something that will ruin his life," I said with a sigh. "If he goes, there's no turning back. He'll have to slip across the border to somewhere. I'll probably never see him again."

Lucinda stared at me. "Are you so sure you have no romantic feelings for him? You sound a little hysterical."

"He's a friend—a really good friend. I'd miss him if he was gone." I tried to shake off the feeling. "It's very hard to investigate when nobody is supposed to know what you're doing." I told her about Jimmie Phelps's wanting to tell me something and how I had to walk away before I heard it because of Kevin St. John's arrival. "Jimmie probably realized how bad what he said about the underage thing sounded and wanted to explain it away."

We pulled in next to Madeleine's golf cart in the small parking lot at Vista Del Mar. By now lunch was over, but the ground still seemed deserted. I figured everybody had left for the softball game. It was nice that the sun had stayed out.

The three of us dragged the boxes of things to our meeting room. We were all going to walk to the game, but I remember what Jimmie Phelps had said. "I might as well see if he left me a message on the board," I said, making a detour to the Lodge.

I crossed the desolate interior to the large corkboard parked near the door to the gift shop.

By now it was covered with papers with messages. I checked the alphabetical area where any message to me would be. I saw my name finally, but when I took down the note, it was only a scrap of paper and the message seemed to have been torn away. All I saw was a curve, a dot and another curve that must have been the tops of some letters.

"Somebody probably grabbed the wrong message," Lucinda said when I came outside. "You can talk to Jimmie at the game."

I was sure my friend was right, even though seeing the paper ripped like that gave me a little chill. The three of us left the hotel and conference center and walked the few blocks to the small park near the lighthouse. The whole way there, Madeleine went on about how excited she was about the dance.

"Everything we went to was always formal and no fun. I've never been to a real dance." I didn't want to bust her bubble, but I thought she might be expecting too much.

"Look, Bobbie Listorie is singing the National Anthem,"

Madeleine said, rushing ahead as we got close to the park. He got to the last note just as we reached the group. Everyone applauded and then sat down in the bleachers. The singer ran off the field as the two teams came out. Dotty Night and Sally Winston started waving poms to get the crowd excited. Kevin St. John had added a baseball cap to his suit and came out in center field. He yelled, "Play ball," and the game began.

Lucinda and Madeleine went to the bleachers, and I went along the fence to the sidelines, looking for Jimmie Phelps in the cluster of people up ahead. Before I reached the group, I saw Scarlett separate herself from them. "Somebody call 911." Beyond I saw Jimmie Phelps leaning forward holding his chest. Even from the distance I saw that he looked white as a ghost.

The game came to an abrupt stop just as it started and stayed on hold until the ambulance arrived. One of EMTs got Jimmie onto a gurney while the other one asked questions.

"He was drinking this," Scarlett said, handing the uniformed woman the can of Boost Up from the bench. The EMT read over the ingredients and then poured the remainder of the drink in a cup apparently to ascertain how much he had drunk. I had gotten close enough to be in the middle of the action and looked into the cup as the EMT did. There was no mistaking hunks of white stuff.

"It looks like somebody spiked his drink with something," I said.

"Just a guess," the EMT said, "but could be he wanted to boost up his Boost Up and added more caffeine. We've been having trouble with kids adding powdered caffeine to their drinks. A guy like him would be more old school and probably use something like NoNap, or Revive tablets."

"Is he going to be all right?" I asked.

"We've had them go both ways," she said. "A guy his age?" she said with a shrug. "I shouldn't say anything. Let's hope for the best."

She took the cup and the can and joined her partner. Jimmie had already been loaded into the fluorescent green vehicle and a moment later the siren wailed as it pulled away.

Kevin St. John and Norman Rathman did their best to get the softball game going again, but without Jimmie, everyone seemed bummed out and they gave up after a couple of innings.

I couldn't shake the feeling that there was a connection between Jimmie wanting to tell me something, the torn message and his apparent caffeine overdose.

By the time we were walking back to Vista Del Mar, the fog was rolling in again. Fingers of it were gathering between the trees and filling the space with gauzy whiteness. The lower light went along with everyone's mood. I felt bad for Jimmie and bad for me, well, really Sammy, as I thought there might have been a chance that whatever Jimmie had to say would have helped clear my magician ex.

Our group headed en masse to our meeting room. There was no coffee and tea setup, and I regretted that I hadn't baked cookies even once for this group. If ever they all needed a lift, it was now. Instead of sitting down at the tables with the rest of the group, Lucinda pulled me aside and offered to see if she could get the café to do something for us. With her restaurant experience, I was sure she would come up with something.

Scarlett and her friend Alys came in just as the group was settling into working on their projects. Everyone seemed grateful to have their knitting to focus on, and for once, no one was talking.

The door opened and I expected it to be Lucinda, but it was Kevin St. John in his dark suit without the baseball cap.

He stepped inside and everyone turned in his direction. "I wanted to let you know that Jimmie Phelps is in intensive care, but it looks like he's going to be okay."

A collective sigh of relief went through the group. Then it became apparent that he wasn't alone as Lieutenant Borgnine stepped next to him. He glanced around the room and his gaze stopped on me for a moment and then moved on to Scarlett. "I wonder if I could speak to you two," he said, quickly adding that it was just part of a routine investigation after what had happened to the baseball player. The three of us stepped outside. I expected him to separate us, but he just said, "I understand the two of you were close to Mr. Phelps when the incident happened." We both nodded and he asked about Jimmie's drink.

All of Scarlett's usual outgoing nature seemed to have evaporated and the dual retreat woman looked worried. "I handed him the open can when we first started setting up," she began. "I think he took a slug and set it down on the bench."

"So then you didn't see him add anything to the drink?" Scarlett answered with a vehement shaking of her head along with mentioning that there was a lot going on. The lieutenant excused her with a wave of his hand.

He was doing his best to keep a benign cop face when he turned to me, but it was still obvious he wasn't happy with the encounter. Before he could ask me anything, I explained that I was going to talk to Jimmie and had just gotten there when he slumped over. "So I really didn't see anything," I said. I mentioned what the EMT had said, that caffeine pills might have been what was added to the drink and looked to him for confirmation.

He didn't hassle me about asking a question this time; he merely ignored it. "Why were you going to talk to Mr. Phelps?" Lucinda, Wanda and Crystal went past us and on into the meeting room while I tried to decide what to say. Because of the situation with Sammy, I was trying to keep a very low profile with the cop and didn't want to give away that I was investigating. But at the same time I thought he should know that the silver-haired baseball player might have been about to disclose some information regarding Diana Rathman's death. Information that someone might not have wanted him to say.

If I said nothing and something more happened to Jimmie Phelps while he was in the hospital, I would never forgive myself. I swallowed hard and proceeded.

"I think you should consider that someone spiked his drink." I hesitated, wondering what else I should say, seeing that he'd already begun to massage his temple.

"Why would anybody want to hurt Jimmie Phelps?" he began. "The guy is a legend, a baseball hero. Everybody loves him. I even have an old baseball card of his."

"You do know about his connection to Diana Rathman," I said.

"And that is?" he asked, being cagey.

"He said her father brought her to all the games and that he'd watched her grow up. He implied there was something between them, but told me that he'd lost touch with her." I debated mentioning the offhand comment Jimmie had made about there being nothing between them when she was underage and decided to leave it out.

"Jimmie didn't tell me any of that. All I got was that her father was their announcer and he might have seen her occasionally at games." The lieutenant seemed upset that he'd admitted to not getting information that I had. "There's more, isn't there?"

"When I saw Jimmie earlier, he told me he'd thought of something. We couldn't talk at the time and he said he'd leave it in a message on the board." I described the condition of the message. "Someone could have torn it off accidentally or not." I let the words hang there before continuing. "I was just going to talk to Jimmie. But of course, I couldn't because he was being rushed off to the hospital." I was deliberately trying to be vague, but then I worried that the lieutenant might not get it so I added, "I think he was going to tell me something about Diana Rathman's death and somebody wanted to stop him."

The lieutenant cocked an eyebrow. "I see what you're doing. You're using one of the magician's tricks and trying to misdirect me. I can assure you, the matter of someone else having added something to the drink will be looked into, but I think he probably added it himself. And if you see the Amazing Dr. Sammy Glickner, tell him I'd like to talk to him." He gave me a last hard look before he walked away and headed toward the Lodge. The lieutenant had never even asked to see the remnant of the note.

28

THE ROOM I CAME BACK TO WAS MUCH MORE UPBEAT than the one I'd left. Lucinda had managed to get carriers of coffee and hot water with tea bags, along with some treats. That, coupled with Kevin St. John's news, had lifted everyone's spirits and they were talking about the dance.

The group broke for a quick dinner than came back to the room. They cleared away their knitting and the room turned into a dressing room. Scott mumbled something about meeting us all later when he saw the tables were turned into hair and makeup stations. Madeleine supervised the unloading of the boxes of clothing.

Lucinda decided to handle my transformation. I couldn't see what she was doing with my hair or face and she refused to give me a mirror. She waited while I changed out of the jeans and shirt I'd been wearing and zipped me into the dress we'd picked out.

The apricot silk dress fit perfectly, but felt strange with the fitted bodice and flared skirt. I had drawn the line at wearing panty hose and stuck my bare feet in the cream-colored sling-back shoes. I was glad I'd chosen ones with lower heels. Madeleine helped me put on the long white gloves, and the look was complete. And then Lucinda walked me into the small bathroom off our room and let me see myself in the full-length mirror.

I gasped. I was sure I was seeing somebody else's reflection. She had managed to turn my dark brown hair into a bouffant-style à la Jackie Kennedy. She'd spread some kind of foundation that made my face look flawless, the eye makeup was all Elizabeth Taylor, and she'd finished by adding bold coral lipstick. And the dress, shoes and gloves looked absolutely foreign. It even looked odder when Madeleine hung the chain strap of a beaded evening bag from my arm and showed me she had one, too.

With her love of designer wear, Lucinda was over the top about wearing a real Oleg Cassini silk shift-style dress. I felt all weird, but Lucinda seemed entirely at home in hers. I was astonished at the change in the group. I'd never seen Wanda in anything but loose-fitting pants and floral print tops. It was amazing what a black shift, some hair fluffing and a makeup job could do.

Crystal had managed to tame her black curls into a bouffant style. The white shift was hers, but the blue bolero jacket with the big collar was from Madeleine. I almost wouldn't have recognized her, but the unmatched earrings gave her away.

The others had done up their hair and makeup and added the pieces that Madeleine had brought and were having fun seeing their looks in the mirror. Madeleine had chosen to wear the actual dress she'd worn on her big night out so many years ago. She'd added a little pouf to her timeless bob hair-style and had some subtle makeup. We all agreed we looked fabulous and went as a group to Hummingbird Hall.

Scott caught up with us and did a whole lot of double takes as he tried to figure out who was who. His khaki pants and blue oxford cloth shirt would have worked for almost any year the group was celebrating.

The fog seemed to have settled, dropping a silvery curtain over the background. Fleece simply didn't go with what any of us were wearing and we'd all gone jacketless. It made us walk through the grounds much faster.

We picked up speed when we got close to Hummingbird Hall and then rushed to the warmth inside. Kevin St. John was standing just inside the doorway acting as a greeter. He was so friendly to me, I realized he didn't have a clue who I was. He didn't really notice who anyone was; he just wanted to watch everyone as they stopped in awe of how he'd transformed the auditorium.

The seats were gone, and the middle of the room had been turned into a dance floor. A big net had been draped from the open rafters and filled with balloons. A band was setting up on the stage, while canned music played in the background.

Madeleine stopped in front of me and gazed around with her mouth open. Then she grabbed my gloved hand, and we went to the back of the room. She was fascinated by the large glass punch bowl sitting amid the plates of finger sandwiches and bowls of chips and dip.

She wanted to try the punch, which looked like a concoction of ginger ale and frozen strawberries with an island of orange sherbet floating in the middle. I tried to get her a cup of it, which wasn't easy with the gloves.

Scarlett came by. She'd gone for a pleated skirt and a

blouse and pigtails in some sort of a schoolgirl look. I envied
her loafers, which looked a lot more comfortable than the
sling-backs. She made an odd pair with her husband, who
seemed dressed in what people thought professors wore.
There were suede patches on the elbows of his jacket and a
pipe sticking out of the pocket.

"Isn't this great," Dotty Night said in her perky tone. She
was wearing a skirt and blouse that looked like it might have
been left over from the wardrobe of *Bridget and the Bachelor*. Madeleine held up her punch cup as if making a toast
before she took her first sip.

There was tapping on a microphone and then Norman
Rathman asked if everyone could hear him. He'd taken center
stage with his assistant, Sally Winston, standing close by.
He welcomed the crowd and raved on about how great the
room looked. He called Kevin St. John up onstage. "Here's
the man who did it all. Let's give him a round of applause."
Kevin waved to the crowd then took the microphone and did
the same thing he'd done at the softball game when he'd said,
"Play ball." Except now he said, "Let the dancing begin."

The band took the cue and started on their first song. I
was surprised to see Dane come in. He stopped near the
entrance and surveyed the crowd. Instead of his uniform, he
was dressed in clothes to fit in and had slicked back his hair,
trying to look very 1963. He made his way into the room and
walked right past me. I tapped him on the shoulder. "What
are you doing here?" I asked. He turned and had a blank look
for a moment before he realized it was me. Even then he kept
looking at me, going from the hair, makeup, dress and finally
the gloves and the beaded evening bag hanging on my arm.

"In answer to your question, I'm here in a professional
capacity. After what happened this afternoon, Lieutenant
Borgnine added security," he said.

"It means he listened to me," I said and Dane answered with a confused look. I told him about my conversation with his superior earlier. "Does that mean he has someone watching Jimmie Phelps's room at the hospital?"

Dane nodded. "I could have had that assignment, but this seemed like more fun." This group had no hesitancy about dancing and lots of them were already out on the floor. "Shall we?" he said. "It's a good cover and a way to keep an eye on things."

I started to protest. In all my professions and schooling, I'd never really learned how to dance. I could get out and gyrate on my own, but when it came to something with organized steps and a partner, like the fox trot or waltz, I really had two left feet. Dane laughed when I told him and assured me he'd teach me as we went. We got the hand part right, but when we started to move, and I tried to follow his steps, I only succeeded in tripping over his feet. Lieutenant Borgnine came in and did the same thing Dane had done. He stopped near the entrance and looked over the crowd. When he saw Dane, there was a disapproving shake of his head. Dane had to be relieved. "Sorry, I guess according to him, it's no dancing on duty," he said. He let go of my hand and we started to go our separate ways. He looked back. "We have to try this again."

"Give it up. I'm a hopeless klutz."

"If I can teach those teens karate, I can certainly teach you the waltz." He paused and got his teasing smile. "But we do it in bare feet." He pretended to limp away and we both laughed.

I might not be able to dance with one person, but I could dance with many. So when the hokey pokey line started, I was right there in the front. Madeleine grabbed on behind me and we waved our arms and legs and sang along as the line got longer and snaked around the room.

When the dance ended, Madeleine and I retired to the

side of the room. Her eyes were glowing with happiness. "This is just what I thought a dance would be like. And Bobbie is going to perform, too." She giggled as she called him by his first name.

She opened her bag and took out a folded-up program. "I found this in the cigar box—it's from the other time I saw him. I was thinking that maybe he would sign it for me and we could take a picture together." She wanted to show the program to me. I nodded as she pointed out how it listed the baseball game and the concert. There was something else, but her finger obliterated most of it and I just saw the tops of the letters. "It's too bad how it ended," she said. "It was even mentioned in the newspaper the next day that the fireworks all went off at the same time. I don't know how anybody who was there could ever forget it."

She stopped abruptly as Norman Rathman took the stage and announced the singer. Bobbie took the microphone and the band began. It was the first time I'd seen him perform, and he was very entertaining. He had all the moves down, crunching forward when he seemed overcome with emotion, pumping his arm for emphasis and of course reaching out to the audience and then pulling his arm in and holding it as he did a final crescendo.

The audience loved him and began to sway to the music. Madeleine looked like she was going to float away. Personally, I wanted a cup of punch and left the swooning Delacorte sister for the food table.

I got my cup of the sweet concoction and considered going back to my spot, but didn't feel like pushing through the crowd. I looked at the clock and noted with dismay that it was almost eleven. Time was running out. Sammy wouldn't really take off, would he?

Bobbie had saved his biggest hit for last, which was also

his first hit from 1963. I thought the lyrics were pretty dumb, but I guess it was a different time.

> *Look into my eyes, honey. You can see I mean what I say,*
> *Words can lie, baby, but you know it's true when I look*
>   *this way.*
> *Remember the eyes have it when I tell you you're the one.*
> *Remember the eyes have it, you're my moon and sun.*

I tuned out the rest of the words as I was joined at the food table by Scarlett and her husband. I offered her a cup of punch but she shook her head. Her husband picked up one of the finger sandwiches and said it might help her headache before he turned to me. "Any more word about Jimmie Phelps? I hope he recovers; he's the real thing." Scarlett fumbled in her purse as Bobbie got to the end of his song. Norman Rathman and Kevin St. John came up on the stage. There was thunderous applause as Bobbie took a bow then held up a punch cup as a toast to the audience. The applause continued as he went to the edge of the stage and out the exit. Suddenly I thought of something so ridiculous it couldn't possibly be true.

29

I CROSSED THE AUDITORIUM AND WENT OUT A SIDE door. The fog had thickened and everything outside the area right around me was veiled in dense white moisture. Being dark made it even harder to see. But I had spent so much time at Vista Del Mar, I knew my way around by feel. I followed the building to the stage exit. A light above the door illuminated the immediate area shining onto the paved roadway which was edged by a low retaining wall.

Bobbie had left the area, but as I'd hoped, he had left something behind on the ledge of the wall. The light reflected off the glass punch cup and the cloudy amber liquid inside. Now all I had to do was grab it somehow without touching it. I looked around for something to use. I'd balked about the evening bag but now saw it could come in handy. I opened the metal clasp and pulled the lining inside wide, kind of like when a snake got ready to swallow something big. Next I got rid of the liquid by using the purse to knock the cup on the side and then began to try to get the purse to swallow the cup.

"Sorry, I didn't mean to be a litterbug," Bobbie said, stepping out of the fog. He held out his hand. "Give me the cup and I'll get rid of it."

I tried to think fast. "It's a souvenir for my friend Madeleine. She's your biggest fan."

"I can give her a much better souvenir of the Bobberino than that." He continued to hold out his hand and gestured with his fingers impatiently.

"No, I think I'll keep this." I'd managed to get the purse all the way around the cup and started to walk away, but he grabbed my arm and tried to pull the purse off it.

"Somebody else is going to figure it out," I said, "Bobbie, or whatever your real name is."

"I don't know what you're talking about," he said. He seemed uncertain what to do next.

"Diana Rathman figured out you were an imposter, didn't she? And you were afraid she was going to let everybody know. There would be no Vegas lounge show. And there would go your gig at the Pebble Beach resort. They wouldn't be happy about being deceived and could press charges against you for fraud. You'd have to pay back everything they'd paid you and maybe there'd be some jail time."

All the good nature had drained from his face, and he looked pale beneath the tan. "She came here to rekindle some old romance with Bobbie. It's not the first time one of his women has showed up. It's never been a problem. They do all the talking, reminiscing about their trysts. I was willing to go along with Diana's plan for the weekend. I'd just keep to generic comments and let her fill in the blanks." His face had grown hard. "I thought I'd been so careful about researching Bobbie's shows. I don't know how I missed the thing about the fireworks disaster at Candlestick Park. I thought saying they were beautiful was a safe response. I didn't even know I'd made a mistake until later."

He paused for a moment. "We'd arranged to meet that night on the q.t. I'm expecting maybe a walk on the beach followed by some cuddling and she lays into me about those fireworks and how my comment made her suspicious. I thought I could talk my way out. You know, said my memory wasn't what it used to be. She cut me off and said the jig was up. That when she saw me at that newsreel thing, she knew for sure I wasn't Bobbie.

"It seems that she and Bobbie were drinking champagne on the sidelines when those blanking fireworks exploded. He was so startled he squeezed the glass in his hand and it broke. He got a couple of weird cuts that left scars she said were kind of shaped like a two. When she saw my hand and there were no scars, she said she knew for sure.

"I tried to calm her down, but she just went off. It turns out she had more in mind than a weekend fling with Bobbie. She kept saying something about wanting to take the road not taken or something. She was hysterical that I'd ruined everything. She said I wasn't going to get away with taking over Bobbie's life and she was going to ruin me.

"I tried to reason with her. I really did, but she just walked off saying, there was no use to me wasting my breath. She went rushing down some path and I followed her. The silk streamer fell out of her pocket and I picked it up. She must have realized she'd gone the wrong way because she stopped. When I caught up with her . . ." His voice trailed off and I filled in the rest.

"You realized that Jimmie Phelps caught the remark about the fireworks, too, and he was going to tell me. You already had the caffeine pills. I saw them the night you had the headache and needed aspirin. I'm guessing it was a last-minute try after you tore the note off the message board." I wondered if I should add that he'd made a mistake by not taking the whole message down. I'd recognized that the curve, dot, and curve were the tops of the *f*, *i* and *r* in *fireworks* when Madeleine had put her finger over most of the word while she showed me the old program. I decided to keep it to myself. I knew what I needed to do was get out of there, but I really wanted to get the rest of the story.

"So then who are you?" I asked, taking a step away at the same time.

"Frankie Listorie. Bobbie's cousin," he said.

"What did you do with the real Bobbie Listorie?" I asked, backing away a little more.

"Nothing. I didn't do nothing to him. He's in a home. He doesn't even know that he's Bobbie Listorie anymore. All my life, people have been saying I looked just like him. I didn't have a dimple in my chin, but a few bucks to a plastic surgeon and I did." His voice turned harsh. "You don't know what it's like to be told that your voice is better than his, but he gets all the fame. We started out as a duo and then some music executive blew in Bobbie's ear and said he was the talent and he should lose me. So when the opportunity presented itself, I took it." He looked directly at me. "You heard them applauding for me. Nobody has complained once. I got the pipes."

"Now that I know how much it means to you," I said, trying to sound upbeat. "It will be our little secret." Before I could move, he'd stepped behind me. I felt something poking through the thin material into my back. It felt like the muzzle of a gun.

"Now I'm finally getting my due. I don't care what I have to do to keep it. The spotlight is finally mine." He pushed against my back. "I think it's time for us to get out of here and take a little ride."

He didn't have to say the rest. I got it. There would only be one of us at the end of the ride, and it wasn't going to be me. What was it they always warned people who were grabbed? Don't leave the location. Maybe I could stall. "Aren't you curious how I figured it out? It might be useful in the future."

"Yeah, now that you mention it. I should know where I screwed up." I could feel the pressure against my back give up a little.

"That night you had the headache. Something seemed off to me. I thought it was because you were in sweats, but tonight something one of my retreaters said made me think of that night again, and then when I heard the line in your song about the eyes don't lie, I got it. It didn't register then and you put on the tinted glasses so quickly. The dimple isn't the only difference. You have blue eyes, not Bobbie's famous green eyes. It's all in the contacts, isn't it?"

"Good to know," he said. I could tell by the pause after that he was going back to his plan. I tried to think of a means of escape and I heard the door to the stage open and the sound of applause and people chanting "Bobbie."

"You can't leave them hanging like that. They've been clapping and chanting for five minutes," Kevin St. John said. "You need to do an encore." There was a pause and Kevin said, "Oh," apparently seeing Bobbie wasn't alone.

"Sorry to interrupt you and your lady," Kevin faltered. In this outfit from the back, he didn't recognize me and it must have looked like Bobbie and I were having a moment. The manager said something about leaving the romance for later and coming back inside. By then I wasn't listening, but instead thinking. Bobbie/Frankie had turned to face Kevin and was distracted.

My mind flitted through possible escapes, hopefully without me being shot. And something Sammy had said about human nature came to mind and I made a move.

"You go on back in," the singer said to Kevin. "I'll be there in a minute." Much as I knew that he wanted to go back in and do an encore, I also knew he was set on erasing me from the scene.

As soon as Kevin was back inside, the singer turned forward, and he saw that his gun was pointed at no one. "Hey," the fake Bobbie yelled, starting to run down the path after me, or so he thought. I had thought of Sammy's story about the falling fire escape and that it was human nature to go forward to try to escape getting hit, when the right thing to do was go sideways. And that was what I had done. I stepped off the path and slipped behind one of the Monterey pines. In the darkness and fog, I was invisible, not that Bobbie/Frankie even looked as he ran down the path.

I was pretty sure he was going to keep to the plan to get out of Vista Del Mar with or without me and was headed to his car. I didn't want to try to stop him myself. I needed help. I went through the brush to the front of the building. Lieutenant Borgnine was still standing just inside the door. His expression darkened when he saw me.

"I know who you're looking for," I said. "And I know where he is." The lieutenant's face came to life.

"Finally, you're showing some sense."

"We have to hurry, though, he's trying to make a run for it." I rushed to the door and the rumpled cop caught up with me. "Follow me."

Bobbie/Frankie would stick to the path that wound through the grounds, but I knew a shortcut. I actually grabbed the lieutenant's hand and pulled him off the path. The heels weren't going to do and I kicked them off before taking him through the underbrush.

I could only imagine what was happening to Madeleine's

beautiful dress as it caught on bushes while we serpentined through the trees. I had too much adrenaline pumping to feel any pain from my bare feet stepping on twigs, dried pine needles and who knew what else.

We finally came out in the small parking lot near the Lodge. I looked over a line of cars around Madeleine's golf cart, but there was no one.

The lieutenant had long since pulled away from my hand and looked around the empty parking lot with a grumble. "You're doing it again. This is some kind of diversion, so the Amazing Dr. Sammy Glickner can do a disappearing act."

Just then there were footsteps on the paved road, and a moment later, Bobbie/Frankie came into the parking lot and sprinted toward a light-colored Corvette.

"Not staying for your encore," I said, stepping out of the darkness.

"There you are," he said angrily. The gun was still in his hand and he waved it in my direction. "Get in the car." I took a few steps and then a noise behind me made me turn back. The low lights around the edge of the parking area were enough to see that Lieutenant Borgnine had stepped behind the singer and had him in a choke hold. After a moment, the singer dropped to the ground unconscious and the gun fell from his hand.

"We're not supposed to use a choke hold, but seeing that he had a gun aimed at you, it was the best alternative." He looked at the figure on the ground. "He'll come to in a minute," Borgnine said. He leaned over the fallen singer and pulled his hands behind him, handcuffing him.

The rumpled bulldog-shaped cop shook his head at me. "Ms. Feldstein, you deceived me. You said you were taking me to Dr. Glickner."

"No," I protested. "I said I was taking you to who you were after—that's Diana Rathman's killer, isn't it?"

There were more grumbling sounds as he said something about evidence.

It turned out not to be a problem. When Bobbie/Frankie came to, he was escorted to the backseat of a cop car. Before the cruiser could drive away, he began to spill his guts, and Lieutenant Borgnine got an earful. Apparently the singer wanted everyone to know that the crowd at the dance had been chanting and cheering for him—Frankie Listorie. So there was no need to get his DNA off the punch cup I still had in my purse and see that it didn't match the real Bobbie's DNA on Madeleine's ancient champagne glass she'd snagged as a souvenir. He admitted to strangling Diana. He repeated pretty much what he'd told me, but the kicker was when he insisted it was really some kind of self-defense because she was look-ing to kill his career. The lieutenant tapped on the side of the car and told the officer to take him downtown.

Eventually, the DA charged him with Diana's murder, mali-cious intent for spiking Jimmie's drink, and fraud for mas-querading as his cousin. He ended up making a plea deal and looked forward to being locked up for a long time. I wondered if they had prison talent shows.

But in the present, I peeled back the soiled white glove and looked at my watch. It was five minutes to midnight. "You wanted to see Dr. Glickner?" I said to Lieutenant Borg-nine, who was headed to his car.

"No, that's okay." The rumpled cop started to move a little faster.

"I insist," I said, linking my arm in his. He pulled free, but reluctantly followed me as I went across the street.

"I thought so," the cop said as I knocked on the window.

"Officer Mangano kept saying he was sure Dr. Glickner wasn't here."

Sammy opened the window. I had never seen him look so forlorn. In the background I saw that he had tied up his belongings into a sheet. His expression froze as he saw Lieutenant Borgnine standing behind me.

"Tell him," I commanded the cop, a little surprised at my own gutsiness.

"You know we could have straightened this all out a long time ago if you hadn't gone into hiding," Borgnine said.

"That's not what I meant." I turned back to Sammy. "What he means to say is that he has a suspect in custody who allegedly did everything." Sammy stood there for a moment as the information sank in. "It means you're not a fugitive anymore. You can go home and live your life again."

"A fugitive?" the lieutenant said. "He was more like a person of interest."

"Whatever, you're free!" I said. It was like Sammy had been holding his breath since the whole mess started and he let out the air all at once. The forlorn look melted into his usual smiley expression and he leaned through the window and hugged me so tightly my feet left the ground.

"I knew you wouldn't let me down, Case," he said, waiting a moment before releasing me.

Just then Dane came up the driveway and shined his flashlight through fog on my bunged-up feet. "It looks like you need some first aid."

"No problem," Sammy said, going around and opening the door. "I'm a doctor."

30

THE FOG WAS STILL HANGING AROUND IN THE
morning, and when I looked out my bedroom window, it
was like looking at the world through a veil. Sunday morn-
ings were always quiet, but with all the moisture to absorb
the sound, it was deathly silent.

Julius had the good sense to cuddle next to me instead
of draping himself across my chest. Madeleine's apricot silk
dress hung on the closet door. It was pretty much a dead
soldier between the dirt, the pine sap and the shredded skirt.
I don't even know why I hung it up.

The adrenaline that had blocked any pain was all gone
now, and I felt bunged up. I was covered in spots of antibiotic
cream and small bandages. Fortunately, the damage was all
minor, just scrapes and a few cuts.

Though Sammy was free to go home, he had decided to
spend the night in the guest house. I sat up and carefully
slid my banged-up feet into my slippers. As I went down the

hall, I looked into the room I used as an office. Madeleine was asleep on the love seat, which had turned out to be a pull-out bed. She'd been too upset about everything to drive her golf cart home and I'd invited her to stay.

I still had the rest of the retreat to finish, but there was no reason to wake her or Lucinda, who was asleep on a couch in the living room. I'm not sure why my friend gave up her guest room for my couch unless she thought I'd need help dealing with Madeleine.

Julius followed me into the kitchen. I needed real coffee and pulled out the bag of grounds. I'd just pushed the brew button when Madeleine came into the kitchen wearing an oversized T-shirt that said *Chicago Bears* and her heels from the night before.

"I'm sorry about everything," I said, but she shook her head.

"You can't go back in time. It was silly to suppose the Bobbie Listorie I saw in 1963 and 1977 would be just the same." She caught herself and her eyes lit up. "I did think he would be the same person, though." Julius had jumped up on the counter and was sticking close to me while staring at Madeleine. I'm sure he was trying to figure what was going on.

Madeleine pulled out a chair and sat. "Wow, this is my first sleepover with girlfriends." Lucinda yawned as she came in right after and pulled out the chair next to her.

AN HOUR LATER THE THREE OF US HEADED ACROSS the street. I'd given Madeleine clothes to wear; it was the least I could do after destroying her dress. She was shorter than me and rounder, but somehow the jeans and shirt fit, sort of anyway. Lucinda raided my closet and settled for some of my no-name clothes, though she managed to roll up the pant legs and add some accessories from my aunt's stash and ended up looking very stylish.

We stopped in the dining hall for breakfast, though it was mostly empty. It had been a late night for everyone. Kevin St. John came in to make the rounds. He stopped at Norman Rathman's table before coming to ours. There was just a touch of bouffant left to my hair. His gaze stopped on it and he looked uncomfortable.

"I'm glad that everything is settled. The good news is that Jimmie Phelps is out of intensive care and expected to make a full recovery." He started to move away and then looked back. "If I'd realized that was you and the singer had a gun stuck in your back, I would have done something."

"I know Diana was your half aunt," I said. His placid face didn't show any emotion.

"I barely knew her," he said before moving on. I had a lot of questions I would have liked to ask, like what really happened to his grandmother and was there evidence that might show she was Edmund Delacorte's mistress, but I knew I might not like the answers. The best thing to do was leave the door shut on that whole inquiry.

Everyone was there for our last workshop session and, despite all, seemed sorry to see the retreat end. I was glad that Wanda and Crystal had made peace and they worked together making sure all the worry doll people got the hair attached to their dolls and figured out how to do their faces.

I slipped out during the free time before lunch and went to the hospital. I was relieved to see Jimmie Phelps sitting up in bed doing some kind of arm exercises.

We talked about how he felt for a few minutes before I got down to why I was there.

"I don't know if anyone has filled you in on last night," I said before telling him about the singer's confession. "You remembered about the fireworks. That's what you put in the note and would have told me. Right?"

He nodded. "I didn't really pay attention at first and then I heard him tell that Delacorte woman how nice the fireworks were and it struck me as odd. Just so you know, I was always polite to Diana, but I tried to keep a distance."

"You mean because there was something between you and Diana when she was underage and you were afraid it would come out now?" He gave me a puzzled look and I mentioned what he had said.

He shook his head in disbelief. "There were just rumors because she hung around the dugout so much. Not that she didn't try to make them true no matter how many times I nicely told her I wasn't interested. The one she was involved with was Bobbie Listorie. They met the night of the fireworks debacle. She was seventeen and her father couldn't stop her from going off with him. I'm just guessing, but I think when she came for the weekend, she was hoping to pick up with Bobbie again."

I nodded to let him know that he was right. Then I wished him a speedy recovery before I left, glad that it had turned out that he was really the good guy everyone thought he was.

I didn't get back until lunch was over and I met up with my group in the Lodge as they and the 1963 people were all checking out. Dotty Night rushed past me, pressing a brochure of her inn on me as she said good-bye to everyone. Sally Winston was practically an appendage to Norman Rathman as he spoke to Kevin St. John. He didn't blame Vista Del Mar or the manager for what had happened to his wife. And he was interested in using the place for further retreats with one change.

"We simply arrange for the rooms and meeting space with you. We plan the program and special activities and special guests," he said. He gestured toward Scarlett's husband and said he was the new co-president. Sally Winston didn't take the news well.

Kevin St. John was caught in a bind. He had made it clear to me that aside from my retreats, which were sort of grandfathered in, he was going to be in charge of any other retreats held there. Was he going to be insistent he couldn't work the way Norman Rathman wanted to? I'm not sure if he used good sense or it was because he saw that Cora Delacorte had arrived looking for her sister. "Of course, any way you want to do it is fine," the manager said.

The early birds were in the middle of my people and the talk was that my future retreats should be longer and they wanted me to add outside activities such as whale watching and wine tasting. I promised I would. Olivia Golden showed me the huge bag of squares everyone had made and promised to send pictures of the blankets before she brought them to a shelter. Scott Lipton was pleased with himself that he had actually given some knitting lessons. Bree Meyers couldn't wait to take the signed baseballs home to her boys and husband.

Cora was horrified to see her sister wearing my clothes and being so familiar with everyone. She was upset that she'd missed church and wanted to make sure she was home in time for their Sunday dinner since the minister and his wife were coming for the meal.

Madeleine let it all roll off her back and suggested that Cora wait by the door for her. She hugged me and Lucinda and thanked me for the most exciting weekend of her life. "Consider me signed up for the next retreat. Whenever it is."

It was hardly good-bye with Lucinda. It was more like see you later. Even so we hugged and she congratulated me on another retreat under my belt. "These weekends are so great. Absence really does make the heart grow fonder. I can't wait to get to the restaurant and watch Tag straighten the silverware," she said with a laugh. "By the way, I used one of the landlines to call him so he'd know I would be there soon. He was thrilled to hear that Sammy was off the hook. And he wanted me to give you a message. He said he was the anonymous tipster who sent Lieutenant Borgnine on the wild-goose chases looking for Sammy. Tag said he wanted to be sure you knew so that you'd realize that he could be involved in the sleuthing, too."

Lucinda and I shared a laugh. "You are definitely having an effect on him," I said before she followed Madeleine out.

The staff went around the room and took down all the posters and pictures from the 1963 group as the large room emptied. I spent the afternoon clearing up the meeting rooms and it was starting to get dark when I finally went home.

When I went up my driveway, there was a figure on the stoop outside my back door, but he wasn't slumped and this time I knew right away it was Sammy.

"Hey, look at my new pal," he said. When I got closer, I saw Julius was sitting next to him eating stink fish from a spoon. "How can I ever thank you for what you did?"

"What I did?" I repeated. "All I did was mess up your life."

"No way," Sammy said. "None of this was your fault." He scooped another spoonful of food for the cat.

"Well, at least when you leave, it won't be on the lam," I said. "After all this, I guess Cadbury must have lost its appeal for you. I suppose you'll be packing up and heading back to Chicago."

Sammy seemed surprised at my comment. "Case, I thought you knew me better than that.

"The Amazing Dr. Sammy is back in business, or so I hope." He glanced in the direction of Vista Del Mar. "C'mon, sit down for a minute." He patted the spot on the other side from Julius.

"I have to get ready to go to the Blue Door," I said. But I sat down next to him anyway. I wanted to tell him what Tag had done for him.

"That's part of the reason I'm not leaving," Sammy said. "I have friends here, work, hopefully my magic job. A life." It was twilight now and darkness was settling in. "I know you have to go to work, but could I show you my new trick?"

"Sure," I said with a laugh. Sammy really was amazing. After all this and he'd come up with a new trick.

"I'll start off with a bunch of patter. Something about how I'm so upset because my heart is missing. Then I'll look over the audience to see if maybe it's out there." He turned to face me. "After I've built up the tension, I'll turn to the person closest to me." He pointed to my lap. I was totally surprised to see something heart shaped and red was pulsing with light. "And I'll say I knew you'd stolen my heart."

I was speechless. "You can keep it," Sammy said, getting up. "You can keep my heart." He started down the driveway and turned back. "You know, anytime you want to rent the guest house, I'm first on the list."

When he was out of sight I looked down at the pulsing red heart and hugged it to myself. Sammy really knew how to get to me. What was I going to do with him?

Julius followed me when I went inside. "Don't try to tell me you're hungry," I said as the cat glanced at the refrigerator.

I called Frank first and told him how things had ended up. "A fake Bobbie Listorie—Feldstein, you get involved in a lot of weird stuff. I'm glad that Jimmie Phelps is okay. Do you think you could get me a signed ball?" I heard the creak of his recliner chair and voices. "Got to go, the boys are here." I wanted to ask what boys and what they were there for, but he'd hung up.

And now to call my mother. "Sammy's free and clear," I said when she answered, even before I said hello.

"Thank heavens," she said, and I waited for what she would say next. I was expecting something along the lines that, after all I'd put Sammy through, I really owed it to him to marry him. But my mother surprised me, by not saying anything close to that.

"I never thought I'd say your name and *detective* in the same sentence. But I have to admit, Casey, that if you got him out of all that trouble, you must be a good detective." I heard her rustling some papers. "You know, honey, there's a detective academy in Los Angeles. You could go to school and get your license. You seem to like it so much."

"I have a profession, actually two," I said. "I put on retreats, and I bake desserts and muffins. Any investigating is really coincidental." I heard myself. Here my mother was actually complimenting me and I was being difficult. I tried to soften what I'd said by thanking her for her confidence in me.

"Casey, I think you can do anything if you put your mind to it and stick to it. You just need to pick it carefully. If putting on these yarn retreats is what you want to do . . ." She left it hanging, which was her way of saying that she thought I could do better. I waited for her to get to the usual ending of our calls, when she said at my age she was a wife, a mother and a doctor and what was I, but instead she said, "Your father is grabbing for the phone. He wants to hear all the details about how you saved Sammy."

I went outside a little while later just as Dane went jogging by. As soon as he saw me, he jogged up my driveway. "Looks like everything is back to normal," he said, glancing toward the guest house.

"Lieutenant Borgnine had you watching me, didn't he." Dane tried to wave it off, but he finally gave me a halfhearted nod. "What about in the kitchen at the Blue Door? You must have known Sammy was in the pantry."

"Really," he said in mock surprise. "I never thought to look. You can't report what you don't see."

"And why didn't you leave the plate of food?"

"It was a trap. Borgnine's idea, by the way. So I merely didn't set it out." He was running in place to keep his heart rate up. "Anybody with any sense would know that Sammy wasn't a killer."

"And you're not trying to get rid of him?"

Dane thought about it for a minute. "You mean because I think if he's out of the way, you'll fall into my arms?"

"Something like that," I said.

"I don't play it that way. Speaking of us, I've come up with a solution. We do the dinner thing somewhere out of Cadbury. I found a great place on the way to Big Sur. It's a complete tourist trap, so no locals to coo over us." He'd started to jog backward. "I'll send you the website." He was gone before I could say anything. The truth was after all he'd done for me, it was the least I could do. Besides I wanted to go. I'd worry later about where it was going to lead.

Julius looked upset when I loaded up a plastic shopping bag with muffin-making supplies and got ready to go to the Blue Door. "I promise, it will just be the two of us tomorrow and you can have a stink fish fiesta." He watched through the window while I walked to my car. I felt bad leaving him, but it was kind of nice feeling that I was going to be missed.

Sunday night everything closed early. The Blue Door was dark when I got there. The lights were off at the movie theater, and the streets were practically rolled up. It was just me, the jazz and the batter this time. No one knocked at the door. I left pans of cream cheese brownies for Monday's desserts and walked out with the plastic containers of vanilla muffins to take around town.

I made my deliveries and was about to head back to my car, but took a detour past Cadbury Yarn. The lights were on in the display window and I laughed when I saw that Gwen had put out a display of mystery bags along with samples of things people could make with them. Her daughter, Crystal, must have just finished her worry doll in time to add it to the window. It reminded me how far I still had to go with mine. I was sure Wanda had supplied the samples of the scarves. A center spot had been made for some of the samples Crystal had brought the first day—her own teddy bear, and a small bag. Why hadn't I noticed it before?

Back home I took out the envelope and emptied the contents. When the picture of the baby girl fluttered down, I grabbed it. All along I had been focusing on her, but this time I looked at what she was holding. The style was unmistakable. Even with the faded colors, I could see that the teddy bear was wearing a jacket of all different yarns with random beads. His body was made of different-colored yarns. There wasn't a doubt in my mind that Crystal's grandmother had made that bear for her own child. I let the information sink in. It meant that Gwen Selwyn was Edmund Delacorte's heir and Madeleine and Cora's niece. Her daughter, Crystal, would be their great-niece. I wasn't sure about all the legal stuff, but if somehow the will could be reopened, Gwen would be the owner of Vista Del Mar.

Now I had to decide what to do with the information.

Patterns

Crystal's Worry Doll

Supplies

BODY

1 skein beige, Lion Brand Vanna's Choice, 170 yds (156 m), 100% acrylic, medium (4) weight

DRESS

Approx. 70 yds of assorted medium (4) weight yarn or 1 skein Rainbow Bright, Loops & Threads Impeccable Brights (Michaels store brand), 192 yds (175 m), 100% acrylic, medium (4) weight

Approx. 12 beads with holes big enough for yarn to pass through

HAIR

- 1 skein black, Loops & Threads Charisma (Michaels store brand), 109 yds (100 m), 100% acrylic, bulky (5) weight, 1 skein black, Loops & Threads Poodle Caniche (Michaels store brand), 23 yds (21m), 61% acrylic 29% wool 7% alpaca
- U.S. size 6 (4mm) knitting needles
- Size J-10 (6mm) crochet hook
- Tapestry needle
- Small piece of thin wire folded over for threading beads onto the yarn
- Black felt for facial features
- Polyester fiberfill for stuffing
- Finished size: Approx. 15" tall

Stitches Used

Knitting—cast on, cast off, garter stitch (all knit).
Crochet—chain (ch), half double crochet (hdc), half double crochet two together (hdc2tog).

Note: Put beads on yarn before you begin to crochet dress. When you want to add a bead, push it down before making next stitch and make sure it is pushed to front. The doll is knitted. The dress is crocheted.

DOLL'S HEAD, BODY AND LEGS AND ARMS (ALL DONE IN THE GARTER STITCH)

Using knitting needles and beige yarn, cast on 40 stitches and knit 30 rows, use a piece of yarn to mark (this is end of head).

Knit 34 more rows for body.

On next row, knit 20 and turn (this is beginning of one leg), put a marker.

Knit 39 more rows (only on 20 stitches), cast off.

With right side facing, attach yarn to other 20 stitches for other leg.

Knit 40 rows, cast off.

Make 2 arms.

Cast on 15 stitches and knit 37 rows, cast off (make 2).

•

PUTTING DOLL TOGETHER

Fold body in half lengthwise, and sew together from top to marker for tops of legs.

Arrange so seam is in middle of back. Sew inside and bottom of legs.

Stuff doll, shaping it as you do. Sew top of head closed. Squeeze doll to shape its neck, and tie a piece of yarn around neck to hold shape.

Fold arm pieces in half, and sew side and end closed. Turn inside out and stuff. Sew last side closed.

Sew to doll just below neck.

Hair: Cut 20 15-inch lengths using a mixture of yarns for hair. Arrange lengths of yarn across top of head and sew to middle of head. If desired, tack "hair" in place with needle and black thread.

Make facial features out of felt, and glue in place.

Dress Front: Put beads on yarn first, reserving two beads for the straps. Using crochet hook, chain 21.

Row 1: Hdc in third ch from hook, hdc across— (19 stitches).

Row 2: Ch 2 (doesn't count as first stitch), turn, hdc across—(19 stitches).

Rows 3–13: Repeat Row 2, adding beads randomly.

Row 14: Ch 2 (doesn't count as first stitch), turn,

hdc2tog with first two stitches, hdc across until last two stitches, hdc2tog—(17 stitches) (this is beginning of armhole).

Row 15: Repeat Row 14—(15 stitches).

Row 16: Ch 2 (doesn't count as first stitch), turn, hdc in first 3 stitches (to make strap).

Row 17: Repeat Row 16.

Row 18: Repeat Row 16, fasten off.

Attach yarn to top of other side of Row 15 (to make other strap).

Row: 19: Ch 2 (doesn't count as first stitch), hdc in 3 stitches.

Row 20: Ch 2 (doesn't count as first stitch), turn, hdc in 3 stitches.

Row 21: Repeat Row 20, fasten off. Weave in ends.

Attach a bead to each strap to work as a button.

DRESS BACK

Put beads on yarn first; Using crochet hook, chain 21.

Row 1: Hdc in third ch from hook, hdc across—(19 stitches).

Row 2: Ch 2 (doesn't count as first stitch), turn, hdc across—(19 stitches).

Rows 3–13: Repeat Row 2, adding beads randomly.

Row 14: Ch 2 (doesn't count as first stitch), turn, hdc2tog first two stitches, hdc across until last two stitches, hdc2tog—(17 stitches) (this is beginning of armhole).

Row 15: Repeat Row 14—(15 stitches).

Row 16: Ch 2 (doesn't count as first stitch), turn, hdc in first 3 stitches (to make strap).

Row 17: Repeat Row 16.

Row 18: Repeat Row 16.

Row 19: Repeat Row 16.

Row 20: Ch 2 (doesn't count as first stitch), turn, hdc in first stitch, ch 2 and skip next stitch (for button loop), hdc, fasten off.

Attach yarn to top of other side of Row 15 (to make other strap).

Row 21: Ch 2 (doesn't count as first stitch), hdc in 3 stitches.

Row 22: Ch 2 (doesn't count as first stitch), turn, hdc in 3 stitches.

Row 23: Repeat Row 22.

Row 24: Repeat Row 22.

Row 25: Ch 2 (doesn't count as first stitch), turn, hdc, ch 2 and skip next stitch (for button loop), hdc, fasten off.

Weave in ends.

Sew sides of dress together, slip on doll, and use button loops to fasten back to front.

Wanda's Scarf

Supplies

Approx. 300 yds (275 m) assorted medium (4) weight yarn

Approx. 60 beads with holes big enough for yarn to pass through

U.S. size 10½ (6.5mm) knitting needles

Small piece of thin wire folded in half to thread beads onto yarn

Tapestry needle

Stitches Used

Cast on, cast off, knit, purl, yarn over, knit two
together.

Approx. length of finished scarf is 5 feet without fringe.

*Note: When changing yarn, make sure to thread beads
onto yarn before attaching to work. Also best to change
yarn at beginning of row.*

Cast on 21.

Add beads as desired.
   Row 1: Knit across (21 stitches).
   Row 2: Knit across.
   Row 3: Purl across.
   Row 4: Purl across
   Row 5: Knit across.
   Row 6: Knit across.
   Row 7: Knit across.
   Row 8: Knit across.
   Row 9: Knit 1, *yarn over, knit 2 together,* repeat
from * to * across to last stitch, knit.
   Row 10: Knit across.
   Row 11: Knit across.
   Row 12: Knit across.
   Row 13: Knit across.
   Row 14: Repeat Row 9.
   Row 15: Knit across.
   Row 16: Knit across.
   Row 17: Knit across.
   Row 18: Knit across.
   Row 19: Purl across.
   Row 20: Purl across.

Row 21: Knit across.

Row 22: Knit across.

Repeat sequence of rows, changing to new yarn as desired until scarf is approx. 5 feet long. Cast off and weave in ends. Use mixed yarn to make fringe.

Recipes

Flashback to the Sixties Cream Cheese Brownies

BROWNIE LAYER

- 6 ounces unsweetened baking chocolate, broken into pieces and chopped
- 3 tablespoons butter
- 2 eggs
- 1¼ cups organic sugar
- 1 teaspoon vanilla
- 1 cup unbleached all-purpose flour
- ¼ teaspoon salt
- 1 teaspoon aluminum-free baking powder
- ¾ cup chopped walnuts

CREAM CHEESE LAYER

    8-ounce package cream cheese, softened
    ⅔ cup organic sugar
    2 eggs
    2 tablespoons unbleached all-purpose flour
    1 teaspoon vanilla

Preheat oven to 350 degrees.

Line a 9-by-13-inch pan with parchment paper.

Melt chocolate in microwave. (Put in small microwave-safe bowl, microwave on high 30 seconds, stir, microwave for 30 seconds, stir. Continue microwaving in 10-second increments and stirring until chocolate is melted.) Stir in butter (heat of chocolate will melt it), and let cool.

In a large bowl, beat 2 eggs until foamy. Add 1¼ cups sugar and 1 teaspoon vanilla and beat until slightly thickened. Add chocolate mixture and beat. Combine 1 cup flour, salt and baking powder and add to mixture. Stir in nuts. Batter will be very stiff. Spread ⅔ of mixture in pan. Pressing with wax paper helps to spread batter. Set remainder aside.

In a medium bowl, beat cream cheese, ⅔ cup sugar, 2 eggs, 2 tablespoons flour and 1 teaspoon vanilla until smooth. Spread cream cheese mixture evenly over chocolate layer in pan. Drop spoonfuls of remaining chocolate mixture on cream cheese layer. Take a knife and swirl to give a marble effect. Bake approximately 40 minutes. Cool in pan on a wire rack. Cut into bars. Makes about 32 brownies.

Out-of-Time Cinnamon Nut Square Muffins

2 cups unbleached all-purpose flour
1 cup organic sugar
1 teaspoon cinnamon
2 teaspoons aluminum-free baking powder
½ cup chopped walnuts
¾ cup milk
2 eggs, beaten
½ cup butter, melted
paper baking cups (optional)

Preheat oven to 400 degrees.

Grease an 8-inch-square pan.

Sift flour into a bowl and add sugar, cinnamon, baking powder and nuts. Stir to mix. In a separate bowl, combine milk, eggs and melted butter. Add wet ingredients to dry ingredients, and stir until just blended. Pour into pan. Bake about 25 to 30 minutes until a toothpick comes out clean. Let cool and cut into squares. If desired, put each square into a paper baking cup to serve. Makes about 12 squares.

Keep on the lookout for Betty Hechtman's
next Yarn Retreat Mystery and Crochet Mystery,
coming soon from Berkley Prime Crime!

FROM NATIONAL BESTSELLING AUTHOR
BETTY HECHTMAN

Yarn to Go
A Yarn Retreat Mystery

Dessert chef Casey Feldstein doesn't know a knitting needle from a crochet hook, but when her aunt dies and leaves her a yarn retreat business, the sweets baker finds herself rising to the occasion. When a retreat regular is murdered, though, she has to unravel whodunit.

Includes a knitting pattern and a recipe!

PRAISE FOR BETTY HECHTMAN'S NATIONAL BESTSELLING CROCHET MYSTERIES

"Fun...Has a great hook and a cast of characters that enliven any scene."
—*The Mystery Reader*

"Delightful."
—Earlene Fowler, national bestselling author of the Benni Harper Mysteries

bettyhechtman.com
facebook.com/BettyHechtmanauthor
facebook.com/TheCrimeSceneBooks
penguin.com

M1435T0214

FROM NATIONAL BESTSELLING AUTHOR
BETTY HECHTMAN

Silence of the Lamb's Wool

A Yarn Retreat Mystery

Dessert chef Casey Feldstein has learned the knitting business, and now she's taken on a bigger challenge: running a new retreat called "Sheep to Shawl." Twenty retreaters will come to a resort on the Monterey Peninsula and learn about sheepshearing, fixing up the fleece, and spinning—and eventually, knitting a lovely shawl. Casey is excited about her big plans...that is, until a murder threatens to unravel them.

"A cozy mystery that you won't want to put down."
—*Fresh Fiction*

bettyhechtman.com
facebook.com/TheCrimeSceneBooks
penguin.com

M1511T0614

Meet Molly Pink, the happy crafter who believes
every mystery should be unraveled in...

THE CROCHET MYSTERIES
by Betty Hechtman

"Get hooked on this great new author!"
—Monica Ferris

~

Hooked on Murder
Dead Men Don't Crochet
By Hook or By Crook
A Stitch in Crime
You Better Knot Die
Behind the Seams
If Hooks Could Kill
For Better or Worsted
Knot Guilty

~

Delicious recipes and
crochet patterns included!